*The River Bend Chronicles*

# There's
# No
## Explaining
# Love

Book 12

# The River Bend Chronicles

# There's
# No
# Explaining
# Love

## Renee Kumor

**Book 12**

ABSOLUTELY AMAZING eBOOKS

# ABSOLUTELY AMAZING eBOOKS

Published by Whiz Bang LLC, 926 Truman Avenue, Key West, Florida 33040, USA.

For information contact:
Publisher@AbsolutelyAmazingEbooks.com

ISBN-13: 978-1949504194 (Absolutely Amazing Ebooks)
ISBN-10: 1949504190

*The River Bend Chronicles*

# There's

# No

## Explaining

# Love

## Book 12

# Prison Reform

What a political catch phrase! It's great as a campaign sound bite. But let me tell you about prison reform. Sounds good but does it work? There are two ways to advance prison reform: 1. Build more prisons and increase funding so that overcrowding and other challenging conditions are corrected, or 2. Reduce prison populations by a. reducing sentencing guidelines, i.e., maybe only ten years for murder instead of life, or by b. releasing prisoners early.

The downside of "1"- building more prisons and correcting conditions is that it costs tax money. The upside is more humane and thoughtful approaches to prison management.

However, review the downside – MORE MONEY.

So we're left with "2"- reducing prison populations. Now option "a" – reducing sentencing guidelines is not a great campaign sound bite – let the bad guys drop into prison for a few years instead of the red meat campaign focus of punishing the bad. The downside, you guessed it – bad guys running loose. But there is an upside to reducing prison populations using Option "b" – let the old guys out early! Let out the over fifty-year-olds who are starting to cost MORE MONEY because of deteriorating health and because they're too old to be too bad and they cost money to feed, clothe and house even if they are healthy.

*There's No Explaining Love*

There you have it. Common prison reform. But wait! If old criminals are going to leave the protection and security of three meals a day, health care and housing, where do they go?

Send them back to the local communities, the places they committed the crimes!

Here's how it works. State legislators, who campaigned to lower taxes and save money and be good managers of state programs, create an early release program to relieve crowding in the state prisons by sending the bad old guys to local communities to handle. For a lot less per day a bad old guy can be managed in a local community, given some housing and help to find a job, maybe some training to give the oldies current job skills. The state calls it a partnership with local communities and the bad old guys are released, like old birds from a cage – a warm, food and healthcare provided cage.

Who wouldn't want that? Well, not every community wants an assortment of bad old guys to babysit. Not all bad old guys want to leave their snug, safe cocoon.

Read on to see how a prison reform early release program plays out in River Bend.

# Chapter One

"*T*his garbage has possibilities," whispered a big, bald, tattooed man, dressed in a T-shirt and sturdy prison work pants. He looked at his friends. "These jerks want to give us help to get back outside. We work with them and have our sentence terminated."

"How can they do that?" asked the skinny fellow. No one was certain who his ancestors were. He looked Chinese and Mexican and in a certain light he looked like Yoda. It was the way his ears sat on his head.

"This state has crowded prisons and we cost a lot of money to feed," grinned the bald man. His size indicated that he probably ate more than his state allotment. "Some bean counter in state government decided us old timers and people with good behavior should be cut loose. They're giving money to groups for training and half-way housing once we're released." He smirked. "They try all this stuff every decade or so."

"Does it work?"

"We're still here ain't we?"

That about summed up a new program coming out of the state legislature. It was a recent law called *Home Again* designed for aging prisoners who might start costing the state more money in healthcare than the taxpayers wanted to pay. As the governor said during his recent campaign, "Let's employ retraining and early release. I'd rather spend healthcare money on our children." That always got approving applause. Everyone was still waiting for the increase in healthcare spending for children. In the meantime, the legislature had earmarked significant funding for local communities to create public-private partnerships to design training and early release programs for their incarcerated citizens.

Most communities had created a local nonprofit as the private side of the partnership and had started their early release programs three years ago. James County and River Bend weren't quite there yet.

~ ~ ~

Dusty Reid, chief of the James County/River Bend Joint Investigation Unit, was on a roll. He entered the office cursing in a rhythm that told his staff the meeting with the Sheriff's advisory committee hadn't gone well. When he could finally speak printable words, he said, "They ignored this program for three years and now they tell me I have to straighten things out." He flipped some pages in the report he carried. "Listen to this, 'form a public-private partnership' —

"What's that?" interrupted Danny Valeri, a young detective in the office.

"It's some sort of group. The commissioners just appointed me to the board along with someone from the DA's office and probation office and the community college."

"It sounds like a smorgasbord," offered Teniquia LaMont, another young detective.

"It is," Dusty growled. "One of everybody and a few citizens. We're supposed to create a nonprofit to do the work and we supervise and the state sends money based on population."

He scanned the report. "All it means is that we have more work."

"Don't you mean you have more work?" asked Martin Healey, the third detective of the unit. "You said they put *you* on this committee, not us." Dusty supervised an office staff of three young detectives. As he got older they seemed to stay young. Martin Healey, Mars to his friends, was a former Marine with exceptional physical skills and a degree in forensic accounting. Younger and smaller than Mars was Detective Danny Valeri. He was part of the long time Italian-American community in River Bend. His relatives had immigrated here about a hundred years ago, bringing good food and music to the region. The final member of the team, Teniquia LaMont, was a twenty-something African American woman. She and her husband had recently adopted three children. Danny and his wife were enjoying their first child. Mars often wondered if marriage and children would ever be a part of his life.

Dusty glowered at his staff and they all laughed. How could they not? It was spring, the days were longer, the afternoons warm, and life was good in River Bend.

"Is there already some group doing this parole thing?" asked Teniquia, "You said the legislation is three years old."

"That's the scary part," replied Dusty. "A local group has been operating for about a year and getting state money, but no one in local government knew it was happening. The state sent in some auditors and now everyone is trying to look organized."

"Why don't you ask Lynn?" suggested Mars. Dusty was married to Lynn Powers, the executive director of the River Bend Philanthropies, a community fundraising and granting organization, with knowledge of all local nonprofits at her finger tips. "She might know about this group. Who are they?"

Dusty flipped through more papers. "The James County Prisoner Early Release Project."

Teniquia began to giggle. "It spells perp." The others looked at her. "The letters of the program – Prisoner Early Release Program – PERP."

Dusty scowled at her and returned to reading the

3

program information. "God almighty, its board is made up of half the ministers in town. And the auditors can't figure out what they did with some of the money?"

"Embezzlement?"

"No, incompetence," said Mars, the detective with the CPA. "It's all here. No solid bookkeeping system. No finance policies, no check cashing policies, no ... well ... no anything in place to watch the money."

Dusty reached for his phone.

~ ~ ~

Lynn Powers swayed into her office, River Bend Philanthropies, loaded down with lilacs. "I love the spring. The aromas, the colors." She turned around helplessly, her arms stretched around the bouquet.

"Yes, dear," came the reassuring voice of her assistant, Nelda. The woman finally grabbed Lynn to stop her from spinning like a top, lifting the flowers from her arms. She gently placed them on a desk and helped brush twigs and bugs from Lynn's sweater. "Where did you steal this batch?"

"I didn't steal them," explained Lynn in a righteous voice. "There were so many blooms at Herbie's office, that I know he won't mind." Herbie was H. Lawrence Grayson, the treasurer of the Philanthropies board and a local River Bend attorney. "He won't even notice they're gone."

"That's what you thought about the Parks and Recreation staff when you helped yourself to their daffodils," Nelda reminded her.

"They were behind some rocks where I jog. You know, on that old washed out road. Besides I helped the rec department and their citizen board and staff with strategic planning – for free," grumbled Lynn. "They owed me." Besides, she told herself, she deserved some reward for getting back into her running routine.

"And the Methodist church?"

"We manage their endowment fund. It's growing." She

thought about how upset the Sunday school class that cultivated the meditation garden had been when some of their azaleas were pruned.

Nelda sorted through the boughs of lilacs. "Where did you get these peonies?"

"They were peeking through the fence from Herbie's neighbor. He won't miss them."

"Who's the neighbor that won't miss them?" Nelda liked to be prepared for complaints.

Lynn thought a moment. "I'm not sure. That old house that's been vacant for several months. The yard is really overgrown. The plants needed thinning."

The phone rang.

~ ~ ~

"Letitia, honey, I got you three prisoners," whispered a voice over the phone.

"What?" Letitia Jacquet sputtered a response taking her eyes off her computer screen with her favorite online shopping site.

"Honey," came the tense voice of her almost best friend, "I've been telling you for months that you need to be supervising some prisoners. I got you three. You have to go up to Craggy and meet them." Craggy Correctional Center was in Buncombe County, about a forty-five minute drive.

"All the way up to the prison?"

"Yes. Then they'll be delivered like UPS."

"But what do I do with them?" asked the confused woman, trying to stay focused on whether she should buy the magenta or mustard leggings.

She heard a long-suffering sigh. "Honey, I've been telling you for months. You should have some jobs lined up, maybe some community college classes. Doesn't your board have any ideas?" Pause. "You do have a board, don't you?"

"Yes, I do," came a whiney reply. "They don't know anything and rarely meet."

"What have you done with all the money I've been putting in the checking account for your office to operate?"

"Wasn't that my salary?"

A long pause. "You just paid yourself the money? Did you take out FICA and taxes and those things?"

"I thought you did."

The woman on the other end of the line concluded the call in a very businesslike voice. "After you meet them at the prison, two men will be sent to your county jail in a day or so. The third will be along in a few days later. They are your responsibility." Click.

Letitia Jacquet stared at her phone. She remembered the meeting when she accepted the role of program director for the prison project in James County. She had grown up here and the people in Henderson County had been happy to send her off to organize the new office. But she hadn't gotten the office organized yet. There had been so much else to do – find a place to live -alone, away from her mother; learn how to use the computer assigned to her – she thought she had mastered online shopping very well.

Now they were bothering her about work. Had it been a year? Where had the time gone? It had been a good year – a salary, living alone, a vacation at the beach. She guessed her chickens had come home to roost as her granny used to say. Prisoners? Classes? She thought she better review that file someone gave her. She wasn't even certain who her board members where. They had been recruited and had come into existence under the sponsorship of the Henderson County early release program that had been acting as the fiscal agent for the James County program. She tried to think of all the things she had done related to her job in the last year. And she thought …. and thought.

She remembered going to a training class several months ago. She also remembered meeting with the board maybe last December. But Christmas distracted them and then wintry weather and then it seemed like, since they were all pastors of mostly Christian churches, they all got distracted by Easter. She looked around her kitchen. She didn't even have an office. What had she been doing all last year? She couldn't remember. Wait. She recalled going to some non-profit roundtable discussions. She even went to an executive directors' discussion group once. She remembered starting the paperwork to incorporate as a nonprofit. She remembered getting the paperwork to apply for board insurance. She did have an agency bank account, although she used it as her personal checking account. She looked at the mess on her kitchen table. Her eyes strayed to the papers stacked on the end tables in her living room. Hmm. I guess I got behind, she thought.

Now that she realized that those paychecks were not all her funds, she panicked. She hadn't spent all the money, and decided that she could use what was left to organize an office, somewhere. Maybe she would have enough to rent a copy machine. She didn't need a computer. The Henderson County office had sent her off to James County with a state provided computer that she had been enjoying all this time as her personal shopping computer and game center. Hmmmm.

Letitia stared out the kitchen window in her small rental cottage. She liked the place. It got her away from a nagging mother and nosey sister. She would do all that she could to keep this oasis as her own. It was a little house built in the mid fifties, part of a small subdivision of homes with three bedrooms, one bath, tiny yard and one car garage. She knew nothing about her neighbors, and that was the way she liked it.

However, she had a feeling things were going to change in this quiet stress-free life she had designed. She had to convince the state that she was working and convince her board that she was organized and productive. She would do anything to keep from returning to live with the mother who saw her as a failure. Survival and self-preservation were great motivators. She did have some talent. She spoke well, sometimes even convincing folks that she knew the score. She opened the computer, found some files that pertained to this prisoner project, studied the notes, scanned the pertinent legislation and prepped for tomorrow.

~ ~ ~

Dusty had the papers spread out on the table in Lynn's conference room. He had been trying to explain his problem to her and she kept asking questions before he could explain the few things he actually knew. "Just stop," he finally barked. "I'll tell you everything I can and then you can figure out what's missing."

"I can tell you what's missing now," she said, smug because she knew it all and Dusty, her husband, was in the dark. "This group may exist in your report, but doesn't exist as a nonprofit on the state website." She pushed her laptop for him to see. "It's not incorporated, has no solicitation license, and no history in town as a local nonprofit."

"How do you know?" he challenged.

She stabbed at the computer screen. "It's all here on the Secretary of State's website."

"Why does the state department care about a non-profit?"

"Not the U.S. State department, but the North Carolina Secretary of State's website." Lynn gave him a dumb and dumber look. "That site manages a lot of non-profit information. Or provides links to information." She stabbed the screen again. "Nothing here referring to a nonprofit in James County doing early release." So there!

Clickety click a few more times on her computer. "I'm also looking for other state websites that might reference this program." She flipped through sites, scanned onscreen information. Click. "Ah."

8

"What?" Dusty moved behind her to study the screen.

They silently read together. Then Lynn said, "Here is more specific information. They are part of the Henderson County program. It says they are working to organize and establish their independent program ... . mmm ... .hmmmph."

"What?"

"They were supposed to be organized and independent by now."

"That's what I've been trying to tell you." Dusty bristled. "They are supposed to be organized and aren't, and the state auditors caught up with them."

"Who's on the board?" He handed her the list. She frowned. "Half the ministers in town."

"That's what I said," he groaned. "So now what?"

Lynn studied the list of board members. "You're right, we know most of them. Maybe we should call one of them and get some more information." She was smug again because she had the idea first. "Let's call Rodney Byers at the Presbyterian Church. He's listed as the chair of this board and he's nice to deal with." Lynn reached for her cell.

"Rodney, this is Lynn Powers." She smiled into the phone as she listened to his cheerful greeting. "The reason I called ... no, no one left your church some money. I'm calling about the James County Prisoner Early Release Project ... Yes, I can. Do you mind if I bring Dusty?"

With a nod from Lynn, Dusty collected all his paperwork from the conference table and followed her out the door.

At the Presbyterian Church they found Rodney working in the church's flowerbeds. Lynn's eyes were dazzled by the azaleas and columbine. And there were white bleeding hearts – a great spring perennial. Her hands itched to grab a clump to transplant into her own garden. Dusty, who had been receiving complaints from all over town, grasped her hands as Rodney stood.

"You can have one clump of the white bleeding hearts for your garden if you help me with this agency," said the gardening pastor.

Lynn hung her head. Did *everyone* know she stole ... er ... borrowed spring flowers, helping to thin out those overcrowded beds? It was free gardening! "Deal."

Rodney ushered them into his office. Once settled he began, "I'm the chair of the board." He shook his head. "I'm not sure how it happened. Our church prison ministry found out about this state early release legislation and joined with a few other churches to start the project in James County. We exist as part of the Henderson County group. They draw down the money, pass it through to us and we run our program." He stopped talking and looked at Lynn.

She knew. "You're all in over your heads," she concluded. He nodded agreement. "And no one really has time to do it right." He nodded again.

"Have you hired a staff person to help?" she asked.

Rodney blew out his breath and seemed to gather his thoughts. "The Henderson County group had a staffer who wanted the responsibility and she lives in River Bend, so she sort of took over."

"But you're already in trouble with the state because of lack of management skill, lack of management plan for the released prisoners and lack of good nonprofit administrative organization." Lynn hammered it home.

"You don't have to tell me," Rodney sighed, "I've taken the Philanthropies' classes on good nonprofit management. Unfortunately, I don't have the time this project needs, and our staffer, Letitia Jacquet, doesn't seem to have the skill or the leadership ability to get the job done." He looked at Lynn and Dusty with relief. "Are you here to help?"

Dusty growled. Not a reassuring sound. "The Sheriff

and a few other law enforcement leaders just got word from Raleigh that we better get ourselves organized to provide this prisoner release service. We're one of the last counties in the state to get on the bandwagon. We were happy to hear that you already exist. I mean, I think we're happy about it."

Rodney moved his hands in a calming motion. "We just need some guidance. If we follow the program as it has been organized by Henderson County and work with local law enforcement and with the community college, it'll work."

"What about your employee?" asked Lynn.

"That's another story," sighed Rodney. "Maybe you could help us with a quick board retreat, like you did for the chamber and the rec department."

Dusty looked at Lynn and she knew she was doing a board retreat for the James County Prisoner Early Release Project. Before they left the Presbyterian Church, Lynn had the board meeting on her schedule and a clump of white bleeding hearts. And all the board members and the executive director, Letitia Jacquet, had been advised of the Saturday morning meeting.

# Chapter Two

*L*etitia Jacquet stared at her email. Not only was the program director in Henderson County mad at her, but her own board members were organizing behind her back. A board meeting and retreat? New board members? Help from the Philanthropies? She was familiar with Lynn Powers. She had taken a class or two, well, maybe just one, sponsored by the Philanthropies for executive directors. She tried to recall what she learned. Not much. She had been too busy doodling in the margins of the handouts. And she had been delighted that she was working on her own, no supervision and with a salary that allowed her to rent a small house – and allowed her to get away from her mother and nosey sister.

Those women had no respect for her privacy. They read her mail, snooped on her computer. The last straw was when they found out she had registered at a dating site. That wasn't so bad, but they also learned that after a month, no one had indicated any interest in meeting her. Of course, they had all sorts of reasons why no one would want to meet her. It was the usual criticism. She was fat, she dressed funny, she was too tall, too big, and too pushy. Letitia liked to think she dressed with an artistic flare. Her mother thought she looked like a gypsy tent in paisley or geometric patterns – with saggy boobs. What was a girl to do when she was big boned and tall?

Her sister was thin, even after carrying two children. Her husband owned a small auto repair shop and he didn't seem to care that she never cleaned or that the children had no manners. Letitia thought he had been interested in marrying her but once he met her sister, Larissa, he changed direction. That was okay. He wasn't any prize. Letitia was looking for more than a boring guy with dirt under his nails who worked hard paying the mortgage. She was looking for adventure and excitement – a bad boy. And maybe some sex. She was almost forty and had never been seduced, romanced, loved.

Well, that wasn't really correct. She had been deflowered, as they say. The first time the guy had been drunk and he didn't seem to remember. He had served his purpose, even if she couldn't remember his name or what he looked like. It happened about eight years ago when she thought about moving to the coast. She drove all the way to Wilmington, found a motel and happened to meet several men returning from a fishing trip. One thing and another and she accomplished one task on her bucket list. Next time she determined to hook up with someone sober – just to get a little feedback. And she had.

Trips to the coast every now and then had honed her intimate skills and helped her self-image. There were sober guys out there who liked a good-sized woman looking for nothing more than a little entertainment – no last names, please.

Letitia felt better just thinking about her adventures. Eight years of sex and sun. She had managed to seduce or overwhelm a number of forty and fifty somethings and leave them impressed with their own skill and stamina. Letitia smirked. If she could troll for sex on the beach, convince losers they were Romeos, she could handle this board, their retreat and any over -the-hill cons.

~ ~ ~

"What do you think?" Dusty asked as he and Lynn settled into a booth at the diner. After their meeting with Rodney, Dusty had suggested that they have a late lunch. He really wanted her to help him think through this new assignment.

Lynn sighed and thought for a moment, recalling all that she had read. "The Prisoner Early Release Program works with inmates in the state prison system who will be released back into James County. A statewide vetting system begins working with inmates while they're in prison. Then the local program takes over as the inmates are released. The local group meets with them and helps set up jobs or training based on education and other factors."

"Like?"

She stared at him, focusing on the question. Finally she quoted, "Factors include education acquired while in prison, behavior, type of crime, criminal history, family support once they're released. It's a comprehensive program based on research and using a template of other successful programs operating nationwide."

"How do you know so much?" he asked as he wondered why she wasn't on the board instead of him.

"I read the information you emailed to me before you got to my office." She closed the diner menu and stared at him. "Didn't you read it?"

"I figured you would." She scowled at him. "Yes, I read it," he grumbled. "Sounds like it gives some guys a chance," said the law enforcement professional, "although I'm a skeptic."

"Don't those guys deserve a second chance?" She tilted her head and he could see a small leaf in her hair. He groaned to himself, she been out stealing flowers again! But he could ignore the crime because she was giving him her time.

"Depends on who's giving the second chance and who's getting it. Nothing is ever black and white." Skeptic through and through. Except where Lynn was concerned. Dusty always ignored the complaints about Lynn's flower antics and always gave her another chance.

Their food came and they continued their conversation. "The program hasn't operated long enough in River Bend to demonstrate any success. I think the woman who runs the program attended one of the Philanthropies' trainings. But she isn't one of the nonprofit regulars. She did ask for some funds once. But we declined the application."

"Why?"

"They had projected nine men and three women coming through the program last year. They hadn't seen any clients. My grant committee asked me to check it out. I called the state program and they told me that Ms. Jacquet hadn't gotten the program up and running yet. They were disappointed because they had several inmates ready for release."

"You mean after one year she didn't meet those outcomes?" Dusty had been married to Lynn long enough to have some idea of nonprofit jargon.

Lynn shrugged. "The state group had no idea what she's doing. And I think the Raleigh group started talking with the group in Henderson County because they act as fiscal agent. I suspect Ms. Jacquet didn't measure up to the performance of other groups around the state."

"That's why the sheriff is so nervous. The state auditors came through and must have blamed him for the inaction." Dusty took a bite of his lunch. "That's why he gave me the job. He knows I'll save his ass – again." Many in James County saw Dusty as a potential political challenge to the current sheriff. But not for a few years. The sheriff had just begun his four-year term a few months ago.

Amelia Shipley stopped at their booth. "How's everything?" she asked. Amelia ran a very successful cleaning service, Amelia's Maids, and had the contract to clean the Philanthropies' office. "I just initiated a new crew at your office," she told Lynn, "let me know if they do a good job." Lynn marveled at how attractive Amelia was. She had blossomed as a successful businesswoman. Her even features were enhanced by the coloring of her Latin heritage – sparkling dark eyes and shiny black hair.

"A new crew?" asked Lynn, "business must be good."

Amelia smiled. "Spring cleaning." As though that explained it.

"I've seen your ads," said Lynn, "convincing everyone in town that they need your help with spring cleaning." She slid over. "Join us?"

"No, thanks, I have a new crew at Dr. Rita's office, too. I only have time to grab an iced tea and chicken wrap to go."

They watched Amelia rush to the take-out counter. "She needs a man in her life," said Lynn.

"Not with your help," warned Dusty. Amelia had been a victim of domestic violence, until her husband was murdered. It had been three years and she had created a business that helped other women like herself find entry-level jobs and move from that cycle of violence. "She's doing fine on her own." Dusty gave Lynn a stern look and Lynn smiled. They both knew she would do what she wanted regarding Amelia's love life.

"Besides," he reminded her, "You have to solve my problem and get this program operating correctly."

# Chapter Three

Before going to bed last night Letitia had gone online to the River Bend Chronicle site and reviewed rental ads. She found the perfect spot, a small house on the edge of downtown. She knew the spot had been vacant for months. It needed some yard work. An idea struck her. Her prisoners could clean the yard while she looked for other jobs for them. She congratulated herself for solving problems as fast as she thought of them.

An early morning call to the listed number got a happy response from a desperate landlord. "I won't do anything," he bargained, "you take care of the yard and cleaning up inside. It's yours 'as is' at that rent you asked about." Letitia was delighted – low rent and chores for the prisoners – win-win.

"Thank you," she replied. And they talked a little about utilities.

"Water's on. Electricity's off. We'll talk about heat if you're still there in the cold."

The deal was sealed. She raced around town picking up keys and making deposits. She walked through the weeds to the derelict structure. She sighed as she opened the door. It smelled musty, but had a few pieces of furniture – a small dining table and several chairs as well as a kitchen with serviceable appliances. In its original life it had been a small two bedroom home, but had evolved into a small business site with a reception area and two small offices, break area – think kitchen – and a bathroom that could use a good scrubbing.

It would do, Letitia decided. She called her Internet

provider and negotiated a cable, phone and online service for a fee available to nonprofits. She spent the morning waiting for the hook-ups and then ran home to scavenge odd pieces of furniture and office supplies. No need to pay for something she already had.

Then she thought about transportation. She contacted her worthless brother-in-law and was able to borrow an old pick-up truck. She used it to move furniture and thought she could use it as extra transportation when her as yet-to-arrive prisoners needed it to get to jobs.

~ ~ ~

The Philanthropies committee for high school alumni fund raising was wrapping up their meeting. Lynn basked in the praise. Robert O'Hara was the Philanthropies board chairman. He reminded the committee members, "Lynn was inspired when she started encouraging all the local high schools to support scholarships for local kids." He nodded toward the Philanthropies financial managers, a regional fund management group, "And you folks have certainly delivered on your promise to grow our funds. This year we'll have more than ever to award for scholarships." It had been a great meeting – more money, more grants!

"Are you meeting with the local alumni groups again this year?" one of the committee members asked Lynn.

She grinned. "I've organized local folks to speak to each group. I'm staying away this year." For the past few years Lynn had made an effort to address alumni groups from the three local high schools, encouraging them to support scholarships for graduates. "Some of the recipients of our scholarships or their parents or some other interested alumnus will speak to each group." Lynn was really happy to relinquish this fund raising task. Visiting boisterous alumni gatherings to ask for money sometimes got tricky, especially if she got there after the beer.

"Great plan," said Robert as he slipped his notes into

his briefcase. He never wasted time at a meeting. It was late on a Friday afternoon. He had better things to do.

As the committee members rushed for the door, one member lingered, Penny Rawlings, a member of the Taft family – a generous Philanthropies donor. "Got a minute?" she asked Lynn.

Lynn nodded. The two women watched as the office cleared. "How's the baby?"

Penny smiled fondly at the thought of her daughter. "She's marvelous. Uncle Nathan adores her, and my husband Buck is wrapped around her little finger."

"Has she met your father-in-law or Nancy?" Lynn asked.

Penny frowned. "We haven't seen much of either of them. Zachary," her father-in-law, "says he's thinking of leaving his job in Texas and finding something to do closer to us. We send Instagrams and other photos almost every day. I hope he does move closer to us. He seems so forlorn."

Lynn sat at the conference table and thought for a moment. "He had a terrible experience when his wife was kidnapped and murdered. It was a horrible time for the whole family."

"Neither Buck nor Nathan talk about it much. Can you tell me anything?"

Again, Lynn thought for a moment. "It was a painful time. Some people decided to rob Taft Manor and surprised Nathan and Cynthia as they were planning Nancy's engagement announcement party. Nathan was attacked and left unconscious. Cynthia was taken, as a hostage, I suspect." Lynn thought about the autopsy report. "She didn't go quietly. In fact, the ME said she struggled and fought so hard that one of the kidnappers probably didn't realize he had killed her until she finally quit moving."

Penny was pensive. This was more information than what she had learned from Cynthia's family. "How did it affect Nancy?" She was Cynthia's daughter.

"It ended her engagement," explained Lynn. "She started dating Mars and we all thought she would settle down in River Bend. But something happened and she ran off to Australia to live with her father." Lynn shook her head in confusion. "We all thought she would return and marry Mars, but she came back to the states when Zachary took the job in Texas and seems to avoid River Bend. I know Mars doesn't talk about her any more, according to Dusty."

Penny sighed. "Yes, she has become an enigma to the family. Pleasant, but unavailable. I don't know her so I can't say anything else." She shrugged as she thought of the mysterious Nancy. "But I'm here to deliver a message."

"I'm all ears," said Lynn.

"Buck says that Taft Manufacturing will take care of shipping all of Yolanda's gifts for the orphans." Penny grinned and Lynn gave her a grateful hug.

Tomorrow night many people would be saying farewell to Yolanda Valeri as she set off on her adventure to South Africa to join her friends and celebrate the opening of an orphanage.

# Chapter Four

The Prisoner Early Release Project board members, new and old, had agreed to a Saturday morning sort of retreat. Lynn had done this often enough with all sorts of community boards. The old board members were committed to the mission of prison reform and rehabilitation. She was certain they had no idea about the goals of the state program or the performance measures that had not been met. The new members attending, like Dusty, were there because of their job requirement. She saw this early morning meeting as a way for the reconstituted board to organize itself and get ready to meet the state mandated requirements.

She had tried to meet with Letitia Jacquet prior to this meeting but had been rebuffed at every turn. The woman was not interested in preparation. Lynn suspected it was because she had no work to show for her time as executive director. Although Letitia had not cooperated, Lynn would make certain that this meeting was not an attack on the director.

Rodney had offered a Sunday school classroom at the Presbyterian Church for the meeting. It was a bright, sunny room with windows looking out into a meditation garden. It was a calm and serene view. Lynn hoped things stayed that way. She looked up as several people carrying coffee mugs entered the room having stopped first at the coffee pot in the church kitchen just down the hall from the meeting room.

When the board members finally assembled Lynn faced eleven people – five ministers or church affiliated folks –

one Presbyterian, one UU, one synagogue member, one Baptist and one from the Congregational Church. And six state mandated participants – Lynn thought of the mandated members as a Chinese menu, one from every column. The six included an assistant DA, one commissioner – happily Lynn's friend Bev – one sheriff's appointee – that was Dusty – one probation officer, one appointee from the community college, one appointee from the James County economic development committee. And coming in late, participant number twelve, the executive director, Letitia Jacquet! A large woman in a paisley sort of dress that came to her knees, accented with magenta leggings.

Since Letitia had not cooperated in planning the retreat, Lynn and Dusty had decided that they would, by default, develop the agenda and goals for the meeting. They had reviewed the legislation over the last two evenings. To start with, Dusty wanted the meeting over by noon. He also wanted to be given no new assignments. So much for program goals, thought Lynn, as she introduced herself and invited all those present to introduce themselves. Once that very basic chore was completed she said, "We have our agenda before us and with the chairman's permission," she looked at Rodney and he nodded with relief, "I'll help guide you through the particulars of this state mandated program and help you set some goals for the coming year." With that very brief opening she proceeded to outline the principle mission of the legislation and what she assumed were the circumstances driving it, such as crowded prisons that were expensive to maintain and dealing with middle-aged and older prisoners as their health became an issue. She went on to outline the legislated goals of the program – early release of older prisoners, job training opportunities, job placement and some sort of oversight to make certain that the program participants were not committing crimes in their off hours.

She allowed Rodney to explain that the James County program was an offshoot of the program in Henderson County and had been working locally during the first year of its existence to address the organizational issues of becoming independent. But that had not been accomplished yet and the Henderson County program was still their fiscal agent.

Lynn then ran through an administrative review of the necessary organizational paperwork that should be completed as the program worked toward its independence from the other county to become a viable nonprofit. Rodney heroically tried to explain where the organization stood. In a mess, was what Lynn thought. She distributed packets of information that she and Dusty had assembled, saying, "Each binder contains your board membership list with contact information, a proposed set of bylaws, a copy of Henderson County's program budget to help you develop one of your own, a copy of the legislation to help you work out your own strategic plan, at least something that gives you some short term objectives, and finally, I've included a list of suggested policies that you should develop. These include finance policies, such as, check cashing, accepting donations, making deposits. I've also included some suggestions for policies that you should consider regarding your prisoner/clients."

"What does that mean?" asked one of the ministers.

Since some of this had been Dusty's idea, he spoke up. "We should have some of our own criteria for selection. We should have expectations of their performance, getting to school, working, level of independence and oversight." He looked at his colleagues. "I contacted one of my friends in Dare County and got a copy of their policies. I'll give them to the committee working on this stuff."

It was soon eleven o'clock and Lynn was pleased with

the discussion. Several members had volunteered to take various jobs. The basics of organization would be dealt with soon. But the operational side of the agency, dealing with the prisoner/clients, hadn't been addressed yet. Then Monica O'Hara, the assistant DA, asked, "How many released prisoners have we accepted?"

The five members of the old board lowered their heads. The new members turned toward Letitia. She had been quiet through the morning exercises. Pulling some notes from her paisley patterned shoulder bag, she stood and walked to stand beside Lynn. Letitia was a big woman and wearing her usual tent type colorfully designed clothing, she looked like a spray painted pachyderm as she glared forbiddingly at her old board members. "We haven't had a board meeting for several months, so let me bring all of you up to date on things I would have reported," she gave them the evil-eye, "had we met as we should." The five old members blushed. She squinted at the new members. "I have signed a contract for our office – the small old cottage next to H. Lawrence Grayson's law offices. I have our banking account in place." She passed signature cards to the chair and treasurer. "And we have the files of three participants from the state prison in Buncombe County who are interested in working through our program." So there, she thought.

Rodney hadn't been the leader of a Presbyterian congregation for twenty years for nothing. Everyone knew how contrary Presbyterians could be and how a skillful pastor could always get the theological ship back on an even keel. "What great news, Letitia! We're so blessed to have you, a proven go-getter, as our director." He scanned the membership. "We can start Monday morning in our new location, work on our assignments and begin to meet our mission."

Letitia scowled. "I have to go interview these prisoners

on Monday."

Connor Davenport, the probation officer, asked, "Who are these prisoners and what do we know about them?" Letitia handed him the folders with photos and summary of the three prisoners. Connor flipped through the information and passed it to Dusty and Monica, the other law enforcement professionals. Once they reviewed the information, they passed the files around the table. Lynn even took a look at the three middle-aged men who, through their applications, were telling the prison release group in James County that they wanted to be reformed.

"Any objections?" Rodney asked the board members.

Dusty heaved a sigh. "They haven't a history of violent behavior or narcotic use. One of them is incarcerated for car thefts. The other two for burglaries." He looked to Connor for comment.

The probation officer said, "If local burglaries pick up we'll know where to look." Members tittered. He continued, "I don't see a problem with Ms. Jacquet interviewing them. We can discuss her report at our next meeting and act on her recommendations."

Rodney smiled at that reply. "Then it's settled. We'll meet in two weeks at our new office and decide on our first prisoners. In the meantime our curriculum committee can design a program for them and our home and hearth committee can determine housing and other living arrangements." Sasha Wren from the UU group smiled at the board members because they had accepted her title for the housing committee. Rodney looked at Lynn.

It was eleven forty-five. She was meeting Dusty's goal. Smiling at the group around the table she said, "Thank you all for being so cooperative. I think you're off to a fine start and within the next few months I'm certain you'll be well organized and operational. Please contact me if there is something more I can do for you." There was a general chuckle as they all looked at Dusty. She, however, nodded to the chairman.

He said, "Thank you, Lynn. And thank all of you for your time today. We are adjourned."

~ ~ ~

Yolanda Valeri's party was at St. Bridget's parish hall. She was taking off for South Africa tomorrow. Her son, Danny, was driving her to Charlotte where she would get on a plane and begin the long journey and anticipated adventure.

During the past winter Yolanda had distributed five hundred thousand dollars to local nonprofits. It had been a bequest from an elderly gentleman she knew from her church. During the process, she learned a lot about giving money away, was threatened by some murderers who had started a fake church, and met the son of her benefactor – Mason Donovan.

And that's why she was going to South Africa – finally. Who knew preparing for this journey would take so much time! Travel documents, state department warnings, health advisories. But most of all, collecting children's clothing. Mason and his soon-to-be-wife were building the Foster and Marian Donovan Children's Home. Once Yolanda had shared the story of the orphans in Africa finding their way to Mason's care, all the churches and nonprofits in River Bend wanted to help. This was their last chance. Yolanda had been shipping clothing and supplies since February. Tonight's farewell party was an opportunity to collect more. It was clear that this was only the first year of support. If Yolanda was involved, everyone knew they would be sending clothing to South Africa for years to come.

"Where will you stay?" Piper asked as she took a package of onesies from someone and tossed them into the cardboard container. Lynn's best friend and sister-in-law was the principal at a local elementary school.

"Mason says that they've added a few suites to the orphanage so that international volunteers can come and spend time to help out and be comfortable."

"International volunteers?" asked Lynn. She was too busy eating pizza to help pack.

Yolanda smiled. "I think that's my suite. He and Riva say they expect me to visit once a year." She hugged Lynn and Piper. "I'm so excited. And Mason says I learned so much about fund raising and grants that I can help them be more professional in their fund raising."

Lynn nodded. "You did learn a lot."

"Like how scary some people can be who want money," offered Piper.

"It wasn't that bad," said Yolanda downplaying her funds distribution adventures.

"Dead mice?" countered Piper. The people from the fake church had sent a threatening letter to Yolanda that included the bodies of several dead mice.

Will, Piper's husband, came by and inspected the carton, pulled it aside and replaced it with an empty while Dusty took the full carton and sealed it with packing tape.

Marianna, Lynn's stepmother, and Teniquia were helping take names because Yolanda planned to have the children send thank you notes back to River Bend. She had learned a lot about fund raising. A thank you note from one of the kids would go a long way to insure a future gift. Lynn was right, thought Yolanda, fundraisers have no souls.

# Chapter Five

*T*o everyone's surprise Will, Lynn's brother, had announced last winter that he was starting a vineyard. And as with all of Will's projects, everyone seemed to be sucked in. So on this lovely Sunday afternoon, Will was directing Dusty and two of his brothers, plus Bri Llewellyn, Will's father-in-law, and the boys, Jeff, Will's stepson, and Ricky, Jeff's best friend, in vineyard development. It was Will's expectation that five years from now he would be making wine from his grapes. Dusty's brothers, local successful farmers, would believe it when it happened. The agreement was that Will helped at the farm on Saturday and Dusty and his brothers helped Will on Sunday.

Piper was happy to see her father involved in this enterprise. He had survived several personal challenges in the last months – knee surgery, a dead man in his barn, and finally having to cease being a full time farmer. In fact, once Bri became interested in working with Will, Piper became a supporter of the hare-brained scheme – if it energized Bri, she was on board!

The boys didn't mind helping too much. Will had gotten a small electric cart to ferry supplies from Lynn's barn to his vineyard. But other than driving the cart, nothing about working for Will was fun. He was a taskmaster. Everyone hustled as Will kept reminding them, "Let's move. We only have today."

Over the weeks the land had been prepped and Will had purchased vine stock. Today they were constructing trellises that the vines would grow on. When the boys looked at the small sticks Will called plants, they doubted they would ever see a vine anywhere close to the top of the trellis. But Will paid well and so they worked. Besides Lynn always had food to offer when anyone made the circuit from the vineyard to her barn.

Sadly the boys looked at the five acres of infant vines and knew what they would be doing all summer. They almost wished school would run right though summer. Bri, on the other hand, thought that the electric cart was a great addition to any agricultural endeavor. He loved being back in the soil.

~ ~ ~

Dusty flopped into bed before Lynn. She wandered into the bedroom from the bathroom rubbing lotion on her hands and arms. Dusty moaned. "I'm too old for this. I can't farm all weekend and work all week!"

"You didn't farm all weekend. We had that retreat Saturday morning," Lynn reminded him as she tugged the blanket free so she could join him.

"That was just as bad." He wrapped his arms around her.

"Saturday night was relaxing," she said as she stretched under the sheets.

"Packing boxes and taking them to Taft Manufacturing, loading them on a truck." His voice told of the undo hardship, working in the Gulag couldn't be worse.

"Poor baby." He got no sympathy from Lynn, she was focused on Yolanda's South African adventure. "Yolanda is so excited about her trip. I'd already received three text messages before her plane left the ground. Janet made certain she had a sim card in her phone so she could continue to communicate with us from South Africa."

"Danny and his wife and baby will live in her house until she returns," said Dusty. "There's been a lot of talk at the office since Tee and Lonzo just moved out of her mother's house and into their own place."

"Maybe Danny and his family should move in with Yolanda, permanently."

"I wouldn't want to live with my mother." He yawned.

"Why not?"

"She would always find things for me to do." Dusty kissed her neck. "And I wouldn't have enough time for you."

Lynn squirmed closer. Dusty always said the right thing. "What do you think Yolanda'll find in South Africa?"

"Orphans."

"Of course she'll find orphans, but I think she'll find that she wants to travel more. Maybe we should travel – you know, take a cruise or go to Europe."

"You smell good."

Lynn knew when Dusty wanted to change the subject, whether she was finished with the subject or not. "I just don't smell like fertilizer or dirt," she said with a pout. "Those clothes you left on the bathroom floor are disgusting." She sort of sniffed at his lack of, well, lack of getting rid of smelly clothes.

"I'm sorry," he snuggled closer. "I just didn't have the energy to put them in the hamper."

She got comfortable in his arms. "You seem to have energy for other things."

"I saved my last strength for you." He nibbled her ear.

She smiled to herself. She could forgive him for dragging her into organizing that retreat Saturday morning when she had wanted to work in her garden because he was so lovable. With a sigh, she said, "I always like -" Was that a snore she heard? "Dusty?"

He was wrapped around her and sound asleep. She kissed his cheek. "Maybe you are getting a little old for somethings." She rested her forehead against his cheek and was soon asleep herself.

# Chapter Six

*L*etitia arrived at work at eight-thirty and there were people standing in the yard of the cottage, newly dubbed the PERP offices. She squinted. Those church people, she groaned to herself. She gave them a half smile as she climbed out of her Bronco. The vehicle sort of sighed as she slid from behind the wheel and stood in the unkempt yard.

"Good morning, folks," she greeted the three people who, she recalled, were going to work on some issues this morning. Was it housing or classes or something? "Let's get you all settled inside. I think you'll like this place – close to downtown and convenient to all the churches."

Because she had to drive to the prison today and meet the early release candidates, Letitia had dressed for travel in a knee length smock of several yards of eye-popping orange and magenta flowers with magenta leggings and green, size eleven sandals. One Congregationalist, one Baptist and one UU gulped at the color assault to their retinae, but managed a tepid greeting for the program director.

Letitia unlocked the door and invited them to inspect the office. Sasha Wren, the UU member, offered, "I can make some coffee."

Reverend Garvey, the Baptist Church representative, waved a bakery bag. "I stopped at Umberto's for some muffins."

Letitia was glad she had taken the time over the weekend to supply the small kitchen with the basics. Sasha took command of the kitchen and coffee pot before the two men had time to glance around.

"We're the home and hearth committee," announced Sasha. "We plan to do a survey of available housing options and bring some recommendations back in two weeks."

Letitia nodded. The two men pulled chairs around the small kitchen table as Sasha set out cups. "I've got work to do," said Letitia, "so you go ahead with your plans." She sidled out to her desk. She had chosen the small office furthest from the door and reception area as her haven.

The committee worked for two hours and Letitia, much to her surprise, found that she had plenty of organizational work to do herself. Finally Sasha came into her office. "We're done for today. I think we have a few options and we're going to do some investigating to make certain our men will be safe."

They're criminals, Letitia thought, safe from what? But she said, "That sounds great. I have to leave now for that drive to the prison." Everyone said good-bye and she locked up as she watched the home and hearth committee leave the neighborhood. With a groan, Letitia climbed into her Bronco and moved out.

~ ~ ~

The Philanthropies scholarship committee was concluding another heart-warming season. It was that time of the year, all the local high school seniors had submitted applications and some of the youngsters who had received grants last year and were already in college or community college, asked for additional support for another year. Everyone had a great story and Lynn was pleased that the Philanthropies had enough funds to give something to everyone who asked.

A year or so ago, she had met with a local Rotarian who was heartbroken that his club couldn't give scholarships to all those who asked. She learned that Kiwanians had the same thoughts. And so did the Elks and several other groups who gave scholarships. With the help of several members of each organization and with a clear commitment to serve kids and not worry about club egos, James County folks managed to organize a secret scholarship group whose members tried to leverage all available community scholarship funds and give awards to as many kids as applied.

Lynn and her friends were overwhelmed. More kids got served with larger grants. And much to her surprise, when it appeared that one or more youngsters who were worthy might be turned away, donations magically appeared. As her board treasurer, H. Lawrence Grayson often said, "Nothing like those bleeding hearts to sweeten the pot."

To which Lynn always reminded him, "I saw your check in the pile." Of course, she kissed him on the cheek and he had to readjust the grip on his cynicism.

This morning the final lists were in, the interviews completed and Lynn was preparing the secret report for the secret committee when Rodney, chairman of the early release board, came into her office. "Thank you so much for helping us out on Saturday," he said as he sat in her visitor's chair. "I think we're going in the right direction."

"What direction is that?" she asked with attitude. She hated being interrupted.

"You know what direction," he sputtered, "You were there."

Enough Mrs. Nice Guy, she thought. "Rodney, you and your board have a hard job ahead of you. You all have full time jobs and you're going to have to rely on Letitia to do a lot of work and take some initiative."

"You think she won't?"

"I don't want to be unkind," Lynn waffled, "but she may not have the experience you need."

"What should we do?"

Lynn flopped back in her chair. "Stay in touch with her.

Make certain you know what she's doing and where she may sneed some advice or direction." Lynn sat forward with her elbows on her desk. "I can't tell you anything specific. She may do fine or just need a little help now and then. Just be prepared."

"Can we count on you?"

"You've got Dusty on you board," Lynn grimaced, "that means Dusty is counting on my help."

Rodney grinned. "I like that kind of support."

Lynn stood and walked him to the lobby wondering how much of her time she would be giving to ex-cons.

~ ~ ~

Of all the things that she had to do, driving to the regional state prison was not on Letitia's priority list. However, her contact from the Henderson County program had insisted that she had to be there for an interview with her prisoners. Her role as executive director was turning into a real job. She struggled to be patient as the pokey prison guards examined her ID and scanned her bag for contraband, and finally made her place the bag in a locker, to be returned as she departed the facility.

All this stress! Meet the prisoners! She understood that the prisoners wouldn't arrive for two weeks. Why did they have to meet now? She had hoped to get to the beach for a few days. She needed time to decompress before this job started to demand all of her attention. But it wasn't going to happen.

She had listened to her home and hearth committee talk this morning. They had some weird ideas about housing. They were looking at scary places in South End, maybe even some trailers or something over in Hanging Oak. She realized as she eavesdropped on their discussion that she could keep more money for herself if she offered her place as housing. Why not pay herself instead of paying some rooming house or other questionable facility – a place she would be afraid to visit? She thought it was a great idea. She had the space. There was no down side in her mind. It was settled. She had two weeks to convince them it would work.

Suddenly she had a thought that surprised her. A house full of bad boys! She wondered how that might work out. She'd look them over and give it some thought. Maybe she wouldn't have to go to the beach to decompress. The guard signaled her through the electronic doors.

She was led into a small room that had a few pieces of furniture and those windows with what looked like chicken wire imbedded inside the glass. The place smelled funny. She wondered if this was the room that families used for visiting. Then she wondered what sort of activity might have happened on the furniture. She decided to remain standing.

The door opened and a guard indicated that two men should enter. "I thought our program was accepting three gentlemen," she stated to the guard.

One of the prisoners responded, "That's Sparky. He's in the infirmary. He'll get released in a few days."

That sounded fine with Letitia because she thought that meant she could delay accepting the men until all three were ready to leave the prison. "I hope he's feeling better soon," she said with what she hoped the guard heard as professional concern. Because she was distracted. She already had her eye on the big bad boy in the room. She marveled at her luck. One of the prisoners was the type of man she always looked for on her beach trips – big, brawny, and his shaved head added a certain sexiness.

A prison official walked into the room as her mind was going in a delightful direction. "Ms. Jacquet," announced the man, "let me introduce you to our candidates. Leroy Wells," big and brawny nodded, "and Pablo Trong." The other man nodded. "We are delighted that James County is

39

going to give these gentlemen an opportunity to work in the prisoner release program." He handed her a folder. "Here is additional information for your files. Mr. Stengle is not available at this time. But I'm certain you'll find him as cooperative as these gentlemen once he joins your program. Do you have any questions?"

She pulled out her new business cards and handed one to each of the men. The prison official scanned it and slipped it into his pocket. The two prisoners held on to theirs. "I'm delighted to meet both of you. My board has been working diligently to prepare our program following the goals and guidelines of the state prison release concept. We know that, since you qualify for early release, we can expect great things from you and look forward to counting you as a success." She smiled her official smile. Three men nodded. "Do you have any questions of me?"

Three men stared at her. She looked over the two prisoners and turned to the prison official. "Is there any paperwork to deal with?"

"No, ma'am," he replied, "that is all handled at the time of delivery."

"Is there anything else?" she asked.

"That's all," the official said. "We'll take our boys back to their afternoon activities and someone will come to walk you back to the front gate." He nodded again, opened the door, and called the guard who signaled the two prisoners to exit the room. The prison official turned to Letitia. "I think you will find these men very cooperative. They have never given us any problems here. Wells has been here three years and Trong, six." He nodded again. "Good afternoon." He walked out and closed the door. Within a few minutes another guard entered and led her back to the gate.

Walking down the prison corridor back to the common room, Trong whispered in that prison way of no lip movement. "That lady looked at you like a side of beef."

"Hmmm," Wells replied, "good, 'cause I like my women big."

"She is that," said the guard who had been around awhile and knew a thing or two about prison communications.

# Chapter Seven

Sitting in her kitchen, Lynn stared out the window. She had a full day planned at work and wanted to have dinner organized before she left the house. Staring out the window offered no inspiration, so she moved to the refrigerator. No ideas. Opening the freezer, she stared some more – nothing. Wouldn't it be great, she thought, if a roast or chicken pieces jumped up and cried, "Pick me!" As hard as she stared – nothing. She was so deep in thought that when the phone rang, she jumped.

"I called to take you up on your offer. You know the widows' advisory group." Sara Margolin, a recent widow, had returned to River Bend to get her bearings – to think about her life and her children's future. She was turning to Lynn for advice. Lynn had mentioned to Sara that there were a few other women in town to help her get a perspective on widowhood for young mothers. Sara had three small children.

Lynn blindly stared at her refrigerator as she replied. "It's just me and Harriette. What can we help with?"

"You've both been where I am now." Sara sounded persuasive and desperate. "Mom and Dad are in New Orleans with the kids. I'm back here to see if I can find a life for us. I could use some advice."

"Let's meet at Frank's about six-thirty." Lynn grinned as the call ended. Dinner problem solved. Dusty could go see what some of their relatives were serving tonight. She left for the office already thinking about the meeting with the auditors. Then she thought about Sara and her children. Losing a husband was something Lynn understood. She

would do what she could to help Sara explore a new
direction for her life.

~ ~ ~

"This is going to work," said Wells. "We cooperate for a
few weeks then we disappear and take off for my family's
place in Kentucky." The two men were whispering as they
sat in the James County jail booking area. "We just go along
with this woman. You seen her. She's a fool."

Trong poked him in the ribs. "She's distracted 'cause
she's thinking about jumpin' you."

Wells ignored him as they sat quietly and watched as
several arrestees were processed. One drunk threw up near
the breathalyzer, two women complain about missing work
and needing to pick up their kids at school. An attorney
walked around trying to ignore the smell while several
deputies sat at computers assaulting the paperwork.

"Wells? Trong?" A deputy motioned to them from the
counter. "We have a note that we are to release you to Ms.
Letitia Jacquet. I can't find her. Do you know how to reach
her?"

The men looked at one another and ambled to the
counter. Wells, the bald man, pulled a card from his pocket.
"We were given this information." The deputy took the card
and studied the information.

"Prisoner Early Release Project?"

The men shrugged. "Someone has been helping us at
the prison to get some training in computers and things.
This group is to help us find housing and jobs." Wells tried
to sound sincere and reformed.

The deputy called the number on the card.

~ ~ ~

Letitia sat quietly trying to look busy as another
committee met in the office this morning. This committee
was working to develop potential jobs for potential ex-cons.
Letitia wondered how long it would take them to realize that

no one in town was eager to hire an ex-con. She knew she had a better idea – yard work, one-day projects that churches or other nonprofits needed. Easy as shit. All those do-gooders would flock to bask in the ex-con aura. And her church-going board members were the best example.

Today's committee was the community college representative, that UU woman, (didn't she ever stay home?), and the county economic development staffer who wanted to be anywhere else. The meeting was breaking up. She could tell by the sound of confusion in their voices that they had not made much progress. The reality was filtering in from the business community.

As the others said good-by, Sasha Wren settled in a chair in Letitia's office. "I can't believe we're having trouble finding work for our men." Our men? wondered Letitia. But Sasha continued, "We have the opportunity to help them reclaim their lives and work on their debt to society. Society has to be willing to cooperate."

Letitia was certain Sasha would have pounded the desk if she hadn't proclaimed to be a pacifist. "We'll have to lead by example," said the executive director trying to look pious and heartfelt in paisley.

"You're correct," agreed Sasha, "thank you for affirming our role in their restoration to humanity."

Hmmph, thought Letitia, but asked, "Will there be more meetings this week?"

"I think the other committees are meeting at their offices or other places but we're grateful that you have this space that we can use." Sasha smiled and left the office to, Letitia was certain, spread blather across River Bend.

The office phone rang.

Letitia paled as she listened to the jail deputy advising her that he had a delivery for her. They're not due for two weeks, she thought to herself as she tried to calm her heart and struggled to say something coherent.

"So, ma'am, when can we expect you to be here?"

"Immediately," she replied. "I'm sorry I kept them waiting." She slammed the phone, cursed, stood gasping for breath. I can do this, she told herself in the same voice she used to prod herself into action during her beach liaisons.

Walking out to the Bronco, she ran through all her ideas, all the plans already in place, any options that might be available for reconsideration. Inside the car she hit the steering wheel. So this was the plan – yard work and house them at her place. The only consolation was that big, bad boy. She wondered how long it would take for the inevitable.

On the plus side, there were no more committee meetings scheduled for the office. The board would meet in about ten days and that gave her plenty of time to do ... whatever it was she was supposed to do.

~ ~ ~

Wells marveled at how easy it was to get out of jail when the system was done with you. He was done with it, too. He was too old to behave in any manner that would get him arrested. With his family needing him and his pure enjoyment of freedom, crime was in his past.

As he watched, that big woman waltzed in and signed them out like dry cleaning. She led them to an SUV and eased herself behind the wheel, assuming he and Trong would know what they were to do. She hadn't said a word to them, even when she walked into the jail.

It didn't matter. The guys were prisoners and used to being ignored. They climbed into the car. Wells got the front seat. In prison he had been the leader, and in this new adventure, he was still the leader. The woman drove the car to her office, invited them inside and said, "I didn't expect you today. I'm a little disorganized." She motioned that they take seats in the reception area. "If you give me a few moments, I'll clear my desk and we'll get you settled at the house." The two men nodded and she left them alone, going to her small private office.

Trong and Wells looked at one another. They were used to this sort of treatment, always waiting for someone else to act. They looked around, smirked at each other and made a few hand gestures that were so common in prison they should have been part of ASL training.

Within thirty minutes the woman returned. "Do you need to use the facilities?" she asked. Both men declined. "Then let's go. We'll stop at the grocery store and then go home." The two men followed, still communicating and still not speaking.

Letitia finally started talking to them. "I'm Letitia and you're going to live at my place." Two sets of eyebrows raised silently. "I didn't expect you for two weeks. I thought they were waiting for the other guy to get out of the infirmary." She glanced at their clothing. "You're wearing ordinary clothes."

Wells thought it might be time to speak. "They gave us each two sets of work pants and shirts" he indicated a small bag that contained all his belongings, "and a pair of work boots." He raised his foot to show off his new boots. "They said you would get us other clothes and things as needed."

Letitia thought about that and thought about the funds remaining in her account. She decided that the men could get extra clothing at one of the nonprofit thrift stores – maybe even for free because of their need and their willingness to help a nonprofit with chores and stuff. "We are to clothe, house and feed you. Our next stop will be the grocery store."

The grocery visit turned out better than Letitia had expected. She thought that the men might be like children she had seen with mothers in the store – always wanting something. They were as they had been, silent and accepting, agreeing to items and demurring when asked for preferences.

The drive to her place was quiet. The men seemed to have nothing to say and she had no skill at small talk, or any talk, that would put them at ease. "Here we are," she announced as they pulled into her yard behind an old truck.

"That your husband's?" asked Trong.

"Ain't married."

Two sets of prisoner eyebrows rose.

"I borrowed that from my sorry-ass brother-in-law to move furniture and for other chores as we figure them out." She climbed out of the Bronco. "Let's get this food inside and see what we've got."

~ ~ ~

Lynn had gotten to Frank's early to claim a corner booth – something quiet where they could hear one another talk, but where Frank would notice when their beers needed to be refilled. She waved as Harriette walked through the door. Harriette had been widowed for two years. Her husband had died in a car accident similar to the death of Lynn's first husband. Unlike Lynn, who had remarried, Harriette had no new man in her life at this time. Sometimes Lynn thought Harriette would never find another man. She was very shy and very attached to her late husband's parents. She had a teenaged son and a very responsible job as the manager of Amelia's Maids, the small business started by Amelia Shipley shortly after her husband's murder.

That made Lynn wonder, should Amelia be included in this widows' advisory group? No, she thought, Amelia had been freed from an abusive relationship at her husband's death. She hadn't mourned as Harriette and Lynn had. She thought more about Amelia, then gave her a call as Harriette stopped at the bar for her beer.

When Harriette slid into the booth Lynn announced, "I invited Amelia, too. She's a widow."

Harriette sipped her beer. "She'll have a different perspective." She slid against the wall of the booth as Sara moved in beside her.

"Hi, this is a real treat. Out with adults and I didn't have to get a sitter." The slender young woman smiled at her friends.

"You know Harriette?" asked Lynn. Sara shook her head. "Harriette Mitchell this is Sara Margolin, Janet Bergman's cousin."

The women greeted one another. "Are you as smart as Janet?" asked Harriette.

Sara laughed. "No one is as smart as Janet, but I do IT consulting also. In fact, that's part of my, well, part of the mix I'm trying to sort out."

Amelia slid into the booth beside Lynn. "It's a good thing I live so close," she said. "I just had to slip on my shoes and dash down the greenway." She wiggled her eyebrows. "I don't have to worry about drinking and driving." She smiled at Sara. "I didn't know you were in town. I was sorry to hear about your husband."

"Thanks." Sara sipped from the frosted mug that had magically appeared in front of her.

"That's why we're here," said Lynn in her call-the-meeting-to-order voice. "Sara is at a crossroads and we've all been there."

"Yes," sighed Amelia, "the widowhood path." She looked at Lynn. "Why do you want me here? I was relieved that my marriage ended."

Lynn nodded. "I know, but you may have some perspective that Sara needs to hear." She turned to Sara. "Why don't you tell us what's on your mind?"

Sara took a gulp from her frosty mug. "It's about eight months since Josh died. It was a terrible explosion on a drilling rig in the Gulf. We live – I have three kids – in New Orleans. The school year ends soon and Mom and Dad are

**49**

suggesting that I relocate here and settle the kids in to start school in the fall. But we have a lot of friends there and the kids have already had one major trauma. Can they handle another? Right now I have a consulting business and have a live-in nanny so I can travel and support us. I make good money but Mom argues that someone else is raising my children." She shrugged. "Talk about guilt." She slumped back against her seat.

"Would you move in with your parents?'

"The house isn't big enough. They sized down a few years ago. So I have to buy a house. And sell a house."

"What about your business?"

"This is where things get strange." Sara leaned her elbows on the table. "Janet is looking for someone to work with her. When she and Tim move to Japan in a few months, she wants to keep her consulting business. I could work with her and keep up my own business and hers."

"Won't that run you in all directions?"

"We've talked about that. She said she could do a lot of thinking and writing code and all the things she does, and I could interact with the clients. And with the time difference, I could send her projects or questions and go to bed and find the work in my mailbox in the morning."

"What's the down side?"

"She does some really sophisticated work. I don't know if I can keep up. I don't want to ruin her business."

Harriette had been quiet through this discussion. "I didn't know anything about running an office and managing people, but Lynn called me to help River Bend Reads after those murders and before I knew it I had a job. It was just what I needed to keep me sane and engaged with people."

"Then I found her and stole her away from that nonprofit..." began Amelia.

"And away from me," added Lynn. "We never told you

that I offered Harriette a job just days after you did. She said she was staying with you."

Amelia gasped, then laughed. "That's why I love you," she told Harriette. "You make my life easier."

"See what I mean," said Harriette in triumph, "You just have to take a chance and people will take a chance on you."

"Did you think about moving closer to family?" Sara asked Harriette.

Harriette shrugged. "My sister wanted me back in Ohio, but my husband's parents are here and they were so devastated by his loss that I couldn't leave them."

"What about you, Amelia?"

"I was born here and there is no family. My brothers are both settled in other cities. But I had a few loyal friends and some new friends," she grinned at Lynn and Harriette, "and they've all helped me make a very comfortable life where I had once been so isolated." Lynn reached out and patted Amelia's hand.

"Are we answering all your questions?"

"Just talking this out is helpful," admitted Sara. She brushed her straight light brown hair back from her face. "I have to weigh what I'd leave behind and which of my clients will leave me because I'm moving away."

Lynn gasped. "There's a guy?"

Sara's eyes bugged out. "A guy? Are you serious? It's only been eight months. I can't see a guy in my life at this moment. Maybe in a few years. I have three kids!" She rolled her eyes at the silliness of the idea.

Harriette put an arm around Sara. "I know what you mean. We can't all be as lucky as Lynn and find another perfect fellow."

"Dusty's not perfect," mumbled Lynn. The other women laughed.

"You're out drinking beer with three single women," Amelia reminded her. "That's got to count for something."

"I got your note," said Dusty as he suddenly appeared beside the table. "What's for dinner?" He looked at the four women.

Sara introduced herself and reached out to shake Dusty's hand. "Everyone says you're a perfect guy." Four hungry women grinned as Dusty signaled for the waitress.

"I guess I'm buying dinner," came his perfect reply.

# Chapter Eight

It had been a hectic two days. Letitia was beginning to think that she needed a parolee day care program. What was she to do with these guys when she had so many errands to run, paperwork to do and board members to flimflam? And this was just the last straw. The third guy was waiting for her at the jail. He was supposed to be here next week, not today. She left Wells and Trong cleaning the office while she ran over to the jail and signed out the new guy.

Letitia brought her new charge back to the office. "Do you know one another?" Three men nodded as they stood together in the office break room – a small kitchen with a scratched table and mismatched chairs. "I've got some paperwork to finish," she told them. "There's some drinks in the fridge," she announced as she continued into her office.

The three men settled at the table as Wells handed out some soft drinks. He looked around the kitchen and was happy to find some snacks – granola bars and cookies. He thought of the oversized cookies as freedom food – something he never saw in prison.

"Good to see you, Sparky," began Trong.

"Fuck you, Yoda," Sparky responded, "I ain't doing this shit work."

Wells stretched out in the wobbly kitchen chair. "Sparky, remember the first time we met? Do I gotta slug you again?"

"This ain't so bad," chorused Trong.

Sparky frowned. "Why'd you get in this scam?"

"I wanted out," said Wells. "I got a lot a years left and I

want to get back to Kentucky. Got a piece of land there."

"Everything OK?" Trong was prison-skilled in facial cues and saw more than hostility in Sparky's face.

"I didn't want to come out," said the new parolee.

"We'll make this work," promised Wells. "We play their game and then you both take off with me for Kentucky. My ma's been waiting three years for me to get back home."

"I ain't got time," whispered Sparky, "I got the big C."

"What!" gasped Trong. "Why'd they let you out?"

Sparky shrugged. "I guess the plan is to not have my healthcare on the prison tab. They let me go because I'm going to cost too much."

"Damn jailers," hissed Trong. "I know what you mean. They hustled us out and I ain't got any skills, too old to learn and too old to even find a job."

Wells munched a granola bar. He had already downed two cookies. "They tell you how you're supposed to get care?"

"They said I was to get to some office and they would help me get Medicaid," he looked at the other two men, "if I qualified."

"What does that mean?"

"I don't know."

Wells was quiet as he ate another granola bar. The other two men had lost their appetites. "Can't you refuse to take this release?"

"Naw, my time was up anyway," admitted Sparky. "I had to leave. They said this was the best way to find the care I need. Just releasing me wouldn't allow me to get care." He shrugged again. "Too bad I didn't carry a gun in my last robbery. I'd still have five years to serve."

"How long they give you?" asked Trong.

"They say eighteen months, max." He hung his head. "If I just carried a gun, things would be better." The three men sat quietly, something they had learned to do in prison.

Then Trong snapped his fingers. "We gotta get you back into prison."

"Shit," scoffed Wells, "that's your idea?"

"Listen," said the Yoda look-a-like, "You rob a bank or something, the feds come in, they got better prisons. You'll get better care." They thought about the idea.

Wells threw his food wrappers in the trash. "I don't want to go back in, even a federal prison. My ma's waiting for me to get home and help her out."

"What is she, ninety?" asked Trong.

Wells grinned. "She's sixty-four."

"But–"

"I know, I'm fifty. She was fourteen when she had me." He anticipated their next questions. "She needs me home to help take care of her father. He's about ninety."

"I wouldn't mind going back inside," mused Trong. "I'd like some nice, clean minimum security place. Out here we're gonna have to find jobs and cook our meals – all that stuff they been doing for us." Two men looked at Wells. He had been their leader in prison and their protector. Wells was big. Not many inmates challenged him. He was cool, though. He just let the general population know that the older career guys in his gang had no patience with the infighting and challenges from the younger, angrier cons. He had kept his friends safe. Now his friends had been dispersed throughout the state with this early release shit. He wondered if the others were in the same mess as Sparky or had the same concerns as Trong. Wasn't it just like the system to screw you every way it could, he thought.

"Let me give this some thought." Wells finished his soft drink.

"Now that we're all together," announced Letitia as she walked into the little kitchen with a bucket of chicken and mountains of sides, "I'll conduct our orientation." She handed out paper plates and plastic utensils. "We have to have employment for you. Since I don't have any plans yet, I've borrowed a truck and some tools from my brother-in-law. We're going to start cleaning and repairing this place and landscaping this lot. It's part of our rental agreement." She looked at her crew. They said nothing. She didn't understand that they had been in prison and were used to listening and not responding. She continued, "I have money to buy you more clothes and feed and house you. I also can help you get a driver's license, and enroll you in the community college. I have money for tuition. For now you'll work on the yard and cleaning this office while I work up some plans for your other options. Is that okay?"

They nodded.

"I've got some work to finish here and then we'll go home. You're welcome to walk around the neighborhood, or stay here until I finish." They nodded. She shrugged, took her two pieces of chicken and a mound of sides back to her desk.

The fried chicken and sides were a real treat. Even Sparky found it in himself to devour his share. Wells belched, "Let's go for a walk."

Three men shambled out the door of the shabby office, glancing at the overgrown yard. They continued to the sidewalk. Wells turned to his right, the others followed. Soon they were standing at the corner gazing at a beautifully restored Victorian style house that seemed to be an attorney's office.

"That's real pretty," said Trong. "My daddy used to do carpentry work."

"You interested in doing that?" asked Sparky.

"Hell, no," growled Trong. "He worked his ass off and died when some lumber yard truck dumped a load of two by fours on him."

"That lady said we can get trained or go to school," Sparky reminded him. "What you gonna do?"

Trong pondered his future. "I ain't interested in working as hard as my old man. The more I think about it the more I think I'd like to get back inside and grow old in comfort."

"What about your freedom?" asked Wells. "I'm so happy to be out and walking with no fences and concrete. I want to get back home."

"I ain't got nothing," said Trong. "When Daddy died, my family sort of disappeared. I was old enough to go in the army and when I came out my mother was gone. She mighta gone back to Hawaii, that's where her family was." He shrugged. "I been on my own ever since."

They had been walking along the sidewalk and came to a halt when Wells sucked in his breath in – anticipation? Surprise? They weren't certain. He said, "Keep walking."

They crossed a street and continued toward a park and some benches. Wells sat and the other two men took places on either side. "Look back the way we came," he said. They quietly studied the street.

"A bank" whispered Sparky.

"Yeah." It was a long sigh.

"What's your plan?" asked Trong.

"If you really want to get back inside," they nodded, "then we plan a robbery, no weapons. You keep me out of it. I'll help, but you two gotta cop to the job," they nodded, "I want to get back home." They nodded again. "We work in the yard like the lady said," he glanced toward the shabby office, "and that will give us opportunity to watch the place and plan the job." Wells knew that TV and movies always used words like 'case the joint' but in his experience, he thought of it as watching the rhythm of his target. That always set the plan. Sort of like dancing with a new partner.

When they got back to the office, Letitia asked, "Did you have a good walk? Is there anything we need to do before I close up?"

Wells cleared his throat. "I'd like to get my driver's license."

"Me, too," mumbled the others.

"That's great," she said, "Let's go to the license place and see what we need to do. It's on the way home."

~ ~ ~

Thursday afternoon found Lynn trying to organize Friday's office work so that she could cruise into the weekend and have plenty of time for her garden. Unfortunately, she looked out her window and saw Piper marching toward the office leading the members of her investment club. She groaned. When Piper marched Lynn was usually trampled. The two women had been friends since grade school and were now sisters-in-law. In Lynn's opinion, that made Piper even more troublesome.

"It's not Saturday morning," said Lynn as four members of the investment club took seats around the conference table. She looked at their determined faces and called out, "Nelda, I'm in conference."

"Yes, dear," came the calm reply. With everything in the office under Nelda's control, Lynn turned to her guests. And waited.

Piper and her friends had formed the investment club over ten years ago. They no longer invested as a club but continued their monthly meetings to discuss finances and had recently been recruited to design a basic budget-planning curriculum for women at the domestic violence shelter. Bev, a newly appointed county commissioner, was the owner of a successful group of day spa's and salons; Janet, very pregnant, was an internationally respected IT consultant, and Annie was a retired school teacher who had recently moved to senior residential housing. She told everyone that at eighty-five, she liked having someone else do the cooking.

"It's Memorial Day," announced Piper as she searched the cabinets and came up with some old bottles of wine. She poured glasses for everyone, except Janet. She found some stale candy for Janet.

"Not for two weeks," replied Lynn while she watched as Bev gulped her wine. Lynn waited for the new county commissioner to speak.

Bev sighed. "I've been asked to give the address at the Memorial Day ceremony. The other commissioners say they've all had a chance and I should do it because I have an election next November." Bev had been appointed to fill the unexpired term of Susan Carmichael who had been murdered several months ago.

"So what's wrong?" asked Lynn, wondering why the investment club was involved.

"I don't have a story. No one in my family has ever been in the military," Bev replied.

"No one?" asked Annie who, as the club's oldest member, could always be relied on for historical perspective, mostly accurate.

Bev shrugged. "My dad was four F, you know, he didn't pass the physical."

"I remember that," said Annie. "Folks didn't look kindly on young men who stayed home when their own sons were being shot at around the world."

"Did they bother him?" asked Bev. This was a part of her parent's history that was in the shadows. She knew that Annie, as a long time James County resident, would have some insight.

"I'm sure he got his share of meanness. But he just kept quiet and worked harder," explained Annie. "Over the years everyone forgot, but during those war days, everyone noticed that he was home."

"He was epileptic," whispered Bev.

Annie gasped. "He never told anyone. He just let folks think what they wanted."

"I guess he thought admitting to his condition was worse than letting people think whatever they wanted," said Bev in a sad voice. "When I got pregnant with my first child, he and Mom came over to talk with me and told me. They wanted my doctor to know in case he saw any symptoms. All my kids were healthy and Dad was relieved that he hadn't passed anything to them."

"The poor man," said Piper. "He served all those men and women who were in the military, even though he couldn't serve beside them." She emptied a shiraz into her paper cup and toasted Bev's father.

"Maybe that's what you should talk about," suggested Janet. She was so pregnant Piper had put the ambulance on speed dial.

Lynn raised her paper cup and toasted Bev. "To a great speech about service, in all the ways we do it."

"Or something like that," said Piper as she emptied a bottle of merlot into her cup and offered a final toast. "To a great speech!"

~ ~ ~

Letitia led the men into her small cottage. They carried in Sparky's small sack of belongings, some groceries and several bags of clothing they had purchased at a thrift store. Letitia drove an old Bronco and was glad that she had something large enough for the four of them and all their purchases. "I'm so glad we were able to renew your license, Mr. Wells. That will make it much easier with a second driver." Trong and Sparky had to get some additional paperwork completed and had to take the written tests.

The men carried in the packages and placed them on the kitchen table. Letitia was unnerved by their behavior. They seemed to anticipate her requests and did everything without speaking. So she added the sound track to this little adventure. "We should take the tags off those clothes and wash them so they'll be comfortable for work tomorrow." Trong opened the bag and begin to sort clothing and remove tags. "Then we can put this food away and think about dinner." Wells removed canned goods and cereal while Sparky sorted the items that needed refrigeration. Letitia blinked at the quiet efficiency. "I'm not a very good cook, but I'm sure I can assemble something for this evening."

Sparky cleared his throat. "Ma'am, I saw you buy some boxes of pasta and sauce. I can get that going with a little garlic bread."

"Mr. Stengle, that sounds great," Letitia trilled. "I'll get these clothes into the washer. Please make yourselves at home."

When she had left the room, Sparky asked, "What's the deal here?"

"We're not sure," replied Wells. "I think this is her place and she houses us because she didn't know what else to do. I think we're her experiment."

"Where do we sleep?"

"That's a good question," replied Wells as he seemed to come to some conclusion. "There are three bedrooms. She has one. And we each had one. We need an extra bed for you. Tonight Trong sleeps on the couch. Sparky, you sleep there tomorrow night. By that time I'll have figured out a different arrangement."

"She's a big woman," Trong muttered. All three men knew what Wells had in mind.

"It's been three years," replied Wells, "And I'm a big man." They all grinned. Because they were used to prison tones, they all spoke in low voices. Letitia was not aware that she was headed for a big surprise.

# Chapter Nine

Marketing a spring cleaning package had created a healthy revenue stream for Amelia Shipley and her staff at Amelia's Maids. They had developed a great one-day inclusive service that helped get any home ready for spring. It seemed that many people thought that regular maid service was a luxury, but a one-day spring cleaning seemed to fit into all budgets. They had taken reservations and were booked until the end of May. Amelia had started her own economic revival in River Bend as she hired some temporary staff to help with the usual cleanings and augment veteran maids for the one-day projects. So when her cell indicated a text, as she climbed into the car with her usual chicken wrap lunch, she thought it was from Harriette, the office manager, with some final scheduling changes. To her surprise it was a note from Zachary Rawlings. It was unusual to hear from him during the day. When she read the text she understood why. *"Making a quick trip to Atlanta – found a few days to stop in River Bend. Dinner next week? Z."*

Amelia smiled. She hadn't seen Zachary for a year. They had been in touch through long thoughtful letters and short electronic exchanges during that time. They had met when Zachary, living in Australia, had come to River Bend to help prepare for his son Buck's wedding. At that time he had confessed to Amelia that he was interested in changing jobs. Tired of working in Australia he wanted to return to the states. The job search was successful. He had found a banking job in Texas, entertaining Amelia through his letters with his adventures as he established himself in his new location. He had invited her to visit him once he had settled in his new location, but Amelia was still uncomfortable in her friendship with one of the wealthiest men she knew. The afternoon they met they seemed to bond over their past history. Amelia's husband had been murdered and so had Zachary's wife. Both murders had been featured in a lengthy review in the River Bend Chronicle outlining murders in the last few years. Zachary and Amelia came together as supporting cast members in a dark era of River Bend history. They grew to be friends when they discovered that they were also victims of sad and dysfunctional marriages. Neither Zachary's wealth nor Amelia's inner goodness had saved either of them from becoming victims of their respective spouses. Amelia was a victim of domestic violence, surviving increasingly violent assaults, while Zachary had endured serial and deliberate infidelities by his wife. Both had felt trapped in loveless marriages because of isolation and social pressure. Both had been set free by murder. In his new freedom Zachary reenergized his international banking career while Amelia became a successful small business owner. Neither one had yet learned to enjoy their new personal freedom.

Over the last year she had encouraged Zachary to date and his letters contained long tales of his dating adventures. Amelia laughed at most of them. He was a target for every single or unhappily married woman in Texas. He seemed to be always escaping with his virtue intact. Amelia had kept his letters hoping that one day she would get him to explain some of his cryptic comments in detail.

Responding quickly to his text, she replied, *"Yes."* He must have been waiting for her reply, because his response popped up, *"Sat at 6 yr plc?"* Amelia replied, *"OK."* She slipped her phone back into her pocket and started thinking about her dinner menu. No one had been to dinner at her place since Zachary last year. Was it really a year ago? She had planned to host a summer cookout, but time flew by, then she thought about doing something in October, but missed the whole month with one emergency job after another. Once the holidays were past, Amelia thought about a spring gathering, and now it was spring and Zachary was returning. After he's gone, I'll think about a summer cookout again, she told herself.

She clutched her chicken wrap as she sat in her car thinking about Zachary. Then Harriette sent a text and Amelia was back to being the formidable small business owner, creating a surge in local job opportunities.

~ ~ ~

The prisoner early release program seemed to be working as Letitia had envisioned. Wells drove the truck and followed Letitia to the office. The men worked all day in the small cottage/office eager to get the rooms cleaned so that they could work outside and watch the bank while mowing, raking, trimming shrubs and cutting low branches on the trees. They took every opportunity to individually stroll toward the bank and watch the daily activity.

As Sparky and Trong began the preliminary bank observation, Wells set his planned seduction of Letitia in motion. He managed time to flirt with her or to be helpful, usually involving some reason to touch her or caress her arm, or to do anything else he could manage without feeling stupid. He kept reminding himself to stay focused. They had a plan and he had to do his part. Now that a bank robbery was in the future, he had more incentive to make certain he was uninvolved and might find a relationship with Letitia a useful basis for an alibi.

This evening they had just finished dinner – another simple offering prepared by Sparky, and the men had settled around the TV for the night. They were quiet, but relaxed in the new – prison free – surroundings. They especially liked being able to watch a program and channel surf – and snack.

Letitia came into the living room. "I'm going to bed. Before I do, do any of you need anything?"

Wells signaled the other two men to leave. Trong cleared his throat and announced, "I gotta walk to that all-night drug store. I think I got poison ivy."

Sparky nodded. "Yeah, me too, I'll go with you." They ambled from the house with a quick smirk toward Wells.

Watching the exchange among her guests, Letitia thought, well, well, Wells. She knew men. Those trolling opportunities at the beach had taught her when a man was interested in sex. She sensed that Wells was interested and had convinced his friends to vanish for the evening. She also had enough experience to know that any interest he had was motivated by some yet undiscovered, or unexplained goal. In other words, she was a means to an end. In any case she was curious, and maybe a little interested herself in some basic exchange with no strings. She acknowledged that he had been off the market for a few years and might be rusty or even shy – and would probably be grateful. Maybe he needed encouragement.

"This sofa of yours is pretty lumpy," Wells stated, knowing he had no real skill at seduction. "Tonight's my turn. I think I'll be mighty uncomfortable." He flexed his large body and gazed at Letitia. She stared back. He unbuttoned his work shirt and unbuckled his belt – almost distracted by the luxury of again being allowed to wear a belt.

She didn't blink. Now what's he doing? Stripping? He sat on the sofa and unlaced his boots. Once they were off he placed them on the carpet beside a stack of magazines. Then, he sat up straight and looked her in the eye.

Letitia hadn't moved. She returned his stare and slowly unbuttoned the three buttons on her bodice. "I guess you could share my room," she said in a businesslike voice. He was stunned. She stared at him as she continued to undo the clasps at her wrist. "I hope Trong can find the drug store. You going to wait up?" She left him in the living room as she marched off to bed, her dress sort of feathering behind her.

Stunned by her response, he wondered what this all meant. So he followed her and asked, "You inviting me?"

She looked him over. "You look like a better option than Trong or Sparky. Together they might weigh as much as me." She walked around him and stopped in front of him after completing the circuit. "I thought I might as well get a little something out of this for my efforts."

"You won't scream rape or something?" He could feel sweat collecting between his shoulder blades. This was very unsettling. Of course, he also thought he might get very lucky.

"You know, Leroy," he winced as she used his given name, "I'm pretty bored with my life. I need a little excitement. And you're my only option as I see it." She closed the bedroom door and began taking off her big tent dress. "I don't see any of you fellows reforming. All three of you'll disappear some day, hopefully without stealing my car, and I'll have no job and have to figure out what to do next. In the meantime, I thought I should have a little fun." She stood naked before him and began to push his shirt down his arms.

"You sure about this?" He still couldn't believe the direction this conversation was taking, even though he was quickly ridding himself of any clothing.

"If you're good enough at this sex stuff," she suggested, as she picked their discarded clothing and tossed it in a pile against the wall, "we might be able to save buying that extra bed." She pushed him onto her bed, stood over him and surveyed his somewhat eager body. She nudged him over and settled herself beside him, reaching out to twirl her fingers in his chest hair. "Show me what you got and I'll see if you're worth my time."

What the hell, he thought, and showed her what he had.

# Chapter Ten

*L*etitia awoke alone in her bed. She could hear Wells talking with the other two. This was different than her usual sexual encounter. There was never a morning after. In fact, there was usually no exchange of any personal information – just an exchange. So how would this work?

And did she want it to work? He wasn't bad. And he was big. She never felt like she was smothering him. He had been warm and kind. And she thought she wouldn't mind another ... exchange.

But he shouldn't move into her room, should he? She heard the vacuum cleaner.

Quickly dressing, she walked into the living room and found Trong dusting the blinds and Wells picking up furniture while Sparky vacuumed the carpet.

"Good morning," she said in a raised voice. Sparky turned off the vacuum.

"Coffee's ready. We waited for you to eat breakfast," Wells said. "In prison Saturday mornings we cleaned because visitors usually came Saturday or Sunday afternoon."

She walked into the kitchen and the men followed. "I don't have anything but the usual for breakfast. You didn't have to wait for me," she said. All this time Sparky and Trong were using their prison skills of not seeing or being seen while listening.

Wells had instructed them that they were to act as though nothing happened. As he put it, "She's no virgin, but she's not too experienced. Don't ruin this set up." Which was all the warning either man needed to act like a gentleman.

The unusual family shared breakfast.

~ ~ ~

Lynn looked over her garden. A vicious spring hailstorm had ravaged her spring flowers. But today she had a small crew to help her get it back into shape and to plant the annuals that she hoped would add color and vitality to her yard until the summer perennials took over. Three teens bustled under her direction. She had managed to recruit, Jeff Hanby, Piper's son, Ricky Mitchell, Harriette's son, and Polly Carmichael, a recently orphaned teen, soon to be adopted by Lynn's relatives.

The kids were sweet. They were all students at River Bend High School. They usually spent Saturday evenings playing video games at someone's home while complaining that until one of them was old enough to drive life had no meaning. It was the boys' usual complaint. Polly, however, was just looking forward to moving to Japan with her new parents as Tim, Lynn's brother-in-law, moved into his new assignment for the Navy. Today they were indentured to Lynn if they wanted to play with her son's games this evening.

Yesterday the nursery had delivered her order – mulch and plants. Today she studied her design and got the kids organized. Ricky was assigned to collect fallen branches. He was pushing the wheelbarrow around the yard and picking up all the debris left by hail and rain storms. Polly was raking dead plants and leaves from the flowerbeds while Jeff collected the piles to cart away and return with mulch that Lynn spread in the gardens.

After a break she was ready to start placing her bedding plants. The kids were distracted when Piper buzzed into the yard. Although she had volunteered to help Lynn with the understanding that the help would be reciprocated, Piper had been led astray by Jason's motorcycle. The vehicle had belonged to Piper's father, had been appropriated by Lynn and Piper as teens, then hidden by their parents after the girls misbehaved – a story their sons loved to hear repeatedly – and finally rescued from the barn loft by Jason. The motorcycle had been repaired by Piper's husband, Will, and all members of the family took lessons at the community college so that they could enjoy the ride.

Earlier this morning Piper had walked into Lynn's barn to begin her job as gardening assistant, but had been lured away by the bike. She had raced off as fast as she could fasten her helmet and start the engine. Now she returned, in time for the kids' break, as Lynn ruefully noticed, and she was promising the kids she would tutor them on the "ride." That's how Lynn lost her team. After running to the barn to retrieve helmets, three kids followed Piper toward the open field at the edge of Lynn's landscaping.

Piper, an experienced elementary school teacher, began class. The kids had a few months before they were old enough to enroll in the highway patrol training classes, but some early practice with a good teacher would prepare them for that day. Joyful shouts and revving engines filled the air. Lynn smiled to herself. She'd wait until this afternoon to take a spin. She had to get the annuals planted now.

~ ~ ~

After cleaning the house Wells had asked Letitia to give them a driving tour of the area. They had all piled in the Bronco and headed into the national forest. Since she never took advantage of the scenery or recreational options in western North Carolina, she had no idea what it offered as interesting or entertaining.

"I brought this flier I picked up at that drug store the other night." Trong shyly passed the paper to Wells who was riding shotgun.

He scanned the notice. "There's a horse show at the

equestrian center in Polk County." He looked at Letitia. "Do you know where that is?" While she thought about it, he asked Trong, "You like horses?"

"We used to have some," Trong said, "when I was real young. I ain't been near a horse since my daddy died." Everyone thought about that.

"I'm not certain how to get there," Letitia finally muttered. She was frustrated – trying to think and drive and sit beside Wells. Sex and its after effects seemed to be staying with her all day.

"There's a map and directions," offered Wells. "Why don't I drive? I could use the practice. And you can navigate."

With that suggestion Letitia pulled into an empty church parking lot and exchanged seats. After that the unusual, but somehow comfortable, little family spent the afternoon looking at horses and enjoying spring.

Once home, like children, Trong and Sparky were too tired to do more than drag themselves into bed. Letitia detected a quicker step as Wells followed her into her bedroom. He had been as surprised as she that they had been able to entertain themselves so successfully last night. Who knew? Letitia decided that tonight there should be a little discussion before the main event. She wasn't so interested in foreplay as she was in some ground rules.

"Ground rules?" asked Wells as he unbuttoned his shirt. "Ground rules? This is just sharing space – you know, so everyone has a bed."

"I'm not disputing that," she said. "I just want us to understand one another."

"What's to understand?" he asked as he dropped his jeans. "A little friendly exchange, always means a good night's sleep for me. You got a problem?" She pulled her tent over her head and stood before him. The big man assessed the big woman. "You ain't so bad, you know? You could firm up those abs, but I like the size of your boobs. And if you was a little more flexible, those long legs of yours could hold a guy real tight."

She looked down at her body clad in white patties and white bra, one of those double double D sizes. She wiggled her toes and thought about his comment. Was that a compliment? No one had ever said anything kind to her, especially her mother or her sister. They had always been willing to point out her faults, from her large appetite to her sloppy dress code to her laziness. "I already had sex with you," she pointed out, "you don't have to lie to me."

"I ain't." He looked her over. "Nobody ever said you ain't so bad?" She looked at him, and he knew. "Come here." He held out his arms. She walked slowly into his embrace. "You can believe me 'cause I already got what I wanted. I don't have to lie." He clumsily patted her back. She rested her head on his shoulder. She was a large woman and seemed to him to be a pleasant change from all those women in his past who seemed skinny and unsubstantial.

~ ~ ~

Lynn snuggled in bed, tired from the physical labor of the day. Her garden was ready – beds were planted and mulched. Her vegetable garden was tilled and waiting for the weather to warm a bit more. She had taken an exhilarating spin on the motorcycle, much to Dusty's chagrin. He had hoped for his own turn before taking a shower and getting to Jim and Marianna's for dinner, but ...

Lynn didn't feel guilty. He could get up early and ride tomorrow morning before anyone else was awake. And that's what she told him.

"I don't want to get up early," he groused. "I had plans for staying in bed."

Hmmm, she thought. "What sort of plans?" He wrapped himself around her, nibbled and caressed. "What's

73

wrong with now?" she asked wiggling closer.

"I thought you might be too tired," he said into her ear. She sighed as she leaned into him and trailed kisses along his neck. But stopped.

"I saw your friend, Letitia, at the grocery store being trailed by those parolees."

"She's not my friend," muttered Dusty flopping on his back leaving Lynn's lips in mid air.

Lynn raised up on an elbow. "They didn't look mean, or evil. They sort of looked lost."

Dusty nodded. "Serving time can weigh a person down. Even a few years. It takes a while for a person to adjust to freedom and to learn to make decisions again."

"Decisions? Again?"

Dusty pulled up and sat against the headboard. "Yeah. Think about it. During the length of your sentence you're told what to do every minute. What to wear, what to eat."

Lynn flopped on her back and stared at the ceiling. And let out a heart-wrenching sigh.

"What's wrong?" Dusty asked, sliding back under the sheets and holding her.

"I was just thinking about all I did today, gardening, riding the motorcycle, having dinner with the family. And I thought about not being able to do that for years." He held her tighter as she continued. "It makes me hope that this release program works out for those men. I can't imagine having to send them back to prison once they've been released."

He didn't want to get into a discussion about the psychology common among older prisoners who were reluctant to be released back into a foreign, open world of freedom. Besides, he had a few other ideas, not related to shop talk. "You want to worry about some parolees or your lonely affection starved husband?"

She snuggled closer. "Where was I?" And began teasing his ear lobe.

# Chapter Eleven

Polly Carmichael sat cross-legged on her bed. She was talking with her mother. She was sketching her mother and talking. That was the way she had figured out to talk with the woman who had been murdered several months ago, leaving Polly an orphan and the legal responsibility of Lynn's father, Jim Hoefler.

"It's spring, Mom," Polly said as she sketched her mother's face with a wistful smile. "I know you always enjoyed the flowers growing in our garden. Uncle Jim says they'll be taking the house down soon. Maybe I can ask Ms. Lynn to take me over and dig up some of your plants." Susan's face smiled at that idea. "She likes to garden. We helped her yesterday." Susan's next face seemed to look favorably on Polly and gardening, maybe it was favorable on helping Lynn. In any case, it was a face that soothed the youngster.

As Polly talked with her mother her hands automatically sketched Susan's responses. Polly didn't understand how it worked but she enjoyed these talks. It had helped her cope with all of the sudden changes in her life since last Thanksgiving. She was happy to see that during her recent talks her mother's responses were always happy, sometimes solemn, but never disappointed as they had been in the early months of her death, as the sketches responded to Polly's hostile behavior.

But today there was a challenging look coming out of the sketches. Polly heaved a sigh. "Yes, I know," she told that challenging look. "I shouldn't keep this talent a secret." Polly was a skilled artist, and with little training she had honed her talent for charcoal sketches of people. She had a secret charcoal gallery of her friends, and sheets of paper with her mother's face in various expressions as a result of their "talks." Polly stared at the most recent face. "I don't know who to tell or how or what I should do with this talent." Polly grinned at her mother. "You always called it a gift." Her mother smiled back with deep affection in the new sketch that appeared on the page and mesmerized Polly. "I promise next time we talk, I'll have figured it out."

Polly placed the sketch paper on the pillow and did as she always did after her "talks," she stretched out on the bed and stared at the many faces of her mother and thought about life.

~ ~ ~

Polly had heard the stories about Lynn and the spring flowers. Thel and Bergy got a kick out of sharing the latest gossip at dinner recounting Lynn's escapades at flower thievery. Or as Bergy liked to call it, 'Dusty's blooming crime wave.' Janet always seemed confused, asking questions like "What kind of flower is a bleeding heart?" Or "Is crocus really the name of a flower?"

Thel would get disgusted and reply, "How can you be so smart and not know anything about flowers. I've grown them for years." Then she would point through the kitchen window and say, "See that's them right next to alyssum."

"What's alyssum?" Janet would always ask and it would start all over. Polly had to admit she found it all entertaining.

She was on her way to visit Lynn this afternoon. Uncle Jim had told her that the house would be cleared from the lot. The explosion that killed her mother had done a lot of damage, but it could be repaired. However, as he pointed out, no one really wanted a house with that kind of history. He said they would clear the lot and put it up for sale. He said it would be another part of her inheritance to help her pay for college and things.

That reminded her of her other promise to her mother. First, get Lynn to take some of the perennials from Susan's old garden and second, figure out how to use her talent. It was comforting to know that she would have money to pay for college. She had time to figure out what to study, or how to study art. She was only a freshman in high school, she had time.

"Polly," exclaimed Lynn as she answered the soft knock at her kitchen door. "Is something wrong? Is Janet OK? How did you get here?" That was Lynn always talking faster than Polly could respond.

The youngster walked into the kitchen surprised to see Jeff and Ricky eating – not surprised that they were eating, they always were – but eating at Lynn's on a Sunday afternoon. "Come in," Lynn encouraged her. "Can I help you with something?"

Polly stared at the boys. Lynn continued, "They've been helping Will with his grapes and stopped in for a snack." Polly nodded. She remembered a dinner some months ago when people were talking about Will growing grapes and making wine.

"I came to talk about flowers," said Polly. The boys groaned. They had heard the stories about Lynn and flowers, too.

"Did she steal something from Bergy?" asked Jeff as he added for Polly's benefit, "She took some stuff from my grandmother."

"Glenda gave me those hostas." Lynn gave him a squinty-eyed look.

"My mom says she thought someone had been thinning her iris while she's at work," added Ricky. He reached for the last cookie on the dish.

"Harriette noticed they were missing? But I was -" She stopped talking because the kids were laughing at her. "I

77

didn't steal from Bergy," she pouted. She turned to Polly and raised an eyebrow.

"Good thing," muttered Jeff, "he probably keeps a gun handy."

Polly cleared her throat. "Uncle Jim says they're demolishing my old house. I thought you might like to dig up some of the plants before everything is trampled and ruined." Was there a tear in her eye?

Lynn hugged her. "I'd love to get Susan's plants. We could make a special garden and when you have your own place someday you can take the plants to your garden." What a thought! Polly smiled. Lynn turned to the boys, "Finish eating, we have work to do."

"But, Will—" sputtered Jeff.

Lynn smirked. "I'm not a slave driver like him." The boys thought about that and agreed. They would disappear with Lynn.

Once they all arrived at Polly's old house, Lynn did a quick survey of the plantings and got everyone organized. Before too long she had more plants and flower clumps than she could put in her car. A quick call to Dusty and he arrived with an old truck and began to load containers.

Lynn walked around the lot and tried to remember what Susan had planted and where. She had the boys digging up several blooming azaleas. There were summer flowers to consider and a few other shrubs. She stopped, a Daphne! She had been wanting one and had thought about taking one from Jim's yard. This would be better and Dusty was here to help.

They took all they could handle and Lynn promised Polly that she would check the lot frequently to see what was coming in each season. And she would make a special garden to preserve Susan's plants for the future when Polly was ready to garden herself.

Polly finally returned home tired and dirty, but she took

a quick moment to "talk" with Susan about the plants and Lynn's plan for a garden. "She says when I have my own place, I can come back and take your plants to my garden." Susan smiled at that proposal with a look that reassured Polly about life and her future.

# Chapter Twelve

*A*lthough Trong had sworn that he had no interest in the kind of wood work and carpentry his father had taught him, he couldn't resist making comments on the condition of the office and offering ideas for small repairs and redecorating as he lounged in the office kitchen early Monday morning.

During the redecorating discussion, Sparky mentioned that as long as Trong had opinions so did he. "I can't eat too much oily food in my condition."

"What condition?" asked Letitia, clearly demonstrating that she had not read his file.

Wells, feeling as though he should protect her and wondering why, offered, "Sparky has cancer and he's supposed to get hooked up with healthcare."

Letitia thought about that information. "I'll do the research today and see what we can line up." She liked the small glint of approval she saw in Wells' eyes. A weekend of sex was having an influence on both of them.

After very detailed discussions about Trong's repair ideas and Sparky's health and menu concerns, the plan evolved: Trong and Wells would take the truck to the building supply store to price out material; Sparky would walk to the grocery store for food stuffs for lunch; Letitia would delve into the miasma of healthcare.

While the men were gone Letitia read through Sparky's file and made initial contact with the local social service agency to begin the Medicaid enrollment process. As she phoned, was referred and made notes, her board chair, Rodney Byers walked in. She ended the phone call and smiled, "Good morning, reverend. Do you have a committee meeting this morning?" She didn't want any board members to run into the cons this week, at least not until she had things under better control.

"No, Letitia," he replied, "I just want to make certain you're all right. I'd like us to have a good relationship. It'll help make our project a success."

Letitia got up from her desk and walked with him into the reception area where they could sit comfortably on chairs she had found at a thrift store. Her goal was to get him out before the guys returned. "Thank you so much," she simpered, and hoped he believed her, "I want us to work together, too. I'm busy today going over the men's files and lining up work and training ideas based on their skills. I told the curriculum committee I would email that report this afternoon."

"Fine, fine," said Rodney as he looked around the dusty space. "Do you need help cleaning our offices?"

"No," she hurried her reply, "I plan on assigning that task to our clients, sort of a training program to see how hard they can work."

"Fine, fine," said Rodney, not knowing what more to say because, as a long time minister, he knew when other things were not being said. He stood. "You call me if you think any of our board members can help you."

Letitia stood and walked with him to the door. She watched him drive away as Sparky came around the corner with his grocery bag. Whew, she thought.

~ ~ ~

Lynn could hardly concentrate at the office Monday morning. All those plants were waiting for her. There were shrubs and mounds of perennials and she even managed to dig up early spring bulbs. They were finished blooming for the season – but there would be next year.

Bev came into her office. "I hear you dug up Susan's

plants."

"Who told you?"

"Word gets around." She stared at Lynn. Lynn folded
"I'll share."

"Great," beamed Bev. "There's a small memorial garden
in front of the public library. I talked with the other
commissioners and we thought we should do something
from Susan there with a plaque. All former commissioners
who have passed have a small plaque and a plant from their
friends. We thought something from her garden would be
perfect."

Lynn smiled warmly. "I think that's a great idea. I have
several azaleas and lots of bulbs and hostas."

"Did you dig up those two azaleas on either side of her
front door?"

Lynn nodded. "You can have one. I promised Polly I
would hold everything until she has a garden of her own."

"It's a deal. Call the county maintenance department
head and he'll send someone out to get it."

Bev left the office but Lynn could hear people talking in
the reception area. She wondered who was going to
interrupt her next. "Father Nick," she gasped in surprise.
She gestured the priest to a chair.

"I'm here because you have some of Susan's plants."

"Who told you?"

He raised his eyes to the heavens.

Lynn rolled her eyes. "What do you want?"

"The parish garden club is working on a prayer and
meditation garden in that shady area in the trees beside the
parking lot. Susan and her family are long time members of
our parish. So we thought one of her plants – -"

"I'm not certain what the garden club is looking for,"
said Lynn, "but I know the spot you mean. I have several
shade loving perennials and some bulbs." She wrote a note
and handed it to him. "Tell them I have Lenten roses and

hostas and spring bulbs. Once the summer flowers are out I'll go back and salvage what I can."

He nodded and held her hand as he took the note. "Are you really saving the plants for Polly?"

She smiled. "I told Polly she can come back when she has her own garden and take her mother's plants."

Father Nick squeezed her hand. "What an act of love." Lynn blushed at his sincerity.

They turned as someone stood in her office doorway. It was the Philanthropies board treasurer. Father Nick stood, looked H. Lawrence Grayson over from head to toe, then commented to Lynn, "God's smiling on you today." He gave the attorney a nod, "Herbie," and left the office.

"How does he know about Herbie," demanded H. Lawrence Grayson. It was a name he earned one drunken night. Lynn looked toward the heavens. Herbie rolled his eyes.

# Chapter Thirteen

Carrying out Trong's decorating and rehab projects meant spending money. Letitia was concerned that her budget would suffer if she met all of his demands. After some thought she drove Trong out to her brother-in-law's place of business and asked if they could borrow some tools. Trong made a favorable impression when he outlined his plans and his needs. Her sorry-ass brother-in-law almost redeemed himself when he suggested that they visit the Habitat thrift store for bits and pieces needed for the project. As he said, "You won't believe the crap people give away that has a lot of life yet."

A visit to the Habitat store had Trong delirious, he found thingies and doodads and wires and old tools that he absolutely needed. Letitia made her nonprofit pitch to the store manager. He checked with Lynn, then offered her a sizable discount on material and supplies. Trong even found cans of paint that he wanted to use to repaint the interior. Letitia was perplexed at what lit someone's fire, but helped him load the purchases into the truck.

Back at the office things were moving along. Wells had taken on the responsibility of the exterior. He started in the back yard wanting to get the trashcans arranged in the alley so that the city pick up would be reinstated. Letitia had called for instruction and he thought he had the area as required.

And Sparky had a warm soup cooking and a tray of sandwiches and a light dessert. He told Letitia that before his illness he had worked in the prison kitchen.

And that's how the week moved along at the office.

Except, of course, that at every opportunity, the men managed a little bank recon and some quiet discussion as they helped Wells with late afternoon yard work.

~ ~ ~

Jason would be home tomorrow. Lynn was frantic. Things had been so busy that she had forgotten to bring in supplies. Once her son arrived from college for the summer there would be a constant flow of other youngsters through her kitchen. They would demand food.

Fortunately for Jason and the other kids, she was able to leave work a little early to strip the shelves bare at the grocery store. She piled snacks and frozen pizzas and soft drinks and trail bars and fruit and breads and lunchmeats and cheeses into the cart. And ice cream – how could she forget ice cream. She raced back through the store to the freezer section. Five or six different flavors should do it for a few days. Then she spied a few interesting frozen snacks and tossed them in the cart. It was now very wobbly. Cereal! How could she forget cereal! Seven different varieties. Adding two gallons of milk to the cart was almost the last straw. She managed to get to the cashier without dropping, spilling or running over anyone or anything. She even weakened and agreed to let a bag boy help her out with her purchases. That was because she staggered when she saw the final total.

Pulling into the yard, she moaned to herself, because she was home alone – no one to help unload these supplies. So she began to ferry bags of food into the house. Luckily her father arrived as she was pulling more bags from her car. She scowled at him and he understood. He picked up some of the groceries. He got inside and began to unpack things. She went out for more bags. Will came into the yard. He was a well-trained brother and took the bags from her arms and carried them into the kitchen – where he found Jim sampling some of the snacks. Of course, Will had to eat his share. Lynn carried in the last of the bags and found her father and brother eating chips, digging into two different flavors of ice cream and opening packages of lunchmeat and a loaf of bread, preparing themselves sandwiches.

"What are you doing?" she demanded, ready to throw them both out the door.

"We got hungry doing all this work for you," explained Will just before he took a bite of his giant sandwich.

Jim only nodded because he was too busy eating a bowl of ice cream and drinking a beer. Lynn was almost speechless – almost. "I bought that food for Jason. He's coming home tomorrow." She began picking up food and putting it away. The softening ice cream cartons she tossed in the freezer as she gave her father a squinty-eyed look. She pulled the lunchmeat packages away from Will and rewrapped them, dumping them into the refrigerator drawer. She was twisting the tie on an almost demolished loaf of bread when Dusty walked in.

"What's for dinner?" He walked straight into the small side pantry and put away his gun and placed his phone on the charger. Returning to the kitchen he said, "I don't remember that we planned having folks for dinner." He dug the meats out of the refrigerator and untied the bread. "I thought you wanted to go out to the Bistro tonight." The words were for Lynn but he was talking to a giant sandwich. He stopped for a moment as he searched the refrig for the mustard. Looking at his wife he asked, "Did you change your mind?"

Piper walked in with her three sons, two of whom had just arrived from college. "We're eating here?" She began making herself a sandwich. "That's good because the boys got in earlier than I expected. There's no food at our house."

Lynn was speechless now. All that food was disappearing before her eyes as Piper and the boys attacked the sandwich supplies, ice cream and assorted chips.

"Hey, Mom, I got out earlier than I thought." Jason came barreling into the kitchen with his usual stuffed laundry bag on his shoulder. He dropped the laundry bag, stuck his hand in a bag of chips and asked, "Is there any left for me? I'm starving." He hugged his mother, leaving salt and crumbs on her back, exchanged fake punches with the boys and threw an arm across his grandfather's shoulders. He grinned at everyone.

Lynn grinned back. She would just go shopping again tomorrow. "I'll call Marianna and tell her we're all eating here tonight."

# Chapter Fourteen

"Bergy," Mars was speaking in a soothing manner as Dusty walked into the office, "You just call an ambulance. This whole town knows about your daughter. That stomach shows up everywhere twenty minutes before the rest of her." Mars pulled the phone away from his ear. Tee and Danny snickered. Returning the phone to his ear Mars said, "I'm only teasing. Pregnant women are all beautiful. Just call the ambulance first and then call me, I'll get right to the hospital."

He slammed the phone down. His colleagues laughed out loud. Mars gave them a threatening look, "I don't want any comment. Bergy is so nervous. He's been bugging all his old deputies. No one wants to take his calls."

"But he feeds you every night," said Danny.

"We all sort of snack and watch Janet," Mars replied. "I can't believe how much she eats." He had been a welcome guest at the Bergman dinner table all through his youth. It seemed to him the old sheriff was calling in his chips. "Either I check in at dinner or Bergy calls me with a million questions."

Dusty cleared his throat. "Unless you all are planning to deliver Janet's baby in this office, I want to see some work done. The commissioners are having their final budget workshop this morning and I'll be tied up." He grabbed some folders off his desk but stopped when a phone rang.

Mars answered. "Yeah …yeah. OK, I'll get her." He hung up the phone and turned to Dusty. "Janet just left the house to take Sara to the airport. Bergy has an old deputy following them. They stopped to visit Lynn and I told Bergy

I'd take Sara to the airport and send Janet home."

Dusty flicked his wrist to get Mars on his way. Tee and Danny laughed out loud.

~ ~ ~

"We had a long conversation with Tim last night," Sara told Lynn as they sipped drinks at the coffee shop in the business park. "Everything seems to be falling into place." Lynn put down her cup. She was all ears as she sat with Sara and Janet having a coffee and in Janet's case, a few Danish, before Sara left for the airport. "He suggested that I live in their house," Sara continued, "you know, the one they bought from Uncle Bergy. Tim said that way he won't have to worry about an empty house for three years. Because he knows Janet wouldn't worry about it." Lynn laughed.

"So you have a place to stay here in town with no pressure to buy right now."

"It will be crowded for awhile. Janet and her baby -"

"If it ever arrives," Janet offered between bites of pastry.

"- and Polly, me and three kids. Thel and Bergy don't want to move to their new retirement apartment until Janet leaves town. They want as much time with the baby as possible. My sons might live with Mom and Dad for a few weeks." Sara shook her head. "You don't need to hear our logistical problems. All should be settled by the time school starts. Tim says Janet, Polly and the baby will be on their way to Japan by August. He'll get there in July to set up their place."

"Couldn't Polly stay in River Bend and live with you?" asked Lynn.

Sara shook her head. "Janet says that young woman wants out of River Bend and the memories of her parents' deaths."

"Yes, Polly has adjusted sort of, but she is eager to leave," replied Lynn. "What about Janet's business?"

"All taken care of," said Janet as she tried to get her bulk comfortable on the tiny cafe chairs.

Sara bobbled her head. "Pay attention, Lynn." And she began to sketch in the air. "Tim has it all worked out. He says I can work from their house because it has all the tech. I can also work at Kevin's office and sometimes help him as Janet did. Tim and Dad are talking about setting up our billing and office management. Dad's really excited. He's only been retired for a year and has been looking for something. Since his heart attack he's had to stay calm and quiet, but this may be just the thing. He'll handle billing and our administration. Set it all up for Tim to take over when they return."

"And Kyle got us our housing already. He says I'm his secret weapon." Janet grinned, a foamy latte mustache riding her upper lip.

"Who's Kyle?" asked Lynn really trying to pay attention.

"A general who thinks I'm perfect." Janet picked at pastry crumbs on her belly.

Sara shook her head. "The general is our contact with this military IT group. He has to do a secret clearance for me so I can work with Janet. But he said he didn't see a problem because he would hold Janet in Japan for ransom if I was a spy."

"That's why he's helping you settle in Japan?"

Janet nodded. "He found us housing close to a secure office and he has day care services ready. Tim's worried they'll put me and the baby in a secure holding cell or something."

"Is Tim still planning to retire after this assignment?" asked Lynn. Janet nodded. "It sounds like everything is working out. Sara, what about your kids?"

"They seem to like the idea and the other grandparents are in Roanoke so we're much closer to them than if we lived in New Orleans." She tilted her head at Lynn, "I do have one question. Since Tim is your brother-in-law and he's my cousin by marriage, what does that make us?"

Lynn laughed and hugged Sara. "I think it makes us best friends."

Mars walked into the coffee shop. "I'm ready."

"For what?"

"Bergy wants Janet home and I'll take Sara to the airport."

Janet opened her mouth to argue, but Mars held up his hand. "It's decided." Sara grabbed her purse, kissed Janet and Lynn good-bye and followed Mars out the door.

# Chapter Fifteen

Jason checked in at the bakery on Friday morning. Umberto said, "It's about time you got here."

"I had to sleep," moaned Jason, "finals were tough."

Umberto shook his head. "You work for me and your tests will always seem easier."

"That's what I'm afraid of," mumbled Jason. He was putting on his bakery shirt and digging out one of the caps Umberto liked him to wear in the kitchen. The day began. Jason was feeling very arrogant – gone for nine months and he hadn't lost his touch. He could still deliver cookies, help prepare wedding cakes, and work the counter.

After school he expected to see his friends stop in – no one. Well, not no one, but a lot of younger kids. He squinted, maybe last year they were the younger kids, but this year they looked like what they were ... a year older. That made him stop and think. He was a year older, too. Did he look different? He was shaving more often and there seemed to be some hair showing up on his chest.

As he thought about hair on his chest and how everyone was aging, he spotted a familiar young girl. She walked out of the kitchen with a bakery shirt on and an apron. She began cleaning up the tables and exchanging comments with the kids who had come in for an after school infusion of sugar. "Polly?"

She looked at Jason, startled, then sort of smiled. She noticed his bakery shirt. "Do you work here, too?"

He nodded. "Did Tim say you had to get a job?" He knew that Polly was moving to Japan with Janet and his Uncle Tim sometime during the summer.

Polly blushed and looked over her shoulder. She moved closer to Jason, "Umberto caught me with some kids and he told Mars and they said I had to work and stay out of trouble."

"What kind of trouble?" Jason tried to imagine what this high school freshman, recently orphaned, could do to get into trouble.

"There were these murders right after Christmas and I was hanging out with some kids who knew one of the dead men."

"Wow." It was a soft statement of awe and respect. "What else did Mars make you do?"

"Not much." She shrugged. "Your mom made me go to a grief counseling group with some other kids. Umberto said I had to work here and your friends, Ricky and Jeff, have to babysit me so I don't get into any more trouble."

"You would get into more trouble?"

"No, but I play video games with the guys." She stopped and placed her hand over her mouth as though she had told a secret. "We use your games. Your mom lets us play at your house."

Jason smiled at her. She was cute and he didn't think Ricky or Jeff thought they were babysitting. "Are you coming over tonight to play games?"

She blushed and shrugged. "They didn't say when we would play this weekend."

"We're all meeting at my house for dinner. Most everyone you met at Thanksgiving."

Umberto had been watching his two employees and finally called out, "I ain't paying for no work." They scurried around the bakery sweeping the floor and wiping tables.

~ ~ ~

Jason texted Ricky and Jeff that he would bring Polly over to the house after work. Ricky was sort of disappointed. Now that the college kids were back home, would Polly even notice him? Jason could drive and he was cool. A high school sophomore was insignificant against a college guy. Ricky grew discouraged as he pedaled his bike to Jason's. Why was he bothering? She wouldn't notice him.

Polly was sitting in the kitchen talking with Lynn as Ricky walked in. "Hey, Ms. Powers," he greeted, trying to look like he might have driven a car over to the house instead of his bike.

"Good," said Lynn "Another pair of hands." She nodded to Polly, "You two know where everything is, start setting out the plates and utensils. Dusty will be here soon with dinner."

The two youngsters followed orders. They had both been at the house often enough, Polly had lived with Lynn and Dusty for several weeks after her mother died. And Ricky had been a part of the gang since meeting Jason.

"Are you dating Jason?" Ricky asked, nonchalant.

"What?" Polly gave him a stare that sort of suggested he were insane. "He's my cousin."

"Your cousin?"

"If his Uncle Tim adopts me," explained Polly, "we'll be cousins."

Ricky grinned, "So he has to look out for you?"

"You mean he wouldn't be nice to me except his uncle makes him?" She scowled.

"No, no, I mean it's nice to have someone look out for you." Ricky scrabbled to save the conversation. "He always looked out for me until I got older."

She scanned the boy in front of her, "Older than what?" Ricky never seemed to have a quick response to her remarks. But today he was saved.

"Good," said Dusty as he walked into the kitchen, "You two go get the rest of the food out of my car." Ricky and Polly jumped to the task.

When they came back into the kitchen they were followed by some of the other youngsters Polly had met during

Thanksgiving and Christmas holidays. Lynn called most of them the college crowd. Polly studied the group. College was correct. They were all older and probably thought she was just a kid. She counted noses – only three high school kids in the crowd, her, Ricky and Jeff. No wonder that Ricky kid seemed so nervous.

"Hey, Polly," Patti Ann greeted the young woman. "I'm glad to see another girl in this crowd." Polly counted noses again – yep, only two girls.

Lynn walked up behind the girls and gave them both a hug. "Glad to have my kitchen filled with kids again." She grabbed two plates from the impromptu buffet on the kitchen counter. "Dusty and I are eating in the office and watching a movie."

Patti Ann watched Lynn take her food out of the kitchen. "They never leave us alone," she said.

"Why?" asked Polly.

"Ms. Powers says it's to stymie temptation. I think they want to protect us."

"From what?"

"I don't know, but I think Dusty sees more than the rest of us." Patti Ann handed Polly a plate. "Get your food now. Once those boys get in here it will vaporize." And they heard the thundering feet coming to attack the food.

Polly sat at the table and listened to the talk. There was a lot of laughter and not too much gross talk. They teased her about working at the bakery with Jason and asked her and the other high school kids to describe how the school had functioned for a whole year without them.

"There was more space," answered Jeff.

"And less noise," added Ricky.

Polly looked at the empty plates. "And more food left over in the cafeteria." The gang howled. Jason pulled her ponytail and it was a great night.

# Chapter Sixteen

Zachary arrived at Amelia's for dinner early. He was slender, a bit under six feet with soft grey tones at his temples feathering into the soft brown of his hair, which matched the soft brown of his eyes. He was tanned and looked much livelier than he had a year ago. He came to the condo with wine and flowers, helped Amelia set the flowers in a vase, uncorked the wine, found the glasses and followed her direction as he set out some strawberries and cheese.

"Did you get my package?" he asked.

Amelia was several years younger than Zachary, but those years had not been easy years. Zachary noticed that the tense lines in her face had softened. He suspected that her life was finally safe and uncomplicated. She was a lovely woman who, if she stretched, came to his shoulder in her stocking feet. She had long black hair that she admitted to coloring and deep brown eyes that sent his heart in a spin, though he wasn't ready to tell her that.

Amelia walked back into her living room and pointed to a large box sitting beside the sofa. "It came yesterday afternoon at the office." Zachary carried it into the kitchen and found a knife to slit it open.

"Now you sit," he instructed Amelia. "I want you to pay attention to these gifts." Amelia was embarrassed to receive gifts from this man. Zachary reached into the box and removed a bottle of barbecue sauce, then he pulled out another, and another. Soon there were six bottles lined up on the counter, each a different brand. With a flourish Zachary explained, "They all claim to be the best and the most popular." Amelia was laughing at the antics of this new Zachary – relaxed and entertaining. "We're going to have a tasting contest tonight," he announced.

"I made shrimp scampi," protested Amelia.

"Not to worry, I can eat it tomorrow. I've eaten your leftovers before." Zachary referred to his visit last year when one meal stretched to two evenings.

"But I don't make a habit of giving my guests leftovers." Amelia was enjoying this evening already. "Does that mean you're taking the scampi home tonight, or are you coming back tomorrow night?"

He inclined his head toward her. "I could do both." He then pulled containers of meat out of the box. The vacuum-sealed containers had the label of a famous eatery in Dallas. Amelia was beginning to think that this was a magic, bottomless box, because right after pulling out meat containers, he presented her with a cowboy hat and vacuum foil wrapped Texas toast.

Zachary had the sauce taste test all planned. He lined up small bowls for the sauce, making certain he didn't confuse any of the brands or mix them accidentally. Then he opened the package and put the chopped beef and brisket on the stove and pushed the scampi aside. "I would have reheated all of this over a wood fire, but we'd starve," he mumbled. Amelia threw her head back and laughed.

"I'll get our plates and set the table on the porch." She stopped. "Unless we're supposed to eat this standing at the stove?" He winked at her and smiled. They worked quietly for some time heating the meats and lining up the sauces out on the porch table. Amelia carried her salad out to the table as an afterthought. When Zachary finished his party preparations, Amelia turned off her stove deciding that she would put the scampi away once Zachary had gone for the night.

"They all taste alike to me," admitted Amelia after she had sampled each of the six varieties of sauce. An empty meat platter yawned back at her.

"Me, too," confessed Zachary as he pushed his plate away. "All of my Texas friends must have different taste buds."

"Maybe they have more refined taste buds, you know, after eating this all of their lives they can tell the difference." Amelia dipped her finger into a nearby sauce. "You spent all your time in Texas eating barbecue?"

"Sometimes." Zachary sampled another sauce. "I've met some lovely people. But Texans are so," he waved his hands, "Texan." Amelia laughed again.

"Zachary, since you came through that door," she flipped her thumb to indicate the front door, "you've kept me laughing. Life must be good to you."

Zachary took her hand. "It is. And you've been so helpful." He held her hand as he lowered his voice. "A year ago I was in a rut, saddened by my marriage history, my wife's life and death. But you listened and encouraged me to move on. I did. I got a new job, made new friends and I'm dating. Can you believe that?"

"Why should it be unbelievable?" Amelia moved closer to him. "You're a good person. And I want to know details about those dates of yours. I have your letters and I've made notes."

"Really?" Zachary was shocked.

"Really." Amelia stood and carried their dishes into the kitchen. "I enjoyed every one of them and thought there were times you should or could have said more. Were you holding out on me?"

"Holding out what?" Zachary followed her into the kitchen.

"Now I know you were." Amelia thumped him on his chest.

"I was what?"

"Holding out." She stared at him waiting for

information.

"You could tell?" asked Zachary in a mystified whisper. Amelia clapped her hands.

"I knew it." She thumped him again. "I want details."

"It hardly seems gentlemanly."

"I'm not a gentleman. Pour some more wine. I'll get the letters." She disappeared and came back with a shoebox in her hands. She took a letter from the box, "Here's the first time you mentioned this Bitsy woman. Is she real?"

"She is and more than I wanted to deal with." Zachary walked out to the porch carrying two glasses of wine.

"How? Why?" Amelia followed him waving the letter.

"She wanted an escort. She said I looked great in a tux and she always picked me up in her limo. Her chauffeur drove." Zachary sat at the table with his wine glass in front of him.

"What happened?" She placed the box between the glasses on the table and sat down.

"One night I caught her with the chauffeur. It seemed that each time we went out, to a party or a fund raiser or some society gathering, she always found a minute for him."

"A minute?"

"Well, usually ten or fifteen, just enough to get the job done, but not long enough to be missed." Zachary toyed with his glass. "They said they were in love, but Bitsy was widowed and her husband had included a clause that prohibited her from remarrying unless she gave up the money. She and the chauffeur never read the will and only took the word of her lawyer." Zachary looked shyly at Amelia. "I read the will and explained that they could still have a relationship, just not marry if they wanted to keep the money."

"How much?"

Zachary sighed, "Tens of millions."

"I wondered why you wrote about Bitsy for weeks and

then, poof, she was gone. Now I understand. They must be grateful." Amelia sipped her drink.

"No," Zachary shook his head. "They split once they knew what was what. Bitsy liked the excitement of flaunting respectability. Once they could be out in the open she lost interest." Amelia was laughing again. "Did she come back to date you?"

"No, she told me I was too uninteresting." Zachary put his elbows on the table. "By that time I was disenchanted with her anyway. I moved on."

"That's right, next was Sweetlips." Amelia pulled another letter from her shoebox.

"It's amazing the kinds of names some of those women had." Zachary frowned at the thought.

"What happened to her?" Leaning on the table Amelia propped her head on one hand as she looked at him.

"She liked women." Zachary laughed and Amelia laughed along with him. "I was shocked. She was a born and bred Texan. She explained her story the first time I took her out. She asked me to help her keep her sexual preference secret by becoming an adoring escort."

"Did you?"

"I told her that unless I was the first man to whom she had proposed this idea, all the other men had talked and all of her friends knew. I advised her to face her life and live with dignity. I told her about Cynthia and my great humiliation. Then I suggested that facing life would serve her better." Zachary looked at Amelia. "Her partner turned out to be one of my business associates."

"Are you keeping notes for a book, Zachary?" Amelia was enjoying the conversation. She poured more wine, emptying the last drop into Zachary's glass. He searched the kitchen and returned with another bottle to help them continue their evening uninterrupted.

"I don't have to keep notes. You have my adventures

well organized." He tapped the shoebox. They talked for the remainder of the evening, laughing, drinking and reviewing a year's worth of letters.

"I should be going," suggested Zachary finally. "I'll return for left overs tomorrow if I may?"

"Yes, but don't you have to catch a plane?"

"I might stay an extra day."

~ ~ ~

It had been a week and Wells and Letitia were an established twosome in the house. Trong and Sparky had learned to ignore them. In fact, Sparky had moved the TV to his bedroom and invited Trong to join him nightly for viewing. As he had whispered, "It don't drown out all the sound, but it's better than nothing."

In the other bedroom, Letitia and Wells had spent the nights in mutual exploration -something neither one of them had ever experienced in the past. Both had been used to sex as random, one night stands. Some nights they even enjoyed talking afterwards. Although neither had any practice in building a relationship, they were progressing at a pleasant rate. Letitia found Wells easy to talk to and had told him about her fractured relationship with her mother and sister. He talked about his own mother and their years together, absent a never identified father. Wells and his mother had lived with her father and built a reasonable family unit also enjoying relatives and friends in their small Kentucky community – a concept of family life that Letitia envied.

He laughed. "We had some good times. My granddaddy said he was never sure who was the parent and who was the young'un. Mama just liked dancing and parties, so when I grew up so tall and big, she just took me along to her parties and bars. We did have some good times." He pulled Letitia closer so he could fondle parts of her body. "Sometimes I did have to rescue her. Ma had no sense."

Letitia sighed. "My mama never took me anywhere. She

always said I was too big and clumsy to be girlie and I would embarrass her."

He hugged her tighter. "I think you're girlie."

"Sounds like you had a good family," she said. "Why'd you go to prison?" "We had a good life, but not enough money. I didn't like my mama turning tricks once I understood that stuff. So I told her I would earn the money. I was pretty good and we survived with that and granddaddy's paychecks and then his retirement from the mines."

"She never had a job?" Letitia wasn't certain why she asked. She was just curious.

"She got a waitress job and then learned to be the cook at the nursing home. That happened after my first arrest. She was getting too old to attract good money and needed steady work. Anyway, she's working as the day cook now and gets to bring extra food home for granddaddy. They're doin' okay. But she wants me to come home and help. She can't leave him all day like she used to."

"Are you going to run out on this program?"

"I think I'll wait around for a few weeks then you can tell them I found a job in Kentucky."

"Doing what?"

"Whatever you want. You can say I got hired by my cousin."

"Do you have to go?" The question hung in the air. When had this mutual exchange gone beyond the present? Letitia was shocked at her feelings. Was this a relationship?

Wells was just as surprised by her question. But also surprised at himself because he really wasn't certain that he wanted to leave her. Maybe it was time to just go to sleep. He yawned. "I'm gettin' tired."

"Yeah," she agreed. They separated and lay stiffly beside one another without touching both wide-awake and staring at the ceiling.

# Chapter Seventeen

Sunday evening Zachary arrived early, as usual. Amelia was prepared, as usual. "It's so lovely today," she proposed, "why don't we walk along the greenway before dinner?" Zachary was delighted. As they walked he commented on the bustle on the greenway and the smells coming from Pedro's Casa when they neared the park entrance.

"Why don't we have dinner there?" Zachary pointed with his nose, grabbing the scent of burritos in the air.

"My scampi?" It was sitting on the stove waiting to be reheated.

"I'll eat it another evening."

"You're staying longer?"

"I have some business nearby. I'll be at meetings and back here in River Bend by Thursday." They walked across the street to dine on burritos in the out door dining patio area that offered a great view of the street and the park.

The evening at Pedro's was busy and Amelia knew everyone. It seemed to Zachary that hundreds of people stopped to greet and gossip, including Jim and Marianna Hoefler who were walking along the street and stopped to visit, leaning against the waist high wall that separated the patio from the sidewalk.

"I can see that the only way to spend time alone with you is to stay at your place." Zachary sounded a little disappointed at the evening.

"We can go back to my place for the rest of the evening, but I had hoped for a banana split." Amelia and Zachary had walked to the ice cream parlor on one of his previous visits.

"Won't we have a long walk ahead of us?"

"Maybe we can go back to the condo and decide then." They walked back toward Amelia's place along the greenway. At some point that neither could recall, Zachary took Amelia's hand. Holding hands seemed to make the walk to the ice cream parlor easier, and in Zachary's opinion, too quick. Again, Amelia greeted and gossiped with friends and clients.

"We've walked off all of our calories this evening," observed Amelia as she unlocked the door to her condo. Her dilemma, ask him in? Would it seem anything more than a courtesy? Would he think she meant something else? Maybe he would say something to give her a hint? Should she just run and hide? Amelia sighed to herself, and said, "I have work tomorrow."

"Does that mean you want me gone now?" asked Zachary. He took her hand as the door swung open and entered the house pulling her in behind him. Amelia looked down at their clasped hands. Something was happening. She felt shy and vulnerable. Zachary continued to stand in the room holding her hand, both of them frozen in the small intimacy. Finally Zachary pushed the door shut.

"Maybe we could sit on the porch for a few minutes," she suggested freeing her hand. Zachary followed her through the kitchen out onto the porch. The evening was cooling as it often did in early spring. He sat on the small settee and looked at Amelia with such a warm and inviting gaze that she moved to sit beside him. Zachary raised his arm to welcome her closer to him, causing Amelia to cower and raise her arm in a self-defensive response – the ingrained self-protective reaction that she had used for many years in her abusive marriage.

Zachary was startled by her response. He jumped to his feet and pulled her into his arms, caressing and promising, "I will never hurt you, Amelia." He held her and she cried, at first whimpers that she tried to contain, but as he soothed and caressed, she gave up to great sobs. When she eventually calmed, Zachary sat down with her on the settee, holding her, neither of them speaking as the night settled in around them.

Finally, "I'll stay here as long as you need me, Amelia."

She swallowed, "I'm so sorry, Zachary. I don't know what happened. I..." She couldn't think of an explanation for her behavior. "You may stay as long as you like. It's very comforting to have you here." She sniffed and swiped at her eyes with the back of her hand.

Zachary said nothing, but continued to sit with his arm around her. With his other hand he took one of hers. In the distance they listened to the train whistle as it signaled at a crossing. "That's the eleven-thirty freight," Amelia said as if hypnotized by the sound.

~ ~ ~

Wells rolled back to his side of the bed. She sure is a lot of woman, he thought. But he didn't seem to be out of practice. At least she wasn't complaining. He wondered if they had made their usual amount of noise. Sparky and Trong teased him about rattling the windowpanes. Fortunately they acted as though they knew nothing around Letty. He thought of her as Letty, but never said it out loud. It sort of made her seem close and personal. But she was just sex, wasn't she?

"I know you're planning something," Letitia whispered.

"What?" He hoped the blood got back to his brain quickly because he suspected this was going to be an interesting conversation.

"You and your friends," said Letitia as she untangled from Wells and the bedsheets. "I know you fellas are planning something." This nightly sex was becoming habit forming. She tried not to think about it. "I hope you let me help so that I can make sure I don't look suspicious."

"It's just a little ... idea." Wells felt comfortable saying that because he wasn't lying. The robbery didn't have a timetable or a rehearsed plan, or anything that would guarantee that it would happen.

"I want to help." She turned on her side and ran her fingers through his chest hair.

In a very uncharacteristic move he took her in his arms and held her, sort of nuzzling her brow. "I don't want you to get in trouble."

"What about you?"

"I'm trying to help but make it look like I'm not involved." He ran his hand up and down her back.

"What are they thinking about?"

"A bank robbery."

"Seriously?" She didn't know whether to laugh or cry, but finally sighed and rested her head on his shoulder. "Those two don't have enough brains to rob a toy box. I think we have to help if we want to stay clear."

She could feel his head nod. "You're right," he said, "we gotta help out. Tomorrow night you sit in on the planning."

# Chapter Eighteen

*L*ate in the afternoon Lynn had her usual quarterly meeting with the Presbyterians to discuss the endowed funds managed in their name at the Philanthropies. She wondered if there were any more flowers growing in the meditation garden that she could use in her own. After all, the fund was doing very well; they should show their gratitude. With that thought she scanned the flowerbeds before entering the church offices.

"Lynn," called one of the Presbyterian finance committee members, "bringing us good news?"

"As always," she replied and he laughed.

"Let's get inside then," he said, "and cheer up everyone with your report."

They walked into the gathering and Lynn proceeded to make them all happy about their funds. She also offered to organize a presentation on bequests and estate planning for members of the congregation.

"Would anyone come?"

"I've helped do one for Father Nick at St. Bridget's." She tilted her head. "Frankly, I was surprised at the turnout. So many signed up that we had to offer a second session."

"But, what did St. Bridget's gain?"

Lynn was never surprised any more that church people got to the bottom line faster than anyone else. "Robert O'Hara and one of his colleagues did the presentation. Anecdotally, he remarked that he was surprised at who made follow-up visits to his office and how they made an effort to include the church in estate planning. I think he was moved by their willingness to invest in their church."

Everyone thought about that and wondered if the Catholics were more committed than the Presbyterians. And someone asked, "But was it only because Robert spoke to the folks at his church?"

"I don't think so," replied Lynn. "He has also met with the UU folks. And he mentioned that he found a similar attitude."

The finance committee members sat up straighter. She could almost hear them thinking that the Presbyterians could match those Catholics and exceed those UU folks in gifts to their churches. Game on, she thought. "Would you like me to organize a program for your congregation?" she asked. "I know that you have several lawyers in your congregation who have attended our estate planning workshops. They have all sorts of gifting information to share."

"Don't folks get nervous, talking about end of life issues?"

Lynn smiled. "I think everyone sees life's end as inevitable, but not happening any time soon. That's why they're generous."

"That doesn't make sense."

"Sure it does," she replied, "they're giving away money they won't need at a time in the future that they feel is far off. Win-win." She gathered up her papers and members of the committee gathered at the back of the room for some whispered discussion.

"Thanks," said Rodney as he helped her carry her supplies to her car. "You gave them some good ideas. I'd heard from Nick about the success of his program."

"It's an easy program to organize," she explained. "The lawyers are happy. It brings new clients through their doors and encourages the old ones to review their wills." She unlocked her car and placed the papers inside. "How's Letitia doing?"

"I visited her last week. I think we get our prisoners next week."

"I thought she already had prisoners," said Lynn. "She asked several of the thrift stores to donate clothing. I verified that she was a valid nonprofit making a reasonable request when they called me for information." Lynn mentally reviewed her calls. "She asked for furniture for her office and men's clothing. She brought the men along to get the correct sizes. And I told Dusty I had seen her in the grocery store with her prisoners."

"They're already here?" he gasped. "How long?"

"Maybe a week," she replied and had a funny feeling in her stomach.

~ ~ ~

Dusty slammed the kitchen door startling Lynn as she stood at the stove stirring something for dinner. "Rodney called an emergency meeting tomorrow morning." He put away his gun and placed the phone on the charger. "He says I knew the prisoners were here and that woman was keeping them a secret and why didn't I say something." He glowered at Lynn.

She gulped. "I told you I had seen them all at the grocery store."

"They weren't supposed to be here yet," he growled.

"I didn't know. Besides, they looked harmless." She placed the spoon on the kitchen counter and followed Dusty into the family office. "Are you arresting her or something?"

"We have to figure out where they've been staying and figure out how we're to pay for their housing and food." He ran his fingers through his hair. "You knew!"

Lynn squinted at him. "I told you! You weren't listening!" He always backed down when she used her low and threatening voice.

Sigh. "Yeah." He surrendered because she was right. It was just that hearing about Letitia and the cons hadn't rung any bells.

"What will happen to the program?"

"We have to meet and figure out what that woman has done. It might just be that she has them staying at the Moorings Inn," a small, run-down motel in South End, "and we just have to organize our finances. It is not what I want to be doing tomorrow. We've got budget hearings with the Sheriff and commissioners." He walked back into the kitchen and Lynn followed.

"What's for dinner?" asked Jason as he came through the door. He was back at his summer job at the bakery, and always came home smelling like sugar and fresh pastry.

Dusty nodded to Lynn. They would talk about this later. "We'll be ready to eat in a minute."

~ ~ ~

Letitia gave a warning glance to Wells as Trong washed the dishes and Sparky poured their after dinner coffee. Wells cleared his throat. "Letitia is interested in our plans."

"What?" challenged Sparky.

"She wants to help rob the bank?" asked Trong.

Wells glared at both of them. He was thinking Letitia might be right, these guys are too dumb to succeed.

She settled at the table as though she were calling a meeting to order, straightening her coffee cup, refolding her paper napkin, and clearing her throat. Three men looked at her. "Gentlemen, I think we have to talk about our relationship and how an unsanctioned activity might cause problems."

"Unsanctioned?"

"Let her talk," warned Wells.

"We all have some personal goals, and my late evening companion," Letitia cut a glance toward Wells, "hinted that by working together we could all succeed."

"What's she talking about?" Sparky asked Wells.

"Just listen," he said, "she's got a way of saying things."

"As I was saying, each of us has a personal goal and we shouldn't jeopardize another's goal as we activate any plans." They stared at her. Letitia went on, "I think it's fair to say, Sparky, that your goal is to find good healthcare."

"Sounds good."

She looked at Trong, "And your goal is what?"

"I want back inside," admitted Trong. He added sugar to his coffee.

"And my goal is that I want to still have a job and a good reputation no matter what stunts you all pull. So you see, we all have goals and by working together we can all reach them." Letitia nodded to Wells.

He took a deep breath and returned her gaze as he confessed. "We've been thinking about a bank job."

"That's what she's talking about?" Trong was still puzzled at the conversation.

But not Sparky who thought about the remark, studied Letitia and concluded, "She's gonna be part of this? I thought she was working for the law."

"It's all a matter of semantics," she replied as she placed her spoon beside her cup. "They think I work for them. I know I'm working for myself." She sipped her coffee.

"As I was saying," said Wells, "we've been scoping this job." Saying it out loud made him feel like an idiot – two old cons taking on the FBI? He took a deep breath, "Just remember," he cautioned all of them, "we don't want the money — we want to get Sparky and Trong back inside." Letitia gave him a signal to keep talking. He laid out the bare bones of the great robbery. "We noticed that little bank over in the next block. Don't need a car or anything. The guys can just walk in and take some cash. They get caught. Case closed."

Letitia looked at the three men. "No wonder you were all in prison. That's no plan."

"We don't want a plan," argued Sparky, "we want to get

caught."

"What if you don't get caught?" she asked.

"How could that happen?"

"I don't know. I'm not a bank robber or the police. But I think you should plan for success," she replied.

Sparky was thoughtful, "If we succeed, I'll have money for my treatment. And if we don't, it's a federal offense and I'd do time in a better prison." He grinned. "Win-win."

"That's your goal," Letitia used finger quotes, "a better prison?"

"Better food, better healthcare, better space," Trong explained, "It's all a matter of taste, I guess."

"You want back inside, too?" Letitia asked Wells.

"Naw, I want to get back to Kentucky with no one looking for me."

Letitia felt her heart sort of skip a beat. He wanted to leave, leave her. No, she couldn't think about that. She had to help these jerks or she would be an accessory to a half-baked robbery attempt. Taking a deep breath, she asked, "So what is our plan?"

The men looked at one another, shuffling and fidgeting in their chairs. Finally Wells said, "We've been watching the bank and haven't a real plan yet."

"We know they get cash on Wednesdays. And that Thursdays are quiet. Fridays are busy days." Trong added more sugar to his coffee.

"Three women work there," offered Sparky. "They order lunch delivered sometimes."

Letitia cleared her throat. "It's a small branch bank and part of a banking system with more locations in the eastern part of the state than around here. I've been inside." She looked at the men. "Have you?" They lowered their eyes. "That's what I thought. But that's a good thing. You're not on security tapes." She got up and found a package of cookies that she placed on the table. "Here's what I think.

The two of you go inside on their slow day and time, tell the ladies you have weapons, go behind the counter, grab any cash you can and leave. Come quickly back to the office through the alley."

"No guns," Trong cautioned. "That makes the FBI shoot at you." Letitia raised her eyes to heaven in a silent prayer.

Wells thought for a moment. "Can you draw me a floor plan of the place?"

Letitia found some paper and pencil and sketched the bank. Wells studied it for several minutes and then he grinned at her. "You might have the basics of our job. Let's give this some thought." He poured more coffee for everyone and led them through a very skillful brainstorming session.

At the end of the evening, with their plan sounding workable, Wells said, "We'll talk about this some more, but I think it's time to turn in now." He and Letitia rose from the table and disappeared down the hall. Sparky looked at Trong for an explanation.

The inscrutable Yoda said, "Young love."

# Chapter Nineteen

*T*hrough the early morning mist Letitia watched from her office window as people and cars moved into her office yard. Wells and the other men ignored them and worked outside. She recognized her board members as they assembled in front and seemed to, with a nod from the chair, march as an invading army into the office.

"Ms. Jacquet," called the board chairman, "I have scheduled an emergency meeting this morning." He looked at the other ten people who had followed him in. "Are there enough chairs for all of us to meet here?" He indicated the reception area that had been the former living room of the small cottage.

"Yes, sir," Letitia replied. "I'll just collect more chairs from the other rooms. She took off, with Dusty and another man following her. They soon had all the seating they needed and everyone settled in for the meeting.

The chairman set the tone with his somber announcement, "We have learned that we have three men assigned to our program and were unaware that we were in full operation." Rodney glanced at Sasha Wren, "As our secretary, do you need a better location to comfortably take notes?"

The slim, birdlike woman nodded and moved her chair closer to a small end table. "This should do nicely."

"Then let me begin," Rodney said. He was skilled as a minister at facilitating group meetings and finding a consensus, but he was also skilled at getting all the information out and the guilty discovered. "Ms. Jacquet, we understand that we have clients in our program even though we had not anticipated their presence for another week. We're concerned that you may need our help but have not included us in the planning and delivery of the components of our program." He looked at all his board members. "I speak for the board when I ask, would you please bring us up to date on our project so that we feel comfortable in shouldering our responsibilities?"

Letitia was still standing waiting for the drama to play out. "What would you like to know?" Back at you, she thought.

"What work have we in place for our charges?" asked the community college representative.

"I borrowed a truck and some tools from my brother-in-law. I have the men working on the inside and outside of our office. It was part of our rental agreement." She felt comfortable explaining this facet and continued, "One of our clients is skilled in carpentry and home repairs. He has been doing a lot of interior work. He's repainted our offices and pulled out the old carpeting and polished the old wooden floors. He's done a fine job, don't you think?" She invited them all to glance at the walls and floor.

"Where do they live?"

The million dollar question. "Since our home and hearth committee hadn't finished their survey of potential lodging, I have taken the men into my home."

"That's unheard of," bristled the Baptist.

"We did our job," pouted Sasha Wren, chair of the home and hearth committee. Her committee had developed a list of housing options.

"Ms. Jacquet," asked Rodney, taking control because he didn't want to get into finger pointing, "Do you think that a single woman inviting three men into her home is the image we want to project for our program?"

"What do you think we do," she challenged, "have orgies?" If they only knew, she thought. "I responded as best I could under the conditions. I thought you paid me to be resourceful. I knew you all had other work and I was expected to be self-directed in working out solutions." She moved into the center of the room. "The three men live at my place. We all share the cooking and cleaning. They come into the office with me every day and work on their projects. The local nonprofit thrift shops have helped me purchase clothing and office furniture and some furniture for their rooms at very low costs, sometimes even giving us those supplies. One of our gentlemen is ill and I have been working with Social Services to qualify him for Medicare and Medicaid -"

"What kind of illness?"

"Cancer."

The board members gasped. "Can we do anything?"

At the risk of having the board get lost in the weeds of micromanaging operations and services, Dusty cleared his throat, "It seems Ms. Jacquet has operated appropriately. Maybe we could give the executive committee the responsibility of delving into details and report back."

"That's a great suggestion," seconded the ADA. "I have to be in court in twenty minutes, but I could be back here at four." The others nodded.

Rodney agreed. "We'll get a fix on where we stand and wrap it up for you all this afternoon." He was feeling as though things weren't as bad as he had imagined. With mumbled farewells most of the members dashed to their cars to get to their offices for their real jobs. The executive committee members looked at Letitia. She thought she had survived the inquisition. But someone asked, "Can we see the living arrangements?" Ooops!

After speaking with Wells, Letitia led the executive committee to her home. She cursed herself all the way for never buying that extra bed. Because one quick look through the small house and the first question, "Are there enough beds for everyone?" asked the vice-chair. "Surely someone isn't sleeping on the couch."

"There are men's clothing and women's clothing in this room with the queen size bed."

Busted!

~ ~ ~

Wells drove the men back to Letitia's place before the board assembled for the afternoon meeting. Over lunch she had given him an earful of the meeting and the investigation at the house. After the group had looked over her house, they had reconvened somewhere else, probably a church where they could pray for her. Now she sat in the office waiting for the meeting to convene.

She watched as the board members gathered out front in the street, climbing from their cars. She stood as they entered. They quietly took the same seats they had occupied during the morning meeting and sat silently.

Rodney called the meeting to order and began, "We have looked over the operations of the Prisoner Early Release Program and report the following; our prisoners have been given useful employment, housing, food and clothing. Our board committees have worked for two weeks and have a list of housing options, our curriculum committee has so far developed a list of jobs for men with limited skills and some early training options, our organization committee has worked on a budget, and other pertinent policies.

"What we have not done is appropriately advise and supervise our executive director. It has come to our attention that Ms. Jacquet has improvised in her housing options and invited the three men to live in her home." He looked at the board members. "The executive committee took a tour of the facility today and learned that Ms. Jacquet and one of our clients have negotiated sleeping arrangements that may be determined inappropriate." A heavy silence. Rodney knew they were waiting for his graphic, sort of, evidence. "Ms. Jacquet has told us that she and one of our clients share her bed every night."

"Sinful."

"Unheard of."

"Can he sue us?"

"Or can she?"

Rodney cleared his throat. "It appears that the relationship is consensual. It may be looked at as a conflict of interest because Ms. Jacquet has also paid herself rent for housing the gentlemen. It casts an ethical cloud over the program. We are recommending that Ms. Jacquet resign. She requests that she continue to rent rooms to the men until we find other housing. That will give her a financial cushion until she finds other work."

"Who would hire her?"

"Anyone who needs an experienced executive director." Rodney stared at the board members. "Because no one will breathe a word of the living arrangements at Ms. Jacquet's cottage or she will have the grounds for a lawsuit since her living arrangements were her own decision and a private matter not part of the conditions of her job. She will spend the next three days cleaning out her desk and training Sasha to act as interim director." He looked around again. "Are there any questions?"

~ ~ ~

Dusty walked into the kitchen, slammed the door and stomped into the small pantry to remove his gun and place his phone on the charger. When he came back into the kitchen Will, Piper and Lynn were staring at him.

"Tough day?" Will asked, no sympathy in his voice.

"Sexual harassment," the detective muttered.

"You? Who's accusing you?" asked Piper, always eager to enjoy trouble in Dusty's life.

"Someone from your past," prophesied Will with a

smug nod.

Lynn sat quietly. Will and Piper always got answers. She thought of them as her proxy interrogators. Her husband glared at the kitchen questioners, noting how much they resembled a dark ages inquisition. His eyes tracked to Lynn. She was trying not to laugh. She knew.

"How did you hear?" he challenged her.

She grinned. Will and Piper sat up straight, waiting to be entertained. "I had a meeting at the Presbyterian church and Rodney told me about the meeting. He said he hoped you weren't upset."

"Upset with what?" Piper could only be silent for so long.

Dusty got a beer, got three more and came back to the table. He distributed the bottles and sat down. After a long swallow, he said, "The early release board learned that our former director has been sleeping with one of the early releasees. That lady from the UU group got everyone worried that she would accuse us of sexual harassment or sexual something and did we have insurance and did we have policies. Then each of the church people had to explain how sex policies played out in their churches." He paused for another drink. "Who would have thought there was so much sex in churches that they need policies?"

Lynn rolled her eyes at him in disgust. "You read the papers," she said, "every place is ripe for sexual intimidation and harmful, insulting harassment of women."

Piper added, "Look what happened with the assistant school superintendent in Buncombe County a few years ago. He was a serial harasser. The Board of Education is settling all sorts of claims."

"Does that mean you're on the hook to pay off this woman who got romanced by the con?" Will liked details. The women hissed their disapproval at his insensitive question. "I understand the issue," continued Will, "but we men are so different. If some women wanted to pat a guy's behind he'd just feel validated that he had a sexy butt." He grinned at the group. They all scowled back. "Come on, Dusty, when's the last time someone grabbed your ass? Didn't it ratchet up your self esteem?" More scowls.

"And who's grabbing your ass?" asked Will's wife.

Dusty rubbed his eyes and then stared at his family. "Are you forgetting that I see what happens when harassment gets beyond a grab and into violence or what happens to victims too young and frightened to seek protection?" Everyone nodded. "The issue is difficult to police, investigating incidents along a social yardstick, somewhat ill-defined, going from clueless to intentionally threatening and harmful."

"I remember once I was at a dinner with my ex," began Piper. "We were sitting with several friends at a round table. The man next to me placed his hand on my knee. I took his hand and placed it on the table, sort of not gently."

"That's my girl," bragged Will.

"All I mean, " continued Piper, "was that I was on my own. My ex was already high. The group of friends we were with would all be high soon and I was the one who had to have my back. I'm sure it's even scarier for young women these days. They can't even trust the men around them or that anyone will believe them."

"Patti Ann says that in college the girls are given all sorts of cautions and advice about situations to avoid and safe locations on campus and emergency phones." Lynn took a drink. "She says that the girls are told to never leave a girl behind. When you leave a party leave with all your friends. Don't leave a girl behind, especially one who has had too much to drink." Everyone was silent as they thought about all the implications of sex and life.

"What was the outcome at your board meeting?" asked

Lynn, upset thinking about Patti Ann being unsafe at school. "Rodney didn't give me details."

"Our director, Letitia, is having an affair with one of the cons." Dusty got up and found some pretzels that he tossed on the table. "It seems that this guy Wells and Letitia are in a romantic relationship." They all choked on pretzel crumbs.

Lynn grimaced. "She's so ... large."

"There's no explaining what causes that spark," said Piper and she glanced at her husband who winked at her.

"Wells is a big guy, too," offered Dusty. "He had the reputation for protecting the older prisoners and keeping the young toughs away from his friends."

"A sort of Robin Hoody guy?" asked Will.

"So that means he isn't taking advantage of Letitia," offered Lynn.

"After listening to all the discussion," Dusty pushed out a sigh, "I can't tell who, if either of them, is taking advantage of the other. I give her credit, though. Letitia took her medicine, never begged for mercy, never tried to blame Wells, and spoke with respect for the three cons in the program."

Lynn thought about that. "That's not what I would have expected. She may have more character than I first guessed."

"Sounds like she's a character, all right," groused Will.

"Like I said," Lynn remarked, "more character than I expected." Maybe she would visit that office.

~ ~ ~

Letitia arrived home after the board meeting and walked right into Wells arms as he was setting the kitchen table for dinner. "They fired me." He held her and the other two men sat in chairs and waited for the rest of the drama to unfold.

"It'll be okay," said Wells as he looked helplessly at his

friends. "We'll think of something."

"They're just mad that we sleep together." She wiped her eyes. "The hypocrites! They know more people than us who fornicate, or adulterate, or things." She rested her head on Wells shoulder for a minute. She turned toward Sparky. "We have to rob that bank, soon. That's your only way to get care."

"Now, we don't have to do anything today." Wells thought he should rein in her eagerness.

"Not today," she sniffed, "Thursday like we planned."

"We don't have it all ready," argued Trong. "We never said this Thursday."

Sparky, who had learned over the years to listen before leaping, said, "Let's hear her out." Three men looked at Letitia.

She sat at the remaining chair at the small kitchen table. The sun was just setting through the trees, dancing off the empty dishes on the table. "I think you can grab cash from the counter like we talked and walk out of the building before the women pull themselves together. Duck behind the small dumpster. Keep your dresses on until you get behind our office --"

"Dresses?"

"We did a little planning in bed last night," Wells confessed. "You're going to wear Letty's big dresses over your work clothes. Put some sort of hats on your heads and cover our faces. Wear latex gloves. I checked the cameras, nothing's pointed at the dumpsters, walk behind them and straight out to the street."

Sparky and Trong were not buying the scenario. Letitia continued the plan anyway. "You can walk away from the bank, down the sidewalk, cut through the property behind the office and be back at work before the alarm is sounded."

The men thought silently, seeming to play alternate ideas in their minds. "If we walk, not run, straight back from the dumpster, so it hides us from cameras," Sparky offered, "we only got to go past two old houses and run between the green house and the yellow."

"Then cross the alley to the office back yard," said Letitia. They nodded.

"Then what?" asked Trong.

She smiled at him. "Nothing. Over the next two days we'll work on the yard, because that's part of our lease with the landlord. We'll just mix your bags from the robbery with the yard waste bags. Believe me, five minutes after the police get the call Dusty Reid will be on our doorstep. The three of you will be in the front yard, in your work clothes, doing yard work." She looked at them triumphantly. "I'll say you had some lunch and have been working all day. He'll see the yard waste. He can walk through the office. Check the truck, my car."

"What if he looks in the waste piles?"

"Make sure the money bags are hidden deep," she replied. "He won't waste much time on you because he won't want to be distracted if he's got real robbers he's got to chase."

"They'll have to pull the security tapes, study them, look for get away cars or people running in some direction," Wells reminded them. "You won't be running, you'll be walking away. No car. You'll have to move fast and not talk. What do you think?"

"I think it'll work," Trong smiled.

They spent the rest of the evening refining the script and determining what information and props they still needed.

About eleven o'clock Wells cleared his throat. Trong and Sparky understood. Sparky gave an exaggerated yawn and the two men left for their bedrooms.

Wells winked at Letitia and nodded toward their bedroom. Once inside, he said, as he undressed, "I'll take care of you if anything happens."

"Like what?" She was already naked.

"If there are any problems, I'll have an escape route for you."

"Like what?"

"I don't know, but I owe you. If they nab us, or we have to run, I'll make sure nothing points to you." He threw back the bedsheets and nodded for her to get under cover. "I'll make sure you have a safe place to move. Maybe some new ID. You don't want to stay here do you?"

She settled into his arms. It was almost like having a real boyfriend when he talked like this. "I wouldn't mind moving away," she admitted. "I don't have a job here."

He patted her rear. "Good girl. I'll have it all worked out. Anything goes wrong I'll get word to you. You'll disappear."

With one energetic squeal from the box springs, the night's entertainment began. She hoped that wherever they ended up, if they ended up together, the next bed would be bigger.

~ ~ ~

"You're still mad," stated Dusty as he sat on the edge of the bed. "I didn't egg Will on. I understand these issues." He knew his response was inadequate.

"I'm sad, not mad," Lynn said as she sat beside him. "I've had random butt grabs in my life, but none of the personal assaults many women are making public today. I wonder if I could have done more for my friends. Did someone need protection and I ignored her because I accepted that women should expect to be harassed?"

"I don't know what to say." Dusty stretched his arm around her. "We are certainly getting a lot of training these days." He thought for a moment. "What do you mean by random butt grabs."

Lynn sort of chuckled. "You know, when you walk into

a crowded bar and someone grabs your fanny. But they're hidden in the crowd."

"What do you do when that happens?"

"You just keep your dignity and keep walking. Who do you accuse? Some phantom? Do you stop for finger prints?" She shrugged. "Women have been enduring this sort of disrespect for as long as we've walked the planet. Although in some ways it's better now because we're all more aware. In some ways it's worse because even though we're all aware, it still happens." She leaned into his embrace. "It's sad, and frustrating, and when Will talks as he did tonight, I can't help but think that men see this as a joke."

He sighed. "I don't know what to tell you. I can't solve this problem. My guys know how to behave. We're taught our boys how to behave. My mother made certain me and my brothers knew how to behave."

"We won't find a solution tonight," said Lynn as she stood and pulled back the covers. "But I am vowing tonight that I will ask women if they need help – one woman at a time."

"What do you mean?"

"I think I'll visit Letitia tomorrow and make certain she's being treated well by those men and by her board."

Dusty took her in his arms and kissed her good night. His wife was planning to save the world tomorrow, one woman at a time, and she needed her rest tonight. He knew it was a mean world and he knew he would do all he could to keep her optimistic and keep her safe.

# Chapter Twenty

*L*ynn made an impromptu visit to the Amelia's Maids' office, located in the rehabilitated Victorian next door to the small, dingy cottage that was the office of the early release program. She wasn't certain what to say to Harriette for interrupting the office routine, her plan was to stop in for a few minutes then nonchalantly leave Amelia's Maids and just happen to call on Letitia at the office next door. It was her flimsy plan until she greeted Harriette.

"Are you here with more news?" Harriette whispered.

Lynn's gossip antennae went on high alert. "What are we talking about?"

Harriette blushed. "I thought you were here because you saw them, too."

Now Lynn was almost dizzy at the thought of someone being seen doing something that had everyone eager to hear more about ... something. "Saw who?"

Harriette signaled for her to come closer. In an excited whisper she said, "Amelia and Zachary Rawlings."

Lynn plopped in a chair. She was really dizzy now. "Doing what?"

"Out to dinner and ice cream." Harriette checked over her shoulder, moved closer still and added, "Holding hands." Lynn gaped, speechless, so Harriette continued, "Didn't Marianna tell you she and Jim saw them at Pedro's having burritos?"

"No," Lynn breathed out a long whisper while mentally telling herself to call Marianna this evening.

"Two of our clients saw them getting ice cream and called me the next day for details."

"What details?"

"That's just it." Harriette was beside herself. "There are no details! Amelia isn't saying anything. She's keeping things private."

"That's not fair," Lynn whined in a raspy whisper.

Harriette nodded, "Sad but true. You have to promise if you hear anything, you'll call me." Lynn nodded. "Why are you here if you don't have anything to add to the gossip?" As much as Harriette loved gossip, she was a professional office manager. She liked to keep the work moving.

Lynn smiled. "I just stopped by to say hello. I'm on my way next door to talk to that new nonprofit." Lynn decided that Harriette didn't need any more details since gossip apparently traveled fast through Amelia's Maids. She said good-bye to Harriette and prepared for her nonchalant meeting with Letitia.

Fortunately for Lynn she saw Letitia talking with a man in the front yard of the offices. Lynn waved as she walked from the sidewalk into the yard. Letitia scowled. The man turned to look at the intruder and seemed to become very protective. Lynn suspected that she was looking at the boyfriend.

"Hello, Letitia," greeted Lynn, "I came to see if I can help you with anything. I understand that there will be some reorganization here." She smiled at the man. "Hi, I'm Lynn Powers." She held out her hand.

"Wells," he replied and extended his hand.

"Mr. Wells is one of our clients," said Letitia in a very formal voice. "The other two men are being interviewed by one of the board members." She stared at Lynn.

Lynn hung her head. "I have to confess, Letitia, that before you rented this office, I took some of those peonies." She nodded toward the lavish bushes across the front of the cottage. Then she looked more closely. "You've been doing a lot of work on this yard and garden. It looks great."

"Mr. Wells and the others have been working on the yard and on doing some repairs in the house." The voice was a little softer.

Lynn grinned at Mr. Wells. "I garden so I know that you've put in a lot of work." He nodded. "What are those?" She pointed to a tall plant topped with a purple spire.

"Silver dollars," said Letitia, moving closer to one of the plants. "They turn into those seed pods that everyone puts into dry arrangements."

"I never saw them in this form." Lynn was charmed by the plant, so different from the stem of dangling disks it would become later in the summer.

"Do you want some?" asked Wells. "We have a lot and they spread."

"Can I transplant them now?"

Letitia moved toward a small clump of greenery coming up in front of some bricks defining a garden. "Take these. We were just talking about throwing them out. This plant blooms with a flower every other year. So these clumps won't have flowers this year."

Lynn was always delighted to get new plants and she thought that this exchange indicated that she and Letitia had reached some sort of plateau, or something. Mr. Wells got a trash bag from a truck in the yard and shoveled up several non-blooming plants that he carefully placed in the bag.

"These should work. I think more shade than sun. Can I put these in your car?"

"I can take them, I've parked my car at Mr. Grayson's office." She smiled at Letitia and Wells. "Thank you. And if there is anything I can do for either of you, please call me." She took her bag of plants and returned to her car.

They watched her leave. "She was sincere," said Wells.

"Her husband is a cop," Letitia informed him.

Wells looked at her. "She'll still help you." He moved

131

closer but didn't touch her. "I worry that if something goes wrong, you'll be alone. She'll help. I know she will."

Letitia looked at him. No one had ever cared about her as much as Wells seemed to. "If you think so."

He nodded.

~ ~ ~

Leaving work Lynn headed straight for her father's place. She had an issue with Marianna – not sharing gossip!

Marianna was in the yard working on the small flowerbeds that flanked the steps to the front porch. She stood and rubbed her back as Lynn climbed from her car. "I don't have any plants," was Marianna's defensive statement.

"I'm not here for plants," smirked Lynn, "I have enough."

"You do?" asked Marianna in a stunned voice. "You mean we're all safe from robbery."

"I don't steal plants," Lynn retorted, "I adopt them. Offer them a better home." Marianna rolled her eyes and Lynn ignored her. "Besides, Polly asked me to collect all the plants I could from Susan's old gardens since Dad plans on clearing the lot to sell."

"What a great idea!"

"I told Polly I would create a garden just for Susan's plants and Polly could take them when she had her own place and started a garden."

Marianna sniffed and dashed a tear from her eye. The tear caught on her gardening glove, which left a small smear of dirt. Lynn hugged her and deftly caught the dirt and a second tear with a tissue from her pocket. Marianna smiled. "You are a perfect stepdaughter, even if you raid gardens. But why are you here?"

"Can't I just visit?"

"But we'll see each other tonight. Remember, Piper is having us over for a wine planning dinner."

Lynn's eyes bulged. "I forgot. And the reason I forgot is because of Amelia and Zachary."

"What do you know?" asked Marianna almost breathless with anticipation.

"Nothing, and why didn't you tell me you saw them?" Lynn accused.

Marianna shook her head as she took off her gloves and sat on the porch step. She patted the space beside her and Lynn sat. "I didn't know what to make of it. We saw them at Pedro's having dinner. I asked your father and he said that they were probably old friends."

Lynn gasped. "That's not true. They only met ...well, I don't know when they met, but it had to be recently because-"

"I know, because socially," interrupted Marianna, "they had no reason to meet."

Lynn nodded. "Even without consideration for the social strata of River Bend, Zachary doesn't live here. He never has, even when he was married to Nathan's sister."

"So," speculated Marianna, "it is something to be interested in."

"Yes," agreed Lynn. "I saw Harriette this afternoon and everyone who saw them around town has been calling the office searching for information."

"And?"

"Nothing."

"That's not fair," moaned Marianna. "Amelia is such a sweetheart. Do you think it's something?"

Lynn looked at her solemnly. "I'll put some feelers out."

"That's all we can ask," said Marianna.

~ ~ ~

Evenings at Letitia's place had become quite cozy. Sparky wasn't a bad cook, and Trong turned out to be skilled at hacking into the cable service so Letitia now had access to all the programming that she couldn't afford.

133

After dinner they cleaned and pulled up to the table for their usual review of the day's recon and the refinement of the robbery plan. "What did you see today?" Wells opened the meeting.

Trong began, "Just like last Wednesday. The truck pulled up, the guards open the back, pick up the money and walk into the bank. This will work." He smiled at Letitia because she had proposed this scheme. "Thursday should be quiet."

Sparky sat up straight. "I timed the escape route. We can be back at the office in two minutes, if we walk fast but don't run. At that green house we leave the sidewalk and walk back to the office. It might take a little longer if we try to pull off our clothes while walking."

"I think it best that you at least get rid of the wigs and hats and gloves," offered Letitia. "Don't pull off the dresses until you come through the back yard. Since you'll have your trousers underneath you can pull the dresses up and sort of twist them to look like shirts. And wear the black oxfords we got at the thrift store." They looked at her. "They are the most nondescript shoe I can think of. We don't want someone noticing any shoes with stripes or your prison release work boots."

Wells nodded to the men. "I'll have the trash bag open. Just toss the clothes in and move fast," he said. "Sparky you close the bag and stuff it in the trash can for the green house. Trong bury that big purse under the yard waste and begin working as quickly as you can."

Letitia nodded in agreement. "I'll also keep the remains of lunch sitting in the break room. It's those little touches that will support our alibi."

"What about your skinny shadow?" They were going to have to do all this with Sasha Wren at Letitia's side. She was still training to take over as interim director.

"Wells and I will keep her distracted as long as you

return fast," Letitia promised the robbery team.

"We will."

With the discussion wrapping up, Letitia wondered what criminals did the night before a job. Did they party? Go to bed early? Have a big breakfast? Then she caught Wells' eye and knew that at least one criminal had sex the night before a job.

# Chapter Twenty-One

*A*melia had been distracted all day. Her spring-cleaning schedule was moving without her assistance. She seemed to be a roadblock whenever she stopped to check on her cleaning crews. Deciding that she was useless checking on her crews, she returned to the office where Harriette said, "Amelia, you're in my way. What's bothering you?"

"Spring fever?" Amelia recklessly diagnosed her problem.

She couldn't drag her mind away from Sunday night. Zachary had stayed until midnight. He had hugged her gently as he left the condo, asking "I'll be back Thursday. What time do we have our leftovers?"

Amelia had said shyly, "I'll be home at five." Thinking again about that night and being reminded that today was Thursday, she bumped into a filing cabinet and realized Harriette was correct, she was in the way.

Harriette looked at her and laughed. "You need a few days away from here. Stay away tomorrow, too. Start your weekend early."

"When did you become the boss?" teased Amelia. Harriette made a dismissing motion and Amelia said, "OK, I'll get out of your way. And I might take your advice about tomorrow." Amelia left the offices she leased in H. Lawrence Grayson's old renovated Victorian house.

~ ~ ~

There was a lot of activity in the early release office this morning. Letitia was being shadowed by Sasha who seemed to have a thousand questions for every office operation. She also had suggestions about reorganizing the files, moving

*137*

furniture and redoing landscaping. Whenever Letitia took a phone call Sasha wandered out to the yard to kibitz with the men, hinting that this shrub should be moved or that shrub trimmed. Letitia always reeled her back into the office so the men could set the yard up for the after-robbery tableau.

If Sasha's presence wasn't enough distraction, several other board members came by. Two members of the curriculum committee stopped in to discuss the analysis Letitia had prepared of the men's prison training, education levels and interests. "But they don't have many skills," said one member, resigned to a daunting task. "Did they all graduate from high school?"

Letitia paged through the files. "They all did. But remember they're not young and tech savvy. They were in high school just before computers. Wells is the youngest. Trong, the little guy, was in the Army. I'm looking into veteran's benefits and training for him." Letitia had grown attached to her houseguests. She had an interest in their future and wanted to help them reach their goals – no matter how limited and strange.

Then that Lynn Powers stopped in again saying yesterday she forgot to ask how the plans that were laid out at the retreat were evolving. Evolving, Letitia sniffed to herself. But Wells liked the woman. Letitia gave her a tour of the office, introduced her to Sasha and kept her away from the men who were stealthily moving their robbery paraphernalia to the alley for a quick departure after lunch.

A representative from the Presbyterian Prison Ministry stopped in to ask about chatting with the men. Sasha challenged him, "Your church doesn't own them," she said.

To which Letitia, thinking quickly, replied, "My plan is to invite a ministry in every Thursday afternoon to allow the men to hear about each congregation. Then they can make their decision about which church they would like to join. Why don't you come back about three-thirty?" The prison ministry person should add the right touch to the post-robbery climate at the office. She smirked to herself.

Sasha seemed calmed by the church offer, especially when Letitia invited her to bring the UU prison ministry next Thursday. "Although, I won't be here after Friday," Letitia stated, "You could consider bringing in your UU friends to talk with our clients. And then you could set up a schedule to invite other churches." Sasha scribbled some notes in a small notebook she had with her for all the information she was trying to absorb.

By this time Sparky came into the office, ready to prepare lunch for the day. Sasha, of course, wanted to help. Letitia let Sparky distract her and let the other men finish the prep while Letitia took care of her own preparations. It was time. "Lunch," she called.

~ ~ ~

Once at home Amelia stood in the middle of her living room, staring at the furniture, at the parking lot, at her feet. She felt restless almost as though she were over-caffeinated. Taking a turn around the condo, she straightened some pillows, ran her finger over a windowsill, walked into the kitchen, walked back into the living room. Blowing out her breath in a loud puff, she threw herself on the couch.

Sitting there with her eyes closed she thought again about Zachary. Amelia was happy with her independence and happy to be alone. She enjoyed her ability to take care of herself, buy new clothes, decorate her place. Why did Zachary keep intruding in her well-organized and safe life? He was rich, but she wasn't clear as to whether that was a plus or not. He certainly had more world experience than she had. He had manners, probably owned a tuxedo, and was about twelve years older than she was. What made him interesting?

She laughed. She knew what made him interesting. He was the only man in her life who didn't want his house cleaned. He was kind, honest, had also survived a hurtful marriage and was more willing to explore new relationships than she was. She had a lot to think about, Amelia admitted to herself. Was she interested in Zachary? Was she ready to be touched again? She hadn't acted that way the other night. She reddened as she thought about her behavior during his visit. Crying? She hadn't cried like that for years. And he held her until she had cried all the tears in her.

But he's rich and classy, am I his idea of a relationship, she wondered? Amelia admitted to herself that this was the other problem. Zachary might enjoy a dinner with her now and then, but was he interested in a hardworking businesswoman with no social standing, or social life? By now her head was spinning. No wonder Harriette wanted her out of the office. She couldn't think straight, had lost her power to think logically and was probably losing her mind.

Right, Amelia snapped her fingers, spring fever. Getting up from the couch, she wandered back to the kitchen looking for some lunch. Nothing looked interesting. Zachary would come by at five, the leftovers looked disgusting. Amelia found her cell and texted Zachary. "Home early, are you busy?" She stared at the small screen – nothing.

"I guess that helps me with a perspective," she said aloud. "He's got a life." Amelia shrugged and ran upstairs to change her clothes. She thought a walk along the greenway might settle her. Coming back downstairs with a jacket, she started searching the hall closet for some walking boots when her doorbell rang.

"No, I'm not busy," said Zachary as she opened the door.

"I was going for a walk along the river. Want to join me?" Amelia stepped back to let him in. "I was just looking for my old hiking boots. I want to get muddy."

"Do you want to get muddy often?" He looked around

the spotless room.

"Don't you know anyone else who likes to get muddy?" Amelia felt as though she were babbling.

Zachary gave her question serious thought. "I know people who like to hike and ride horses and race cars. But I don't think I know anyone else who just goes about getting muddy."

Amelia dropped down on her knees and rummaged through the bottom of the hall closet, triumphantly recovering the hidden boots. "Here they are. I was going to the river near the moorings where I used to play as a child. Or we could go over to Indian Hill and walk along a small tributary that has a swinging bridge and a little pond that should be filled with migrating ducks and hatchlings about now. Or we could walk the old logging trail up to Taft Museum." She looked at Zachary.

Standing in the middle of the room, Zachary stared at the furniture, at the parking lot, at his feet, finally throwing himself on the couch and blowing out a large breath. Then he sat staring at her. Amelia sat down on the bench by the window, waiting for him to speak.

"I have to go home and borrow some hiking shoes from Buck," he said.

~ ~ ~

When Sparky and Trong arrived at the bank parking lot in their robbery regalia they saw a young man with some white bakery-like boxes enter the building. Nodding to Trong, Sparky sidled over to a bench and sat for a moment. They would wait for the young man to leave. As the fellow left the building and walked toward the edge of the parking lot, the men heaved a sigh, it had been a quick delivery. Sparky signaled. It was a go!

The two men, dressed as really ugly women sashayed into the bank. The layout was just as Letitia had sketched it. No air lock or foyer, they were right in the main area. The three women were gathered around a desk in a corner away from the teller counter. They were admiring the dessert pastry that the young guy had probably just delivered. Sparky walked over to the desk and slammed a baseball bat down hard. The women screamed and the pastry crumbled.

"Be quiet and stay put," he ordered. Three women froze. Their training had been explicit. Never argue.

Trong had already moved to the counter and was opening drawers taking handfuls of cash and whatever else he could grab. Wells had told them that the amount didn't matter – get in and get out. Trong opened the last drawer, grabbed – he looked at his hand – lollipops? He threw them to the ground and dashed to the door. Sparky swung the bat in the air. "No alarm for ten minutes." And they were gone.

Following Letitia's instructions, they walked quickly behind the dumpster knowing that the cameras would lose them. Then they proceeded down the street to the green house. All the while they were changing their looks.

Sparky had tossed the bat in the dumpster and had pulled off his hat and wig, stuffing them into his big purse. Trong had pulled up his dress to look like an ugly shirt, tucking it into the trousers he wore underneath.

At the trash containers parked in the alley for the green house, they found the black trash bag Wells had provided. They quickly rid themselves of all the clothes and other parts of the disguise, including the shoes and latex gloves. Trong held on to the purse stuffed with money. As Letitia had warned, "Keep the evidence, or there's nothing to prove you did it."

Once they were back at the cottage property, Trong threw the purse under a pile of leaves and yard waste, and slipped into his work boots. He picked up the rake, moving to the front yard to make himself look busy. Sparky walked into the house and into the bathroom where he slipped on his work boots. He flushed the toilet, ran some water over his hands and slowly walked out into the office trying to look like his bladder was empty and he hadn't any other problems.

Letitia and Wells were working with that Sasha woman doing heaven only knew what. He cleared his throat and walked into the office. "Can I help?"

Wells checked his watch. Seven minutes. He winked at Letitia.

~ ~ ~

Driving to Palmer Mansion with Zachary, Amelia held her breath. She had a contract to clean the mansion and the guesthouse twice a month. Her staff fought for the privilege of getting the assignment. Today she was entering the grounds as a guest. Maybe Zachary would just tell her to wait in the car.

"Come on," he said as he stopped the car. "We can ask Cook to pack us a picnic." Reluctantly Amelia followed him to the house.

"Amelia?" Cook asked in surprise. "This isn't..." She stopped as Zachary walked into the kitchen behind Amelia, placing his hand on her shoulder. "Miss Amelia and Mr. Zachary can I get you something?" asked Cook.

"We're going hiking and I told Amelia we might convince you to pack us a lunch." Zachary turned to Amelia, "Excuse me while I look for some shoes." He left Amelia in the kitchen with Cook. The two women looked at one another.

"Thank you for being so courteous," said Amelia, not knowing what to do with herself as she stood in the familiar kitchen.

Cook smiled at Amelia. "It's easy to be courteous to you. Besides, I was wondering who was making Mr. Zachary so cheerful." Amelia stared at Cook wide-eyed. "Come now," said Cook, "he's been seeing you, hasn't he?"

Amelia nodded. "But he must see other women. We just

talk because we had spouses who were murdered."

"You two had spouses who were evil." Cook told Amelia a sad truth.

Penny, Zachary's daughter-in-law, came into the kitchen with her toddler. "I'm sorry, Cook, I didn't know you were busy." The young woman turned to leave.

"You bring that baby here," ordered Cook, "I haven't had a minute all morning to play with this child." As she took the baby, she added, "Miss Penny, this is Miss Amelia, a friend of Mr. Zachary's." Cook and the young mother exchanged a glance that made Amelia nervous. It was the kind of glance two people share who have found the answer to an intriguing question. Amelia didn't like being an answer, especially since she wasn't certain about the question.

Zachary came back. "Penny, I found these old boots in a closet. Can I use them this afternoon?" She nodded. Zachary turned to Amelia. "Have you met Penny and our baby, Olivia?" Cook was holding Olivia and beaming with pleasure at her role as the baby's chief fan and worshiper. Olivia wrestled to get down to the floor, where she could crawl and explore the dark cupboards of Cook's exciting kitchen.

"We play empty the cupboards every afternoon," announced Cook. "This baby rules. Mr. Nathan doesn't care what I use for cooking as long as our princess is happy." Three doting adults beamed as the little girl opened doors. Amelia grinned at them. This was a side of Zachary she had never seen.

"Do you have time to fix us a picnic lunch, Cook?" Zachary pulled himself away from the baby.

"Just give me five minutes," said Cook as she took a wicker basket from a shelf and began opening the refrigerator. "Why don't you show Miss Amelia the place?"

"I know, get out of your way." Zachary took Amelia's

arm and guided her into the main part of the house.

"Zachary," Amelia confessed reluctantly, "I know this house. I have a contract to do heavy cleaning here twice a month." He looked at her. "I guess you have to decide if you want to be seen with the help."

"Is that what you think of me?"

"I don't know what I think, nor what you think, Zachary." Amelia stood facing him. "I just want you to know who I am."

"I know exactly who you are." Zachary moved close and cupped her face in his hands then pulled her lips to his for the sweetest kiss Amelia had ever received. When they parted he took her hand, "Now let me show you Nathan's house."

When they got back to the kitchen Cook was playing with Olivia while Penny ate a quick lunch. The basket was on the kitchen counter. A bottle of wine nosed out of the hamper. Cook winked at Amelia.

Zachary grabbed the hamper, "Thank you, Cook. We won't be home for dinner." They were gone, leaving Penny and Cook to an afternoon of speculation.

~ ~ ~

Things were quiet in Dusty's office. He thought everyone must have had a big lunch because he was certain they were all asleep behind their computer screens. He heard a titter. It sounded like someone got an entertaining text. "All right," he cautioned, "share or put it away."

Teniquia held up her iPhone with a shot of her son giving his kindergarten teacher a hug. "Moses' teacher brought her new baby in to meet her class." Mars and Danny moved from their desks to check out the happy pose.

"He's really fit in," observed Danny. "How are the girls doing?"

Tee smiled. She always had time to talk about her children. "They're great. They've started to talk to everyone.

Last Sunday Esther even sang in her Sunday school class."
The three abandoned children had found a home with Tee
and her husband. Life couldn't get any better for all of them.
Saving those children from a child porn ring had been one
of the highlights of a successful year for Dusty and his staff.

But there was not enough time to think about that
success because suddenly all the phones in the office rang —
desktops and cells. Mars picked up a phone and listened for
a few seconds. "Robbery at the bank at the corner of
Jefferson and Park." It was a regional branch bank located
at the edge of the downtown close to an older neighborhood
with several older houses repurposed as offices. The unit
raced for their cars.

Arriving at the bank lot, Dusty directed all the law
enforcement personnel through their practiced responses.
Once everything was under control and progressing he
paused to give attention to a thought niggling at the back of
his mind. "Mars," he called, "come with me. Tee, you're
managing this scene." All support personnel within hearing
nodded at Dusty's directive as he and Mars raced from the
parking lot.

"What?" gasped Mars as Dusty took a corner on two
wheels.

"Those cons," was his cryptic response. Within what
seemed like seconds he pulled into the yard of the early
release project. Three men were working in the yard. One
was running the power mower while one was clipping
hedges. The third was raking debris from the shrubbery.
They stopped to watch Dusty and Mars climb from their
cars. With a nod to Mars, Dusty walked into the office as the
other officer stayed in the yard.

"Detective Reid," greeted Letitia, "I'm cleaning out the
office and will be gone by tomorrow." Her voice was frosty.

"Has your crew been here all day?" he asked as he
wandered through the rooms. He noticed the remains of

food in the break room.

Letitia followed him on his tour and spoke from behind. "They finished lunch and returned to their chores." In a confident hauteur, she continued, "You may not like my methods, but these men have done everything I've requested."

"Why are you here, Detective Reid?" Sasha walked into the small office behind Dusty. Looking at her he remembered that she was training to be the interim director.

"There's been a robbery," he explained, "and I'm checking on our clients."

"You see, detective," began Sasha, "how can people repent and reform when the community remains suspicious? I've been here all day and so have they."

Dusty calmed his temper and asked, "Why don't you tell me what has gone on here for the last two or three hours and that way we can allay our suspicions about the clients."

"Certainly," said Sasha who began by checking her watch. "We all met in the kitchen for lunch about twelve thirty. I asked Mr. Wells about one of the peony plants out front and he and I went to see if it could be moved. We came back in, and Letitia wanted me to help her take some books into the other office. I heard Mr. Wells in kitchen finishing his lunch with the others. Letitia and I rearranged the books we carried into the smaller office. Mr. Wells helped us move some furniture. Mr. Stengle came in and used the washroom. Letitia suggested that we have some coffee and dessert before the men ate it all. We went back to the kitchen and the men went outside, but they had left us two brownies. Very delicious and I looked for Mr. Stengle to praise his cooking and I found him in the yard raking out the old flower beds." She looked at Dusty.

He looked at Letitia. "Is that a fair rendition of the last few hours?"

She nodded.

He looked around once more. "Thank you for your time," and he walked out to his car. He and Mars returned to the bank. And never noticed the triumphant nod Letitia and Wells shared.

# Chapter Twenty-two

Zachary suggested a trip to Indian Hill because he had never seen that part of the county. The sun floated in and out of white clouds. The air carried a hint of spring blossoms and all the trees were sprouting leaves with the fresh green of new growth. "Do you like being a grandfather?" Amelia asked.

"That's a strange question," replied Zachary. "Doesn't everyone?"

"No, I mean you never speak about Olivia. Yet, I could tell you enjoy her."

"I never know what to say about her." Zachary pulled into the Indian Hill recreation area. "And I'm always surprised at how much joy she gives me."

"What a sweet thing to say." Amelia patted his arm. "She'll blossom under all the love in that household."

Getting out of the car, they studied the display map of the walking trail. Amelia pointed out the path to the suspension bridge and they moved off on their adventure. When the path was narrow Amelia led the hike, when the path was wide Zachary walked beside her and held her hand in a companionable silence. Arriving at the bridge, they stood for sometime watching the small tributary bubble through the rocks and under the bridge, bending out of sight on its way to the river.

"Did you ever have children?" Zachary asked. He was holding Amelia's hand and felt her tense. Then he saw tears trickle down her cheeks. "I'm sorry. It's not my business." He put his arm around her shoulders.

"I was pregnant once. It was after my mother died. My

husband was so angry that she had no money to leave us at her death that he beat me up. I was four months pregnant. I was never able to get pregnant again." She brushed tears with her fingers. "I think there was too much meanness in my marriage for any kind of love or child to grow." Zachary was silent while Amelia cried softly on his shoulder.

"I'm sorry that I always seem to cry when I'm with you," Amelia said softly, "because you make me happy."

"Maybe you trust me." He dabbed her eyes with his handkerchief.

"Let's cross this bridge," urged Amelia as she handed back his handkerchief. "I want to show you a view of the river." He did as Amelia suggested, walking along an old path that led them through low thickets and blossoming dogwood and a dusting of spring wildflowers. Amelia ducked under a low branch and waited for Zachary, then led him to a small knoll at the river's edge, about fifteen feet above the current. There was a small bench and a trail marker relating a short history of the location where they sat quietly and watched the river and the wildlife and the pleasure boaters on the water.

Amelia heard Zachary's stomach growl. She laughed, "I guess that means it's time to eat." They walked back to the car and their picnic hamper. Cook had supplied wine and glasses, cheeses and breads, and things Amelia didn't recognize.

"She sent us off with some pate. She must like you," Zachary observed as he dug out other supplies. Cook had also included some strawberries and pieces of chocolate. "The only thing not here is an orchestra," said Zachary as he pulled the last item out of the hamper.

They worked at setting out their food on the picnic table. Zachary poured the wine as Amelia chased down a small napkin that was captured by the breeze. It was a lovely and relaxing afternoon. "Too bad we can't do this tomorrow," said Zachary as he shook the last drops of wine into Amelia's glass.

"Why not?"

"Don't you have to work?" He clicked his glass to hers in a playful toast.

"I started my weekend early." She grabbed the napkin before it took flight again.

Zachary was thoughtful for a few minutes, then he took Amelia's hand. "Would you like to take a little trip this weekend?" She stammered and blushed. "I have a place about three hours from here. It's not secluded. It's in a small village but not busy this time of the year." Amelia was flabbergasted. She had no idea how to respond. She wondered what he would expect of her. She wondered what she expected of him.

"It has two bedrooms." He read her mind. Moving closer to her, "My things are already there. We just have to go by your place and we could be on the road. We could have dinner on the veranda overlooking the lake." He ran his fingers across the top of her hand. "You can get muddy."

"You didn't say that a lake was included," Amelia tried to control her shaky voice, "that makes a difference. The mud will be really good."

~ ~ ~

Lynn could hear sirens and saw a few cars racing somewhere. Big deal. She'd hear all about it over dinner – whatever 'it' was. But right now she needed a chai tea. She walked out of her office and down to the coffee shop in the business park. A young woman stepped out of an office. "Going for tea?" she asked.

And Lynn's gossip antennae zinged as she smiled at the niece of Nathan Taft's cook. "Chai."

"Want company?"

Lynn nodded and could hardly resist dragging the young woman along the walkway. Once inside the coffee shop, Lynn called out, "Two chai." Then turned to the young woman, "It's about Amelia isn't it?"

"How did you know?" asked the very professional looking young woman, assistant to the owner of the Stylish Home Design Center.

Lynn shrugged. "Zachary and Amelia have been seen around town. Your aunt would know something."

The young woman nodded. "You know my aunt keeps her lips sealed about anything happening at Palmer Mansion, but -"

"This is too big."

The young woman nodded. "Auntie just packed them a picnic lunch."

"He brought Amelia to the house?" The young woman nodded. "Anyone else at home?"

"Mrs. Rawlings."

"Penny?" Lynn gasped. The young woman nodded. The cat was out of the bag and running amok in River Bend. The two teas were brought to their table. Lynn said, "Put them on my tab." She turned to the young woman. "See you later, I have to make some calls."

"Thanks for the tea," the young woman called out.

"It was worth it," Lynn grinned and she dashed toward her office.

~ ~ ~

That evening while the reformed cons, as Letitia thought of her team, sat for their usual daily wrap-up after dinner, she said, "See, he came to look for you first."

"You were right," acknowledged Sparky. "We was in place and he couldn't say a word. And that Sasha lady was the icing on the cake." They all chuckled. "Now what?" Sparky and Trong looked at Letitia, but Wells spoke.

"Tomorrow we work the yard again and help her finish moving her things out." He turned to Letitia. "When did they say you had to move us out of here?"

She grinned. "I told my board chair that since I didn't work for them any more, you could stay here and they could pay me rent. That wouldn't be a conflict." She snickered. "He didn't know what to say, so he agreed that you stay here until they find other lodging."

"We'll be gone by then," prophezeised Wells.

"You will?" Letitia held her breath. She wasn't supposed to feel this way – this loss.

Wells winked at her. "We all will. I'm working on it." He pulled a vibrating phone out of his pocket and scanned a text message. "Shit. I gotta go to see my mama first. Granddaddy died. I'll leave tomorrow night. I'll take the truck. This won't change anything."

"What do we do while you're gone?" asked Sparky.

"Just look busy. Work around this place. But pack up."

"But we gotta get caught. We didn't steal enough to pay for cancer treatment," Sparky reminded the team. They had counted the money when they arrived at Letitia's place. Three hundred dollars! Sparky had been disgusted. "That won't cover five minutes of chemo," he complained.

"Don't do anything until I get back," said Wells. "I don't think they'll come after you. They've got nothing and the FBI probably hasn't even found this town on a map yet." He turned to Letitia. "If you're coming with me, you gotta decide what you take and what you leave. Once we take care of these guys, we're leaving. We ain't coming back."

She nodded.

Wells continued with his plan for phase two. "I'll get back here for sure Monday, but I hope Sunday night."

"I'm sorry about your grandfather," said Letitia. She patted his knee.

"So am I," he said. "I hoped I would get to see him before he died. Mama never let on it was so serious." Wells found himself looking forward to the comfort Letitia would provide this evening. It made him wonder why he felt that way. He didn't understand, he just knew his loss would not be as painful once he crawled into bed beside her.

~ ~ ~

Driving through the countryside to Zachary's lake house was a new experience for Amelia. For most of her life she had lived in River Bend, not venturing any further than a neighboring county. As she got older and her marriage became more abusive, she stayed close to home. Her husband had never shown any interest in seeing any other part of the state. He stayed in town, drank, had his girlfriends and hurt Amelia. She was apprehensive as Zachary drove her toward this new, frightening experience.

Amelia felt ill-equipped to be any man's companion. She had been married at twenty to her high school steady. There had been no other men. She never dated throughout high school as many of her friends had. Although her infrequent evenings with Zachary had been pleasant, she had no idea what two adults did when they had extended time to spend together. Did they watch TV? Did they sit quietly and read? Or have sex? She was uncomfortable as she tried to fathom what role sex would play in this arrangement. Did it have any role? What did Zachary plan to do? Would he expect anything?

All sorts of ideas swirled in Amelia's head as she studied the scenery along the drive. She watched a hawk circling in the sky before he settled on a tree along the roadside. He was a beautiful bird, in charge and disinterested in the traffic speeding by. Amelia saw old barns catching the late afternoon sun, creating shadows and shapes inside and outside of the structures. There were billboards advertising the next interchange, the nearest small town and the fastest food stop along the route. All of the images along the way made her begin to see a new and different world. Something was changing. Something inside the old Amelia.

Zachary exited the highway and followed a two-lane

country road. "We'll be there in about thirty minutes," he said. "I called ahead and they've brought in some food and cleaned up a little."

"Do you and your family come here often?" Amelia asked the question as she became more curious about this man and his appeal.

Zachary didn't answer at first. Then he said, "I've only been here twice since Cynthia died. I used to come here often to get away from her social life. I guess you could say this was my hideout." Amelia couldn't think of a response to that confession.

Her first view of the village was a treat. It had a storybook quality, lovely gardens, green lawns, small touches to make the town center recall bygone days. "I bought this place about ten years ago," Zachary offered. "I enjoy the restaurants and the shops." He turned into a neighborhood that proclaimed that it was lake front. "Do you like to read, or wander through antique shops?" He turned to Amelia anxious to hear her answer.

The look on his face unsettled Amelia. In a flash she understood that he was as apprehensive as she about this escapade. "I like to do both," she replied in a whisper.

Zachary pulled into a short drive and clicked a garage door opener. Amelia watched as the door rose on a garage attached to a charming, two story lake front residence. It was very similar in style and design as the many homes of her clients at River Bend Country Club Villas. Zachary steered the car into the garage, turned off the motor and sat with his hands on the wheel. "I'm glad that you came with me, Amelia." He turned to face her in the dusky garage. "I hope you'll enjoy your visit." It was a very formal statement that some how put Amelia at ease. Zachary left the car and unlocked the door into the house. He came to open the car door for her. She stepped out and watched Zachary collect her bag and the picnic hamper with the remains of their lunch. With a nod, Zachary followed her into the kitchen.

The entire house was all that Amelia expected, expensive cabinetry, beautiful views and comfortable decor. "This is lovely," she said as she walked through the rooms and finally stood at the windows to enjoy a view of the lake.

"I have a boat. We can get it at the marina tomorrow." Zachary stopped, considered, then said, "Unless you want to get on the lake this evening."

"Tomorrow will be fine."

"Here's your room." Zachary walked into a bedroom at the far side of the living room. Stepping inside Amelia found another large set of windows to view the lake, a bed, writing table, and a large functionally designed bath suite.

"Wow!"

Zachary placed her bag on the bed. "I'll show you the rest of the house." He left the room and Amelia followed. Going up the stairs, Zachary pointed out a bedroom he used as an exercise room, a bathroom and the other bedroom. This bedroom had a balcony also overlooking the lake. "You may stay in this room if you think it would be more comfortable."

"Which room do you stay in when you're here alone?" she asked. Zachary's face gave him away. "I'll stay up here, Zachary, you take your usual room." She glanced toward the windows. "This room is beautiful and I can see more of the lake."

After cleaning and dressing for the evening, Zachary announced as Amelia came down the stairs, "I've made a reservation at my favorite cafe. We dine at eight-thirty." Amelia looked at her watch.

"Am I dressed appropriately?" She had no idea what to expect in this strange new place.

"It's near the marina, and very casual." He walked over to the sliding doors and out onto the balcony. Turning back to Amelia he said, "Come out here, I'll show you. We can

156

walk there." She joined him and studied all the sights he pointed out along the shoreline.

Walking to dinner, Zachary took Amelia's hand as had become his custom recently. They walked slowly, viewing the lake from all the turnouts along the way.

~ ~ ~

Dusty was late for dinner. He had texted Lynn so she was prepared with a simple sandwich when he walked into the kitchen late in the evening. He followed his usual routine and stowed his weapon and placed his phone on a charger. Plopping down at the kitchen table, he blew out a breath, and stretched out his arm. He drew Lynn in closer and nested his head on her waist.

"Tough day?" she asked, knowing the answer already.

"A bank robbery."

"I heard all those sirens."

"I thought it would be easy," he admitted. "I thought I would find out that those early release guys had done it." He released her and grabbed the beer she had placed beside his sandwich. After a long swallow, he said. "They were all at that office working in the yard. And one of the board members was there to swear they had been working all day."

"What about Letitia?"

Dusty groused, "Has she become your friend?"

"I'm just asking. She gave me some plants for my garden." Lynn leaned against the kitchen counter. "She'll have difficulty finding a new job."

"She was there and just confirmed what the board member said." Another drink of beer. "I hope you're not taking her on as some charity case."

He munched on his sandwich, finishing in four bites and gave her a look that suggested if he didn't get another soon he would die of starvation. When Lynn placed the new sandwich on the table she asked, "Will the FBI solve this case?"

"They'll be here in the morning. A team is coming up from Charlotte. They'll collect information and help the bank review security measures." More beer. "And in general they'll try to work with us." Lynn nodded at Dusty's underlying philosophy – work with all levels of law enforcement, turf wars don't keep a community safe.

She scooped out some ice cream and placed the bowl on the table. "There hasn't been a bank robbery since we got married," she mused. "Is River Bend going down hill?"

"No, someone just didn't have anything else to do today."

"So they robbed a bank?"

"So they did something to keep busy. It wasn't a big deal. The ladies in the bank did a quick survey before the auditors got in. They don't think the robbers netted more than a thousand dollars."

"Why bother for so little?"

"Maybe for fun, maybe to test the security, maybe for some reason not obvious yet." He yawned. "Thanks for waiting up. I'm going to shower and get some sleep. Will you take out the dog and lock up?"

"Sure." She gave him a hug and called for the dog.

~ ~ ~

Back at the lake house after dinner, Amelia went into the kitchen for a glass of water. Zachary walked into the living room and opened the doors to the deck, letting in the soft smells of spring and water. Dinner had been companionable and relaxed. Now was the time Amelia had feared. Standing at the kitchen sink, she filled her glass with tap water, then stood staring out the kitchen window at another view of the dark water with lights twinkling along the shore. She picked up her glass and her hands started to shake. She couldn't drink; she couldn't control her hands. She dropped the glass and started to sob. Zachary was at her side immediately.

He embraced her, holding her gently as he stroked her back and whispered, "You're safe with me." He led her back to the living room and settled her on the couch as he sat beside her. "Why are you so upset?"

Amelia looked up at him, curious that he appeared to have no clue. "I don't know what you expect of me, Zachary."

"Do you think I brought you here to harm you?" He slowly slipped an arm across her shoulders.

"No."

"Do you think I plan to force you to do anything you don't want to do?" He gently took her hand in his.

"No."

"Do you think I have sex on my mind?" He began to rub her shoulder with a slow, soft caress.

"Is that a trick question?"

Zachary laughed. "I see the real Amelia coming back. So I'll be honest. Yes, I've thought about sex. But, I've waited a long time, I guess I can wait until you consent."

"What if I don't?"

"Am I that terrible a prospect?" Zachary's voice carried the hurt he felt.

"No." Amelia didn't know what to say to repair the misunderstanding. "I ... it's not you. I don't know if I'm ready to trust someone yet."

"Asking you here was a risk. I'm not a young man and you're young and lovely and exciting and..."

"But you have all the women in Texas and all the women in all the places you travel." Amelia couldn't believe she was Zachary's choice.

"I've spent my entire life with conniving, selfish, pampered women. Other men find good, caring women. Why can't I?" Zachary squeezed her hand. They sat and listened to the lake current lap against a retaining wall and to motorboats out in the dark night and to laughter coming across the water. "Here's what we'll do tomorrow," said Zachary, clearing his throat, "We'll walk through town and visit the shops, have lunch packed at the deli, take the boat out to motor around the lake and eat lunch. For dinner we'll go to a jazz club with great hamburgers." He rubbed her hand, "And if you think you want more from me than food and shelter, all you have to do is put your arms around my neck, I'll take care of the rest."

Amelia sat for a few more minutes. "I think I have to get some sleep." She kissed Zachary on the cheek and climbed the stairs to bed. The house became quiet and two people crawled into their lonely spaces, wondering...

~ ~ ~

Wells and Letitia found that sex wasn't important this evening. They were distracted by events and seemed to find comfort in each other's arms without trying to break the bed.

Wells, for his part, had two concerns. One, he wanted to make certain that no fallout from the robbery hit Letitia. And two, he wanted to get to Kentucky and mourn his granddaddy. He could feel the loss in the depths of his heart and soul. He had thought that old man would live forever.

Wells knew he had disappointed his granddaddy by getting into trouble and getting arrested. But the old man never criticized, he stood by the young man he called 'his gift to the future' no matter what Wells did. That kind of support, that kind of love, gave a body courage and strength. He vowed he would take this early release opportunity and make a life that was a gift, just like granddaddy wanted.

Letitia was too sad to do more than cling to Wells this evening. It was over. He was going. He might plan to return from the funeral, but it would be a matter of days before he was finally gone. He talked like he wanted her to go with

*160*

him, but things were moving too quickly. She and her feelings were going to get lost in the shuffle. And she had feelings. He was a man she wanted to stay with, someone she wanted to build a life with. How did that happen? She knew how. If she was honest with herself, she knew. He listened to her. He worried about her and, when nothing else worked, he just held her like he was doing tonight. And soon he would be gone.

She burrowed deeper into his embrace and finally went to sleep.

Wells, on the other hand, stayed awake most of the night wondering how he had gotten so attached to this woman that he was content to just lay beside her and hold her. Imagine that?

# Chapter Twenty-three

*A*melia awoke early to watch the sun rise over the lake. It was a new and exhilarating experience. She had seen the sunrise on the river all of her life, but all the sun did was shine a searing light on the reality that was her life before her husband was murdered. She shuddered at the thought of those unhappy and painful years.

This was different. This was safe.

After preparing coffee she made herself comfortable on the deck where she sat in her pajamas and bathrobe reading a book. There was a sound at the other end of the long deck that stretched across the back of the house overlooking the lake. Zachary came out to look at the new morning. He was in a t-shirt and boxer shorts. He saw Amelia and ducked back into his room and returned wearing sweatpants over his shorts. He smiled at her as he came closer. She sat very still, embarrassed to be caught in her pajamas. "I made some coffee," she said. He patted her shoulder and kissed her on the top of her head as he continued his walk to the kitchen.

Soon he reappeared with a plate of rolls and the coffee pot. He set out dishes, butter and jam. When Amelia began to leave her chair, he said, "You're my guest."

After a leisurely breakfast they got ready for their boating adventure. They walked through an area of small shops in the village. As had become his custom, Zachary took Amelia's hand. He noticed her squinting in the bright morning sun. "Do you have sunglasses?" Zachary asked as they stopped in front of one of the sundries shops along the way.

"I left them at home." Amelia's eyes watered as she returned his gaze. Entering the shop Zachary walked to a display of sunglasses, he spun the case, selected a pair and slid them over her eyes. Leaning his head he straightened the glasses on her face. He removed the first pair and selected another, going through the same inspection again.

"This is the pair for you." He spun the display case to find the small mirror.

"If you say so," Amelia shrugged. She liked his choice but felt uncomfortable with his unexpected attention.

"And you need a hat. The wind will blow once we're out on the lake."

"Won't the wind blow the hat?" Amelia wondered what sort of boat trip he planned.

Zachary ignored her question and walked toward another display. "This is what we need." He handed her a straw visor that hooked at the back of her head, under her hair. "Now you're ready for my boat. Let's get some food."

Holding her hand, Zachary walked into a small deli where he ordered two sandwiches and some drinks. While the sandwiches were being prepared he walked around the shop and collected a few snacks to carry with them. The proprietor placed everything into a large sack, thanked Zachary and wished them a good day.

As they neared the marina they followed a path alongside a small children's park where several youngsters played on the slide and climbed on a contraption designed to look like a pirate ship. They watched the children for a few minutes then climbed down to the dock.

"Which one is yours?" asked Amelia, marveling at all the craft, shiny and clean, tied to the docks bobbing in slow rhythms on the quiet lake.

"I only have a motor boat," Zachary seemed to apologize. "I don't sail well and have never had any companion who could help me."

164

Amelia wasn't certain what he meant until she realized that some of the craft had tall masts and must be sailboats. "I've only been in a row boat." She was keeping her eyes open for the boat that belonged to Zachary.

"Here it is." Zachary stopped at a medium sized craft named *Alone*. Amelia almost cried as she read the word stenciled across the stern.

"Hey, Mr. Rawlings," called a young man coming after them along the pier. "I got your message. She's gassed and ready. I'll help you cast off."

"Thanks," Zachary looked at his watch. "Can you be back here about four-thirty to help tie us up?"

"Sure thing." The young man smiled and helped Amelia onto the deck. Then he handed Zachary the lunch bag. Before Amelia had settled herself, the motor came to life and Zachary was maneuvering them away from the dock and out into the lake, with the young man waving at them as he grew smaller.

~ ~ ~

"Where's your boss?" demanded a trim, fiftyish blond woman with a side arm and a pocket badge that identified her as Claire Conti, agent in charge of the bank investigation in River Bend. "This town's so small we couldn't even find it on our GPS."

Three detectives stared at her and at the three agents following behind. "Claire," grinned Teniquia. "It took a robbery to get you here? I thought you'd come to visit my babies." The two women shared a warm embrace. "Thank you for the Christmas gifts. They were thrilled."

"Sweetie," Claire said as she held Tee's hand, "I was delighted that you and that handsome man of yours stepped up to love those youngsters."

Dusty came into the office and cleared his throat. "I thought you were here to find some bank robbers."

Claire grinned at him. "We'll have it done by noon."

Her team gasped, but recovered and gave him a nod indicating Claire was correct.

Dusty placed a bakery box on a desk. "Coffee made?" he sort of asked the air.

"Yes, chief."

"Why don't you introduce your staff," Dusty invited Claire. "And then we can all have breakfast."

Once the preliminaries were taken care of, the FBI settled around the desks with the James County/River Bend Joint Investigation Unit. Agent Wilson, one of Claire's serious subordinates, began a presentation of assembled information. "We have collected the security tapes from all cameras at the bank lot. We have requisitioned security tapes from some of the nearby establishments. We have identified all the cars in the parking lot and those going through the ATM during the time of the robbery and a fifteen minute window on either side." He yawned. Dusty's staff guessed that none of Claire's agents slept last night.

Another agent, Ms. Anselm, opened her computer and set up a projector to display footage on the office white board. She stated, "We're going to show you the tapes from the bank cameras and ask that you offer us preliminary identification of the citizens walking into the bank. We'll then review the names of the citizens using the ATM drive thru." With that brief explanation, she dimmed the lights and began a review of the tapes. The detectives shouted out names as the agents took notes and attached identifiers, matched the names with cars in the parking lot, and prepared lists for interviews.

Suddenly Mars started to chortle, then Danny. The agent stopped the tape and Claire walked to the front of the white board. "What is it?"

Dusty sort of growled because he didn't know whether to laugh or swear. "That's my stepson."

"Where?"

"Run that part over again, slowly," Dusty requested. He joined Claire close to the white board. "Here he's walking into the bank with bakery boxes." Dusty's shadow fist and elongated shadow finger pointed to Jason on the screen.

"He works for Uncle Umberto," offered Danny. They watched the screen as Jason came out of the bank and walked past two women sitting on a bench. He kept walking toward the security camera reviewing the messages on his phone and thumbing replies. Behind him all the investigators watched as two ugly women jumped from the bench, hurried into the bank and, within minutes, just as rapidly came out. Through it all Jason walked slowly toward the security camera, still texting on his phone and obscuring portions of the view of the camera, making parts of the ladies appear to be dancing on his shoulders as they scurried behind a dumpster.

"Shit." That was Dusty's comment as everyone else laughed.

The agent managing the tapes said in a very professional voice, "We have other camera angles with unobstructed views. We believe those women are the robbers, based on the descriptions given by the bank employees."

"That's some handsome fellow," said Claire. "When can we interview him?"

"Do you really think he saw anything?" asked Dusty.

Claire grinned at him. "I was going for the entertainment factor."

Dusty thought working with the FBI might become challenging. "Why don't we work on some of the other witnesses first?"

With that as a goal, the detectives helped the FBI review the remaining tapes and compile a list of potential folks to interview. They also reviewed the list of cars going through the ATM drive thru.

"Zachary Rawlings?" asked Dusty. "I didn't know he was in town."

"What makes him special?" asked Claire.

Dusty sipped his cold coffee and sort of shrugged. "A few years ago his wife was kidnapped and murdered. I thought he was working in Australia." He looked at Mars.

The young detective took a breath. "He took a job in Texas about a year ago. Right after Buck's wedding." Because Mars saw the question on his colleagues' faces he added, "He and Nancy left Australia together. She's doing museum consulting around the country." That kind of explained to his friends why she wasn't in town and left a lot of questions out there about the status of his relationship with her. But the detectives knew that this was not the time to intrude into Mars' private life. In that respect Mars was grateful that the FBI was camped at the office.

"Is Mr. Rawlings important?" asked Claire.

Dusty cleared his throat. "Mr. Rawlings is the brother-in-law of Nathan Taft, one of the more prominent men in town. Buck is Mr. Rawlings' son. Buck and his wife have a baby. The three of them live at Palmer Mansion with Mr. Taft. Mr. Rawlings is probably in town visiting his family. Nancy, the woman Mars mentioned, is the daughter. Evidently she's not in town." Mars nodded. Dusty looked at Claire. "I'd like to interview Mr. Rawlings alone. Those days of the kidnapping were hard on the family."

Claire grinned. "You know I can't refuse you, you charmer. Just get the information for our morning report tomorrow." Which Dusty understood meant he was interviewing Zachary tonight.

~ ~ ~

Today was Letitia's last day as the director of the early release program. She packed up the few personal things that had migrated from her house to the office and placed them in her car. She reviewed the office procedures one more time with Sasha, ran through some paper work with each of the cons, and tried not to cry.

Sasha had organized a small farewell lunch with Sparky's help. Several board members dropped by to wish her well. Sparky, Trong and Wells behaved like respectable fellows, exchanging comments with board members, teasing Sasha on her upcoming responsibilities.

In an impromptu set of remarks Rodney, the board chair, announced that the organization committee with the help and advice of their counterparts in Henderson County had developed a job description and would be advertising for a new executive director next week.

Since most of the board members present were those who represented local congregations, Rodney was asked to close the small farewell with a blessing. As all ministers can when called upon, he had an appropriate and thoughtful prayer to share as they bid Letitia best wishes in her future efforts.

The board members moved to the front porch, Letitia handed over the keys, Wells climbed into the truck and left the yard, and she followed in her Bronco with Trong and Sparky. Rodney locked the office, handed the keys to Sasha and wished everyone a good weekend. In general it was a melancholy afternoon. But it ended. No drama, no tears.

~ ~ ~

After a slow turn around the lake, stopping for lunch near the shaded shoreline, and a scenic tour for the rest of the afternoon with a stop at a lakeside coffee bar, Zachary finally approached the marina as the young man arrived at the dock. Amelia had enjoyed every minute of their time on the water.

On the way back to the house, she said, "I can't wait to look at the lake from the house now. I feel so familiar with it that I want to see if I recognize any landmarks across the lake." As usual Zachary walked with her hand in his. During

169

the entire walk, he smiled and nodded while Amelia talked about the day's adventure. She had enjoyed the ride, the quiet lunch on the water, and had been dazzled when Zachary allowed her to captain the boat.

In the house as Zachary was closing the door, Amelia asked, "Do Buck and Penny and little Olivia visit you here?"

"No," Zachary answered.

"Olivia has to come." Amelia stood in the middle of the living room, shaking out her hair as she removed her hat. "We have to take her to that little park, then take her for a ride on those little paddle boats and in your big boat." Amelia was excited about the prospect of hosting Olivia at the lake house. She was talking rapidly, but stopped when she saw Zachary smiling. "What?" she asked.

"You said *we*." Zachary looked at her with amusement. Amelia put her hand over her mouth as though she had said something offensive. "You said *we*," Zachary repeated. This time he bobbed around as though he were doing a victory dance. Amelia turned her back on the room and stood staring out at the lake. Zachary came up behind her, placing his arms around her waist and burying his face in her hair, he whispered, "You said *we*." He found her neck through her hair and brushed his lips along her skin. He felt Amelia tense, so he released her.

She turned around to look at him. "You're very persuasive," she said in a low, anxious voice. She moved toward the door to the deck, as though looking for an escape route. "I think I'd like to sit on the deck and enjoy the evening for a bit."

"May I sit with you?"

"Yes." She stared straight ahead as she left the room, perplexed by the delight she felt at Zachary's touch.

He followed her to a small glider that was off to one side of the decking. "Can I get you anything to drink?" She shook her head. He stretched his arm very carefully along the back of the glider and moved it down across her shoulders. He placed his other hand on top of hers as it rested on her leg. Amelia placed her head on his shoulder. They sat in silence until the sun set.

"Do you want to go out for dinner?" Zachary asked.

"How can you be so patient?" Amelia asked him in a whisper.

"I'm fifty–four years old, Amelia, and I think I've finally found what makes me happy." He held her tighter. "I spent thirty years in a painful, life draining marriage. All I ever wanted I've found with you in three or four evenings together over the last year. I can be patient."

"But the risk?" Amelia sat forward to look back at him. "I might not be what you think. I might decide that I want your money and your boat, but not you. I might hurt you."

"You can't possibly hurt me as much I've been hurt in the past."

When he said that Amelia knew that Zachary would never hurt her in the way she had been hurt in the past either. They were two wounded people, one of them willing to take a chance again, because being alone was not what he wanted.

What did she want? Amelia wasn't certain. She knew Zachary; he was open and honest. She didn't know Amelia. Could she be touched again? Did she want to be intimate with Zachary, or any man again? Remembering life in her marriage made her shiver. Zachary pulled her closer. She thought about all the times in the past she would have treasured such concern and protection. Instead she had suffered hurt and humiliation. And she had never truly been loved. She had only been physically used and abused. She knew being close with Zachary would never hurt and would always bring her pleasure.

Wait? Pleasure? What was she thinking? She was thinking about sex. Yikes, she might be willing. Was she eager? Did she even remember how? What if she didn't? What if she couldn't perform? What if Zachary didn't like having sex with her? She'd be so embarrassed. How would she get home?

"Can I get you anything?" He stood waiting. Amelia turned to look at him and shook her head. No matter how gentle and affectionate Zachary was, Amelia couldn't command her body to relax.

She jumped off the glider. Why was she thinking about Zachary and sex? Her brain had taken her to a place she had been avoiding. Was she ready but unsure about her ... her what, her ability, her style, her charm? There was so much to think about – Zachary and his family, his past, her past. She wished she had another woman to talk with, someone to help her think this through. She thought about Lynn. Amelia was certain she knew what Lynn would say. Didn't Lynn have a new marriage with Dusty?

Amelia walked over to lean on the deck railing with her back to Zachary. Staring at the dark calm water, she thought about her painful marriage and then about the freedom of widowhood. She also thought about her new life, new freedoms, yet a persistent loneliness. But was that a reason to cling to Zachary – fear of being alone? She had good friends and her brothers and, of course, her business. But here at the quiet lakeside there was a new option – a man who wanted her, a man who was willing to be patient. He came up behind her.

"Why don't we have a little snack?" he suggested.

"Am I so ...?" Amelia didn't know what to ask as Zachary placed his arm around her waist and walked them into the kitchen.

He kissed her on the cheek and then opened the refrigerator. "I want you to want to participate in a loving relationship with me."

"I'm sorry, Zachary. You have no idea of my past." Then

she leaned against the kitchen counter as he looked into the refrigerator. "I don't know how to ... ah ... er ... participate."

Zachary pulled out some eggs and bacon. He handed Amelia some butter and jam. Ignoring what she had just said, Zachary offered, "We can have an omelet and toast, or we can go out."

"Please talk to me, Zachary. You're asking me to make a radical change in my behavior."

"I thought I've been very clear about what I'm offering." The sound of his voice indicated his own frustration.

"A fling?" The pained look on his face told Amelia she had been unkind in her retort. "I'm sorry." She didn't know how to make amends. They stood in the kitchen in an uncomfortable silence.

"I think I love you, Amelia. I spent a year in Texas and thought about you every day." He took her hand. "I dated every woman who was available. I never touched one of them and many of them were willing to do whatever I asked. I'm quite a catch, not too old, wealthy and not ugly." Zachary stopped unable to think of anything else that might make him acceptable in her eyes.

Tears ran down Amelia's cheeks. She wanted to run away, lock herself in the upstairs bedroom and wait for morning. Daylight might make this conversation easier. Zachary didn't move. Amelia traced her fingers across his face and lips then kissed him softly. Zachary said, "That's participation." She pulled back to sniff and look for a tissue. He took her hand and kissed it. "Maybe we should just watch some TV." Zachary placed all of the food back in the refrigerator, took her hand and led her to a small office. Amelia couldn't look at him.

# Chapter Twenty-four

*T*he last chore Dusty had to complete before heading home for dinner, and some relief from the intense FBI presence, was to call on the folks at Palmer Mansion for his interview with Zachary Rawlings. On his arrival he was led into the family room where the adults were being entertained by little Olivia. He had to grin; this baby had done a lot for the family in just a few short months. Everyone knew that Nathan Taft, leading River Bend businessman, had learned to change diapers within weeks of her arrival.

"Dusty, welcome," Nathan greeted his friend. "Can you join us for a drink before dinner?"

"I'm here on business," the detective replied. Eyes darted. Buck and his wife, Penny, moved as one to protect the baby from ... what? ... marauding River Bend law enforcement?

Dusty took a seat, hoping that the others would relax. "There was a bank robbery yesterday as you've probably read in the paper. We're working with the FBI to interview potential witnesses. We've reviewed the security videos at the bank and Zachary's car is on them." Dusty looked at Nathan and the rest of the household at Palmer Mansion. "I'd like to speak with him."

"He left a message that he was going away for the weekend," replied Nathan. "Do you think he's in danger?"

"The robbery occurred about the time he was at the ATM outside." Dusty shrugged. "And now you can't tell me where he is."

"You think my father robbed a bank?" Buck was

outraged that Dusty suspected Zachary of such a deed.

"No, he may have seen the robbers. I want to be certain that he's safe and hasn't been taken as a hostage or --" Dusty's cell rang. "Yeah ... yeah ... OK." He turned back to the family. "There's been some activity on his credit card. Up at Cedar Mountain Lake someone bought dinner last night and this morning bought a pair of women's sunglasses and a hat. Then they bought a lunch." Dusty looked at his watch. It was almost six in the evening.

"Now you have me really worried," Nathan accused Dusty. "Zachary wouldn't purchase things for a woman." Penny shifted in her seat, drawing Dusty's attention. He raised his eyebrows.

Penny swallowed under his gaze and the intense interest of Buck and Nathan. "He was here yesterday with Amelia Shipley." Now Penny *really* had everyone's attention. "Cook packed them a lunch. Zachary said that they were going for a hike. He borrowed some boots he found in a closet and left." Penny tried to keep her smile in check as she delivered her information.

"With Amelia?" Nathan and Dusty asked together.

"Yes." Penny looked at all three men, letting them know that she thought Zachary and Amelia alone together was a great idea.

"Why would they be at Cedar Mountain Lake?" asked Dusty.

"Dad is one of the investors in the Village at Summer Point. He has a place there," said Buck.

Nathan sucked in his breath then looked to Penny for more information. "Are they seeing one another?" Nathan liked getting to the heart of the matter and in his experience women always knew the real status of relationships.

"He's been seeing someone." Penny nodded to Nathan. "You know that the last two times he's been in town he's disappeared for several evenings. This week he and Amelia were seen out to dinner at Pedro's and getting ice cream." Dusty was impressed because his detectives hadn't found that information yet. "I think," continued Penny, "that this may be the weekend the relationship will..." She made a movement with her hands and three men nodded.

Dusty closed his notebook. "When he returns, could you brief him on the robbery and ask him to contact me?" They all nodded, smiling at the thought of Zachary and Amelia. "I wouldn't mention all that you learned about his spending this weekend. In fact, I'd wait for him to tell you about his weekend." Dusty sounded like a therapist as he continued, "Those two people have had some bad times. They need some privacy." Everyone agreed, but they hoped Zachary would be ready to talk sooner rather than later.

~ ~ ~

Dusty walked into the house in The Heights, kissed Lynn and said, "You'll owe me big for this information." He kissed her again and continued, "I can't decide whether to tell you or collect first." He kissed her again. Lynn's hair radiated from her head as though it were trolling for microwave signals.

"There's no discussion." She kissed him back. "I have to know if the information is worth missing dinner, being late for our plans with Piper and Will, and explaining it all with some big lie I have to manufacture and they won't believe," she took a big breath, "then have Piper browbeat me until she learns every last bit of gossip I learned through dirty sex."

Dusty caved. "Amelia Shipley is dating Zachary Rawlings."

She scowled at him. "I'm glad I waited to evaluate your information. Everyone saw them at Pedro's the other night."

"Everyone who?"

"Let me think." Lynn held up her hand and with each

name threw up a finger. "Bev told Piper at a United Charities breakfast, Cook's niece who works in the office next to mine came in to tell me; Penny told Michelle who told Sophie Grayson who called Marianna. But she already knew because she and Dad had stopped to chat with them at dinner." With this last revelation Dusty was waving a kitchen towel in surrender. Lynn shrugged, "So you see, you were trying to take advantage of me with bogus gossip." She kissed him again.

"I want to know what you meant by dirty sex." He grabbed at her as she placed dinner plates in his hands. Dusty put the plates on the table and completed the rest of the table setting, saying, "I'm impressed with your data collection. Maybe I should have asked you first where Zachary was, because I made Buck angry when he thought I was accusing his father of bank robbery."

"I thought you knew that you should always ask me first." Lynn was smug about the success of her gossip network.

"So where are my bank robbers?"

"They aren't on my radar unless they work for a nonprofit or date one of my friends." Lynn brought dinner to the table. "Piper and Will are joining us." Dusty looked at the table and realized that he had set it to feed four people. At that moment Piper and Will barged into the kitchen.

"So?" Piper demanded as she looked at Lynn.

"Ask Dusty," said Lynn.

"Ask me what?"

Lynn translated. "I told Piper I'd give her an update on Amelia and Zachary this evening. I thought I might hear more from Cook's niece." She turned to Piper. "Dusty came home with the news."

Dusty knew better than to toy with Piper, for as small as she was she would get her information out of him with one scary principal look. Capitulating before her gaze, he sat meekly at the table as he said, "It seems they may be spending the weekend at Cedar Mountain Lake."

Piper kissed Dusty on the cheek for behaving correctly. "You were right," she said to Lynn. "Why did you suspect?"

Lynn demurred under Piper's praise. "I suspected Amelia was seeing Zachary because of the chat I had with Harriette. Once I learned that they were seen having dinner, it was the obvious conclusion."

"Why do the taxpayers pay you to be a detective?" Will asked Dusty.

~ ~ ~

In his office, a room at the front of the house, Zachary had a sofa arranged in an area with reading lamps and a small TV. He led Amelia to the sofa and sat beside her, handing her the remote. "What do you watch on Friday night?"

Amelia looked at him puzzled. "I usually find a movie, sometimes I read."

"We can sit here and read. Didn't you bring a book?" he asked.

"It's in my bedroom. I'll go get it." She ran from the room and raced up the stairs. When she returned Zachary was already settled on the couch with his book, his shoes off and his stocking feet resting on the coffee table. She sat back on the sofa, slipped off her sandals and placed her bare feet on the coffee table.

"Are your feet cold?" he asked as he noticed her toes curled tightly as they rested on the coffee table. "Put them under me." He pulled her legs around so that her feet were on the sofa, then he tilted forward so that Amelia could slide her toes behind him, resting her back on the sofa arm. They returned to their reading, although Amelia's heart was racing.

Studying Zachary over the top of her book, she wondered what he would do next, but he stayed focused on his book, even turning a page now and then. Amelia continued to look at his profile, the shape of his head, the form of his ear, his hair, the crease lines around his eye. She was burning his profile into her memory. Then she wiggled her toes against him. He looked at her and she grinned.

"That's participation." He patted her leg and returned to his book.

By now Amelia was suspicious of his game as she stared at her book with her toes still tucked behind him. Her heart was beating faster than she thought necessary to sustain life. She looked over her book at Zachary again as he quietly turned another page. There he was, Mr. Patience. She'd see about that!

Pulling her feet out from under him, Amelia put her book down and stared at him over the tops of her knees. He didn't move, but turned a page, again. Amelia said, "I think I'd be more comfortable leaning against you and covering my feet with a blanket." She rearranged herself on the sofa with a throw she found nearby, putting her back against Zachary, pushing him into the arm of the sofa.

"Maybe you'd be more comfortable sitting here by yourself," he offered squirming against the pressure from the sofa arm against his ribs.

"No, this is very comfortable." Wiggle, shove.

"May I make myself comfortable?" he asked.

"Certainly."

Zachary put down his book then surprised Amelia by pulling her onto his lap and cradling her in his arms. He looked at her very seriously and said, "My feet are cold. Do you mind?" She slowly shook her head. He pulled his feet onto the sofa, arranged the blanket over both of them, then wrapped his arms around her. In a soft voice he said, "Now we can't read. Do you want to watch TV?"

Amelia's heart was ready to explode and the rest of her body was starting to desire the pleasure of a loving touch.

She reached up, laced her arms around Zachary's neck and pulled his lips to hers. She was shy and tentative, but Zachary had been waiting too long and responded with reckless enthusiasm. They tumbled onto the floor, startled when gravity ruled as they sprawled across the floor laughing.

"That's participation?" asked Amelia.

"Yes." Zachary, in Amelia's opinion, was handsomest when he smiled. He was smiling now and she participated herself right back into his arms.

Waking in the middle of the night all tangled in Zachary and the sheets, Amelia rested quietly thinking about the evening. It had been a struggle with her old self to give in to Zachary's warmth and love. And it was love. Amelia had no doubt. She didn't care what happened next. She needed time to adjust to this new relationship. Weekends away at the lake for the foreseeable future seemed perfect to her. She fell back to sleep.

~ ~ ~

The backyard of Letitia's rental was a secluded area. The adjoining neighbors had either put up fences or shrubbery barriers to preserve a little privacy for their small lots.

Letitia and Wells had found this to be a quiet place to spend the evening. They didn't talk much because thinking of something to say was a challenge to both of them. Trying to explain how they felt about their unexpected attachment proved more than their communication skills could surmount. So silence – crickets, tree frogs – but human silence.

Inside the house they could hear Trong washing up the dinner dishes and Sparky commenting on a sporting event. He was an all season sport fan – he knew what was happening in any sport at any time and always had an opinion.

Out in the dusk and quiet, Wells sighed, huffed, and finally spoke. "I gotta get to that funeral.

"When you leaving?" she asked.

"Tonight, late," he replied. "It's about six hours from here."

"You coming back?" She hoped she didn't sound needy, or attached, or involved, or any of those things that hinted at caring. She added, "You know those folks expect you to keep your bargain about working."

He wanted to reach out and hold her hand. He wanted to ask her to go with him. Instead, he said, "I'll be back probably Monday, maybe Sunday. Will your brother-in-law care if I take the truck?"

She nodded in the darkness. "If you take it, you better come back. I can't afford to pay for it if you steal it."

"If you wasn't so cute," he smiled into the night, "I would steal it. But I wanna come back here and keep you outta trouble."

More silence as the night noises filled the void.

"You tired?" he asked.

"I guess," she replied. "We could rest for a bit before you leave."

"That's what I was thinkin'."

# Chapter Twenty-five

Zachary awoke early, eager to make love to Amelia. The sun wasn't quite up and she was breathing softly beside him. He threw his arm across her stomach and rested his head on her shoulder, trying to awaken her without seeming to do so by blowing in her ear and tracing patterns along her hip and stomach. Amelia slept. Zachary began kissing her neck and moving his hand over more of her body.

Finally she said, "I thought you told me you were old."

"I thought I was," murmured Zachary amazed at his body's eagerness to greet her this morning. He kissed her slowly and brushed some hair from her face. "I like waking up with a younger woman in my bed. How do you feel about cavorting with an older man? Are you ready to go home?" He was certain nothing could dim his outlook today.

"Please don't tease me." Amelia kissed him back, moving into his arms as she pulled at the bedsheets to keep them warm on this crisp spring morning. "I'm embarrassed to admit that I was so skittish. Now I don't remember why." She was seeing a bright day ahead, too.

Zachary settled them more comfortably as he said, "Here's today's schedule. Because I'm old, we'll make love first since, as you've noticed, I'm ready. Next we'll take a rest until after sunrise, have breakfast, go for a boat ride, scope out the playground for Olivia's visit, go to dinner and come home. I reserve the right to make love to you anytime and anywhere this old body is ready, so I hope we don't shock the children at the playground." Amelia giggled as Zachary began to follow the day's schedule.

~ ~ ~

Dusty's office had been overrun by FBI agents less than twenty-four hours after the robbery. They had collected a lot of preliminary information within hours of their arrival. The FBI data along with additional information and identification of banking clients by Dusty's staff had helped the investigators develop a list of potential witnesses. Yesterday as the interviews were assigned for those witnesses, Dusty had asked to interview Zachary Rawlings alone. He recapped Zachary's past with his department when the unit had investigated the kidnapping and murder of Zachary's wife.

Claire Conti had agreed to Dusty's request and asked that he report his findings at the Saturday morning meeting. Late Friday afternoon the FBI investigators had been able to add some information regarding Zachary's credit card activities for the time just after the robbery.

"Did that data on your potential witness help with your interview?" Claire asked Dusty as she sipped her coffee and stared at a tempting pastry. Her team had found the trail of Zachary's credit card activity from Thursday after the robbery through Friday afternoon.

"Thanks for letting me do the interview." Dusty shrugged, a little uncomfortable with his report even though he had known Claire for years. "Zachary Rawlings is away for the weekend and hasn't checked in with his family."

"They verify he could be at this lake?" She had the credit card report in her hand.

"Yes, he's one of the investors." Dusty sipped his coffee.

"Come on, Dusty," coaxed Claire, "I've known you too long. What's the rest of the story?" Claire had a long and exemplary career in the FBI, and was known for her skill at ferreting out the real story.

Dusty smiled at her. She had recently remarried. Her

first husband had been killed on September eleventh in the Pentagon. Her new husband was a federal prosecutor. "Zachary has gone off for a weekend with a lady friend. Our little investigation blew his secret wide open." Dusty chuckled. "By the time they get back to town, even his granddaughter will know all the gossip."

Claire moaned in sympathy for the couple she didn't even know. Dusty filled her in on their stories. "Two shy, hurt people, it makes my romantic side smile." Claire's romantic side only had a shelf life of three seconds. "I still need to question him. Was she in the car, too?"

"I don't know." Dusty put his cup down. "At least let me be with you. You can even question them at my house. I don't want to call too much attention to them."

"Deal. See if you can get them over to your place this evening. That should give the lovers enough time." Claire put her hands on her hips as she continued, "I don't know why I always let you charm me. And I want to meet that wife of yours." Then her eyes twinkled. "And that stepson."

Dusty groaned.

~ ~ ~

"I guess Wells took off," Trong stated as he ambled into the kitchen for breakfast.

Letitia glanced up from reading the morning paper. "He left about three this morning."

Trong knew that. It was when the headboard quit banging against the bedroom wall. "Did he have any cash?"

"I gave him some," she replied.

This discussion was very awkward. Letitia turned her eyes and interest back to the newspaper. Trong buttered his toast. Sparky joined them in the kitchen.

He looked terrible. He needed to get back to his treatments.

"Can I get you anything?" Letitia asked. She had never cared about dealing with sick people. They were always so needy. But Sparky seemed sort of heroic.

"You don't worry about me," he replied. "As soon as Wells gets back we'll get on with our plan."

"What plan?" asked Letitia, all of a sudden worried that the men were planning something and she might be left with the dirty end of the stick.

Trong smiled at her. "Now don't you worry. Wells is a good man. He's got a way to help us and protect you."

Sparky pulled a cup of hot tea from the microwave. "Yeah, he'd kill us if we hurt you."

Letitia stared, then blushed, then looked back at the newspaper.

Trong laughed out loud. "I've known him a while. He keeps his word. And he likes you."

The sun brightened the kitchen, the birds sang, Letitia had never been told that a man liked her. Maybe he meant some of those silly things he said when sex was making him speak. She'd wait to see what happened when he returned. Maybe...

~ ~ ~

Sunlight reflections from the lake were dancing across the bedroom ceiling. Amelia threw her arm across the bed and was startled to find that she was alone. Opening her eyes, she saw the sun high over the lake and could hear noises coming from the kitchen. Scrambling out of bed, she followed the noise and the smell of bacon and coffee.

Zachary was scanning his cellphone screen and making notes on a small note pad as the coffee gurgled into the pot. He rubbed his chin, frowned and put the phone on the table. Lifting it again he stared at the screen, scowled then put it back on the table with a thud. After staring out at the lake for a few moments, Zachary picked up his phone and walked toward the bedroom.

The frown on Zachary's face made Amelia stop as they met in front of the fireplace. "Is something wrong?"

"Read this." He handed her his cellphone. Amelia scanned the message.

"What?" She almost screamed the question, upset at its implication. "Why does Dusty want to see us?" She looked at the message from Buck and the later message from Dusty. "And how did he know?" At that question she blushed and hurried past him into the kitchen.

Zachary laughed. "River Bend is a small town. Maybe there was nothing else to talk about this weekend." He walked over and took her in his arms. "His request is very courteous. He said when our weekend is over, not to come immediately."

Amelia rested her head on his shoulder. "I was hoping for some time to get used to this idea." She slid her arms around his waist. "I don't even know what I'm getting used to." Now she sounded forlorn.

"I'm not sure either." He leaned against the refrigerator with Amelia in his arms.

His comment startled her. She pulled away looking at him with a hurt expression. "I said that badly," confessed Zachary. "I'd been thinking, before this message," he poured them each some coffee then sat at the kitchen table, "I know where I want to be in six months. I don't know about you." He stirred cream into his coffee, studying the eddies in the cup. "I want us to be a married couple. I want us to be in the middle of a cruise to some place you'd like to see. I want us to be laughing and loving from now on." Finishing his speech, Zachary sat quietly, staring at her.

Amelia took a seat at the table, placing her cup in front of her. "I'd be happy to spend weekends here with you and during the week be my old self." She looked at Zachary. "Marriage? What about my business? My condo?"

"That's why I told you that I'm not sure about *us*. I know what I want, but we're a couple." She frowned at him. "I mean I want us to be a couple." They sat and drank their coffee.

"I know that your business and your condo are your decisions," said Zachary, "but I have some suggestions." Amelia raised her eyebrows at him as she sipped some coffee. "I think your business can continue. You have your friend, Harriette, who can step in. If you raise her salary and ask her to be a part of the transition planning, I think she'll take the challenge." He tilted his head and watched Amelia think about his suggestion. "And the condo. We need a place to live in River Bend. I find your place comfortable and charming. We'll have this place and I also have a place in Steamboat Springs and in Florida." Amelia's eyes grew wide. "If those places don't appeal to you, we can always find whatever you want."

Amelia frowned. "I'm poor. I had no fancy upbringing. I've never been to any of those places, nor to a fancy dinner, nor worn a fancy dress. I won't fit into your life, or your family." Now she was pacing the kitchen. "And Mr. Taft, he'll never accept me. And your children?" She stood in front of Zachary. He had turned in his chair to follow her path around the kitchen. When she stopped talking he eased her onto his lap and kissed her over and over as she wept softly.

Zachary held her as he spoke. "Nathan will be delighted. Buck married an environmental attorney. That's worse than a business woman." He pushed her hair aside and traced his lips along her neck. "Nancy may be a challenge, but I think she'd be a challenge no matter what I did."

"Was she attached to her mother?"

"No, but she's become a person I don't know." Zachary let Amelia stand up as he thought about Nancy. "She became a different person when she lived with me in Australia. Each time I see her, she reminds me more and more of her mother. I think young Mars is going to be hurt. Nancy isn't the girl he thinks she is." Zachary stood. "But that's a discussion for another time." He found a pencil and paper. "Let's craft our response for Dusty."

After a lot of debate, they finally settled on the shortest and most direct response to the request for an interview. Zachary sent the message, *"Arrive at Lynn's 4 PM."* For the rest of the time at the lake, they cleaned and packed and found time to make love.

~ ~ ~

With Jason coming home last week and the house disrupted by work and a bank robbery, Susan's garden had been a lost cause. For almost two weeks Lynn had been watering and tending all those orphan plants she had taken from the Carmichael place. Today she had the time and a semi-plan. She stood at the curb surveying the spot for Susan's garden. She had acquired so many plants from the Carmichael lot that she had lost her roving eye. There couldn't be a plant she didn't now have – but she wouldn't turn down something interesting if she ... but, she just had too much work to do before she looked for any new plants and flowers. She wondered if she should join a gardeners' anonymous because she had met plenty of others in town who had the same itch. She'd give it more thought, maybe in winter when there weren't so many blooming distractions.

The roadway into The Heights meandered through the stately old subdivision that had been laid out and built by her father's family. It was platted when the family finally decided to take the wealth of their farmland and convert it to housing – something farmers have been doing for ages. When the road reached the old family homestead, it ended in a small cul-de-sac. The only other home this far back was now owned by Lynn's brother, Will. She stared at the edge of the roadway and at the shabby, tangled growth that separated Lynn's yard from Will's. Because her ancestors had kept about ten acres at the end of the road, there was plenty of space between her driveway and her property line along the arc of the cul-de-sac – maybe one hundred feet.

Lynn staggered at the thought – that would be a lot of gardening! On closer look, though, she saw the possibilities. There were several solid mature trees – pines and hardwoods. Those azaleas she had rescued would thrive near the pine, and those hostas would enjoy the shade of the hardwoods. In addition she had a vision of a small arched trellis for the climbing plants she had retrieved, and maybe a stone paver walkway from the road through the trellis into Susan's Garden.

Lynn grinned. That was it – her vision stunned her as it came together! This would be a beautiful garden, it would honor Susan, lift the sorrow from Lynn's heart and keep her promise to Polly to protect and nurture the plants for Polly's future. But she was working alone today. All the kids seemed to have other plans and Dusty had a robbery to investigate. So she would start small, clear out the space under the pines and get the azaleas planted. Maybe Sunday she could work on the hardwoods and clear a space for the hostas. It would come together. She had all summer.

She heard gravel crunch. Polly hopped off her bike. "Need help?"

Lynn smiled at her. "I'm planning Susan's garden." Together they walked through the space and Lynn explained her ideas. They wept. They hugged. And they began to work the plan.

~ ~ ~

Amelia and Zachary arrived in The Heights before Dusty and Claire. Lynn was delighted to see them and found it difficult to contain her pleasure in this new relationship. For their part Zachary and Amelia were uncomfortable and shy about their first public appearance after their very private and intimate weekend. Trying to respect their privacy, Lynn talked in a rambling incoherent patter until

Dusty arrived. When he walked into the kitchen Dusty found them sitting at the table looking as guilty as two teenagers who had been caught in the back seat of a car late at night. He greeted everyone as he walked through the door taking time to kiss Amelia on the cheek and shake Zachary's hand. "I want you all to meet Claire Conti. Claire, this is my wife." Two of Claire's agents walked quietly into the kitchen and began setting up their gear.

"I've wanted to meet you. I've worked with this heartbreaker for years." Claire ignored the witnesses and poured all her attention on Lynn.

"We'll have to find some time alone and exchange gossip." Lynn liked Claire immediately.

"My thoughts, too," agreed the agent.

"And this is Zachary Rawlings and Amelia Shipley." Dusty looked them over and added. "Claire's the regional director for the FBI." Amelia's eyes bulged as she tried to control her panic.

"By the looks on your faces," began Claire, "I guess you didn't read a newspaper this weekend." She walked away from the table then turned to stare at them. "We had a bank robbery here in River Bend on Thursday afternoon. The security cameras caught Mr. Rawlings' car going through the ATM line while the robbery was occurring inside."

"You think we robbed a bank?" Amelia was outraged.

Dusty was appalled that Amelia thought so little of him, so he got even. "Would you rather confess to bank robbery or a weekend together?"

"Dusty." By the sound of her voice Lynn let him know that he better change his tactics.

"I thought I was the heartless one," commented Claire as she took over the discussion. "We wanted to show you the security tapes and ask about people that you may have seen. Your friend, Dusty, wanted to keep your interview quiet so that you didn't have to explain to everyone that you two have been, well by the looks of you," she surveyed Amelia and Zachary over the tops of her glasses, "you've been making whoopee." Zachary burst out laughing.

"That's a fair deduction." He took Amelia's hand. She was blushing.

Claire said, "We appreciate that you interrupted your holiday. We have the security footage and we want you to look at all the camera scenes for about fifteen minutes on either side of the robbery." One of the agents booted up his laptop. Everyone gathered around the little screen as the blurry black and white film clicked through its cycle. Soon it became a name game as Lynn and Amelia identified friends moving through the footage. Again, Claire's staff took notes, confirming identities of the people on the screen as verified by other witnesses.

"I should think you and your detectives would know all of these people," Lynn said to Dusty.

"They knew a lot of them, but some where unfamiliar. Amelia and Zachary are our last witnesses." Claire let Amelia and Zachary look through the remaining footage as she explained to Lynn. "We have most people identified. The bank staff is compiling a list of customers through that time period. The unnamed start to look like potential suspects."

Lynn smiled at Claire in sympathy. "I've been married to Dusty long enough to know that investigating is often detailed and tedious." She turned and paid attention to the screen while all the investigators worked on their notes. "Isn't that interesting?" she commented almost to herself.

"What? Someone who shouldn't be there?" asked Claire. As an experienced interviewer she was familiar with that tone of voice.

"See that paisley dress on that woman?" An agent froze the frame and Lynn pointed to a person in the lower corner. "That's Letitia's dress. That's the outfit she wore to the board retreat."

"Why shouldn't she be at the bank?" asked Claire, staying focused.

Dusty looked at Claire, trying to organize his information. "I interviewed her right after the robbery." He went on to explain the early release program, the clients they had been assigned, and his role as a board member. "Letitia was with a board member through the entire time span of the robbery." He blew out his breath. "And she and the board member vouch for the three cons in their care."

"She doesn't look right." Lynn squinted, still focused on the screen. "She looks too small. And I don't think Letitia wears hats."

As the discussion and investigation started to become more detailed and proprietary, Dusty turned to Zachary. "Thank you for coming by. I appreciate your cooperation." He ushered them out of the house.

Claire was on the phone with her other agents to ask them to follow up on the information just revealed in the kitchen. Lynn was still studying the security shots, looking for some other scenes showing the paisley dress.

Suddenly she screeched, "That's Jason!"

"Who's Jason?" asked Claire putting on her professional face.

"My son."

Claire startled Lynn by asking, "Would he rob a bank?"

Lynn screeched even louder. Claire laughed. "Did you call me, Mom?" Jason slid into the kitchen on his socked feet – an old habit. Because of the wooden floors in the house, he could slide from the front door to the back door with one good shove off. He stopped at the kitchen table and looked back. He frowned at Lynn. "You aren't waxing these floors the way you used to."

"Maybe you're getting too fat," she countered.

"Or you have all that money from the robbery holding

you back," offered Claire.

Jason grinned. "You think I robbed the bank?"

Claire turned the computer screen and clicked the keypad. She pointed to Jason walking out of the bank. "You were there."

"Wow," he was transfixed. "Was I there during the robbery?" He squinted at the screen as Claire froze the images.

"I think you walked out just before the perps entered. What do you remember seeing?"

Jason couldn't think without food so he dug a bag of cookies out of the pantry and poured himself a glass of milk. Sitting at the table he stared at the screen. "I was making a delivery. One of those women in the bank had ordered some rolls and dessert for a dinner she was having that night."

"But did you see anyone as you left the bank?"

He squinted at the screen again. "See, I was texting the guys. We were planning our soccer game at the park."

Claire sighed. It was what youngsters did – communicate, oblivious to life around them. "Did you drive to the bank or walk?"

"Walk."

Claire raised her eyebrow. Jason responded. "I work at a bakery. I need all the exercise I can get."

Claire laughed. "You saw nothing and you're not fat."

"And I didn't rob the bank."

"You convinced me, Handsome." She patted his cheek. Then she turned to the two agents who had accompanied her. "Pack this up. I told the others to meet us here." The two agents packed their gear and left the house as silently as they had entered. Dusty helped them carry everything out to their car.

Once the kitchen emptied Lynn poured herself a glass of wine and raised it to Claire in a wordless question. Claire nodded and Lynn poured her a glass, too.

Claire sat beside Jason at the table sharing the cookies. "So, Handsome, tell me about yourself." She had enjoyed a productive and successful career, but sometimes wondered what motherhood would have added to her life. The two of them sat and talked while Lynn puttered around the kitchen. Four agents and Dusty returned to the kitchen as Mars walked in with beer and pizzas.

Dusty helped Mars with the food and drink, signaling to the agents to join Claire at the table. "Did she go crazy when she saw him?" Mars asked.

Claire laughed and tousled Jason's hair. "She got a little screechy."

"You knew?" Lynn was not happy about being set up.

"I can't believe it took you so long to notice him," said Dusty as he handed out plates while Mars passed at the beer.

"I guess I got distracted by Letitia's dress."

"But it wasn't her in it, right?" asked Claire.

"Correct," replied Lynn. "She has a unique style. I've seen that dress. She wore it to the retreat, remember, Dusty?" He kept drinking his beer. Lynn continued. "It looked like her dress, but the person in it was smaller."

"That must be some big woman," muttered one of the agents.

"You got that right," agreed Dusty.

# Chapter Twenty-six

Zachary took Amelia by the hand as they left Lynn's house. Outside Amelia, patience exhausted, huffed, "I'm so embarrassed." She pulled her hand from Zachary's grasp and began wringing her hands together. Zachary opened the car door and helped her in as she continued her agitation in pantomime.

"Well, that's it," he grinned as he got into the car. "We're not secret anymore." Amelia turned at him with flashing eyes. She had gone from embarrassed to angry in about a second.

"What if we're not ready to be un-secret?" Her eyes flashed and she pounded the console with her fist.

"Unsecret. Is that a word?" Zachary started the engine and drove from The Heights while Amelia boiled. "Besides I'm ready." He was delighted with the day's events.

As he turned the car on to the highway she asked, "Where are we going?"

"To get my things," he replied with a grin.

"Why?" she asked in a low threatening voice.

"So I can stay with you."

"What?" Nothing of her anger and anxiety was getting through to him. Amelia quietly stared at him for the remainder of the drive to Palmer Mansion as he drove along whistling a happy tune. When they entered the mansion drive she finally said, "I can't walk in with you. What will they say? Won't your family be angry or something?"

"They know we've been away together." Zachary stopped the car on the parking pad. "Who do you think told Dusty how to contact us?"

"I thought he used some secret police stuff." Amelia was no longer angry. She was frightened.

Zachary patted her hand and said. "Dusty just asked my son."

"How did he know? Did you say something?"

"Cook and Penny had us figured out in two minutes." He turned to face her. "I even saw Olivia wink at them when she caught on to our secret."

"I'm staying here." She crossed her arms and pushed herself deeper into the seat.

"Then I'll bring everyone out to greet you."

Giving him a threatening look, Amelia climbed out of the car. Walking up the path to the kitchen, she pushed her hands into her pockets as he said, "They saw us drive in. They'll be waiting in the family sitting room, because Nathan will have told everyone that we will be treated as welcome family members." Amelia glared at him and he winked at her.

Walking into the family sitting room, Zachary said, "We just got back to town. Are we late for dinner?" Nathan put down his book and smiled at them.

"I asked Ted to set out a light buffet. We're ready when you are." Nathan walked over to Amelia. He held out his hand to her. "My dear, we are delighted to finally meet Zachary's friend. Please call me Nathan." Buck and Penny joined him and waited for their chance to greet her.

"I'm Buck. I don't believe we've met." He looked at Amelia. "Have we?"

Before Amelia could answer, his wife said, "I'm Penny and we have met." She gave Amelia a kiss on the cheek. "And you remember Olivia." The little girl smiled up at Amelia.

"I remember you," said Amelia in a very soft, pleasant voice.

Zachary picked up Olivia and said, "Grandpa wants to

show you our lake." He kissed her and she giggled. "We'll have fun at the park and on grandpa's boat." Olivia giggled again and he put her down. The little girl crawled over to Amelia.

Kneeling down to talk directly with Olivia, Amelia said, "We want you to play in the park and ride in the boat. We'll have so much fun." Throughout the exchange the other adults in the room watched, each one of them delighted in this new phase in the family's life. Olivia pulled herself up and indicated that she wanted to be held by Amelia. It was soon clear to all that Olivia intended to give Amelia a test on her ability to be entertaining.

Penny interrupted, "Honey, we'll play after dinner. Let's take Amelia into dinner. Can she sit next to you?" Olivia nodded.

By nine-thirty, the family at Palmer Mansion had enjoyed a light evening buffet, read three books to Olivia and tucked her in bed while Zachary packed a few things for Amelia's place. When they were in his car, Zachary said, "See no one noticed." He nodded toward his overnight bag.

"They all noticed," replied Amelia. "Even Olivia winked at me when she understood."

He reached for her hand. "They loved you. Nathan said that he has some good memories of your family. What did he mean?"

Amelia blew out her breath. "I'm touched that he still remembers. My father was the lead firefighter when Taft Manufacturing had a fire years ago. He died in the fire. Mister, I mean, Nathan always sent a gift to my mother at Christmas and on the anniversary of Father's death." A tear escaped, and Amelia brushed at it.

"I guess I don't know anything about your family. Any murderers or insanity?" Zachary coasted to a stop in front of the condo.

"I have two brothers. One is a painting contractor and

one is a surgeon." Amelia dug her key out of her purse. "I don't know what to tell them about you."

Once inside, he pulled her into his arms. "I don't think I've ever seen your bedroom," he whispered as he tugged her toward the stairs.

Their lovemaking was still exploratory and Zachary still had to encourage Amelia to participate. "All in all, things seem to work pretty well," Zachary assessed in a happy whisper. Amelia nuzzled his neck and relaxed into her pillow. "I guess you agree?" asked Zachary.

"Mmmmm." She pulled the sheets around them.

"Do you think we should talk about tomorrow?" he asked.

Amelia threw herself back on her pillow and stared at the ceiling. "I haven't answered my phone since Thursday. I left shrimp scampi in the oven. It's probably rotten. I haven't watered my plants. I didn't pick up my dry cleaning. And there's no food for breakfast."

"I was thinking we had to talk about a few things more long term, you know, life changing."

"There's rotting food in the oven, dying plants in the living room and no food for breakfast. That's not life changing?" Amelia ran a finger along his chest, lowered her voice as she put her head on his shoulder and said, "I don't have a clue about anything else." Her voice sounded sad and perplexed.

Zachary turned on his side and kissed her cheek. "To start with, I'm here to stay. Do you want marriage or some sort of bohemian relationship?" He felt Amelia shrug. "Second," he continued, "I have to be back at my office sometime this week. Do you want to come with me married or in some sort of bohemian relationship?" Amelia didn't move. "Third, I'll be closing up my apartment in Texas and resigning my job, then I'm moving in here. Do you want me here married or in some sort of bohemian relationship?" He wrapped his arms around her. "That's what I meant by life changing."

He held her until she stopped crying and then said, "Come on, let's go water the plants and clean out the oven."

In the kitchen Amelia couldn't look into Zachary's eyes. He teased and cajoled. She worked on cleaning, moving her focus from her oven to include the refrigerator and then her pantry closet. Zachary worked beside her, never asking for direction, washing shelves, cleaning old food containers, putting items into the dishwasher.

"Living alone for so long," he said absently, "has given me some marketable skills. Since I'll be out of work, I might start up a maid service here in River Bend." Amelia ignored him and kept working. "I could call it *Manly Maids*. Do you think I could attract clients? Maybe *Men in Gloves*?" He glanced over at Amelia and saw that she was smiling. Walking up behind her, Zachary placed his arms around her waist and burrowed into her neck. It was a pleasurable act that Amelia enjoyed. "I could stay home and you could support me." His lips moved along her neck.

"I thought you said you were rich." Amelia moved her head so that he got all the spots that mattered. "Zachary, I don't know what to say about our future." Amelia moved away from him putting the kitchen work island between them. "You just proposed. I've met your family and they were welcoming. But you haven't met my family."

"It doesn't matter. Nathan approves of you and your family. I trust him."

"I have a business that employs people who need their jobs." Amelia clutched the counter top edge.

"We'll keep the business running." He moved around the island to stand behind her again. "So married or bohemian? I do have to warn you, if we aren't married I don't know what we'll tell Olivia. I'm sure she has standards." Zachary waited for Amelia to respond. She allowed his arms to stay around her but she said nothing. "Why don't you go to bed? I'll finish cleaning." He gave her a kiss on the cheek, then pointed her toward the stairs. "Go to bed, and think about how much nicer it is to have me here than to be alone." Amelia took his advice, leaving the kitchen with a pensive look on her face.

# Chapter Twenty-seven

"*I*'ve come to a decision," Amelia announced as Zachary squinted at the morning light. "I want to be your wife, but," she raised her hand halting Zachary's grab, "I want a few days alone to adjust. So why don't you move back to Nathan's, go back to Texas and when you return, we'll set a date?"

Zachary moved closer and took her in his arms. "You want me to stay away how long?" He had learned all of her vulnerable spots in the last few days.

"Until Friday." He kissed and caressed. "Maybe you can come back Thursday." He continued his persuasion. "Maybe Wednesday, OK, maybe Tuesday night." His hands skimmed her body. "I'm firm on tomorrow night." Zachary removed her nightgown. "I don't have any plans for this evening," sighed Amelia.

Amelia didn't understand her behavior. Even after lovemaking, she couldn't let go of Zachary. She had to stay wrapped in his arms, burrowing into his neck, intertwining her legs with his. He sighed. She knew him so well now that she recognized a sigh of concern. "What? Something's wrong?"

He held her tighter. "I think I should leave today."

She moved away quickly, understanding that this is where the story ended. He pulled her back into his arms. "I can tell what you're thinking," he whispered into her ear. "I'm not leaving, I'm just going to return to Texas sooner than I had planned. Close out my place and resign my position. I'll be back in this bed with you by Thursday, unless you find someone else to replace me."

She burrowed deeper into his arms and sniffled.

"So it's settled," he announced. He kissed her nose, threw off the covers and said, "Let's go see what we can make for breakfast." He checked the bedside clock. "I can book a flight and be in Texas this evening. You can take me to the airport." He hopped out of bed and started collecting items for his shower. "While I'm gone you can clear out some closet space for me," one more kiss, "I'll be sending my things to your condo." He grinned and dashed into the shower.

~ ~ ~

Zachary was unable to get a flight out until Monday. They had found enough food to make themselves a pancake breakfast with a little fresh fruit. He told Amelia he would spend part of the day at Nathan's organizing and packing his things and getting some work done at the small office he maintained there. As he helped clean up the remains of breakfast he said, "I hope you go shopping while I'm getting organized. I need more food than a half of a banana and two pancakes."

She hugged him. "What do you like to eat?" She pulled back. "Does that mean you'll expect me to cook every night when I return from work?"

"Hmmm," he gave her question some thought. "We can always stop at Nathan's for dinner. Cook always has plenty.

"We can't just walk in every evening and demand to be fed," she exclaimed.

"No, we just stop by for some innocent reason, and he'll invite us to stay." He finished putting away the clean breakfast dishes.

Amelia started to laugh and Zachary gave her a hug. "We'll figure this out as we go. Right now I want to get started packing my things. I'll be back with dinner." One more hug and he was gone.

Amelia was alone in her condo and began to pace, much

as she had done a few days ago. And her thoughts were still the same – all about Zachary. She cleaned out some closet space and emptied some drawers in the bureau. She moved some of her clothing to the spare bedroom and cleaned out the drawers on one of the bedside tables. She moved downstairs and cleaned out some excess clothing from her coat closet. Soon she had a pile of things that she planned to give to the shelter's thrift store. But she was still mystified by Zachary. There was only one solution – a visit to Lynn. Her good friend would help her put the events of the past weekend into perspective. She walked into Lynn's kitchen on a quiet Sunday afternoon.

Seeing Amelia, Lynn rushed to hug her with delight. "I'm so happy for you and Zachary. What are your plans? Can I do anything for you?" Hoping for all the gossip, Lynn steered her to the kitchen table and a convenient chair.

Amelia blew out her breath and plopped down. She stared at Lynn who looked as though she would burst with excitement. Amelia laughed. "I guess it's not as scary as I thought."

"What do you mean scary? It's wonderful!" Lynn bent down and kissed her on the top of her head. "I'm so, we're, so happy."

"You and Dusty?"

"Me and everyone." She filled her coffee maker.

"Everyone?" Amelia moved uneasily.

"We all suspected something."

"We all?" It was getting scarier for Amelia.

"Everyone at Palmer Mansion knew Zachary was seeing someone." Lynn leaned back against the kitchen counter. "Dad and Marianna saw you at dinner. Piper and Sophie Grayson..." Lynn stopped. Amelia was laughing.

"I was hoping to have some time to get used to my secret before it became public knowledge." Amelia shifted in her chair.

"What's the problem?" Lynn brought cups to the table.

"I'm not sure. I just need you to listen." Lynn nodded at Amelia and waited. "I know he loves me." Amelia beamed. "His whole body loves me."

"I don't think Zachary wants me to know that much." Lynn got her grin under control.

"He keeps saying that he's surprised at it for a man his age." Amelia was happily honest. Lynn bit her lip to keep herself from smiling. "He's wonderful, but I don't fit into his world. I've never traveled or eaten expensive foods, or dressed up, and I don't know a thing about fancy entertaining."

"What do you mean? You just be yourself. Your parents raised you to be polite and respectful. That's all it takes, along with some common sense." Lynn stood and paced the room launching into her pep talk. "We'll all be here to help you. I know Nathan will always treat you like a queen."

"He's so kind." Amelia had found her reception at Palmer Mansion reassuring yesterday evening. "I know you and Nathan and everyone want to help me. But Zachary wants us to live other places, too." She looked around the room to make certain they were still alone. "He has three houses," she whispered.

"I'll help anyway I can." Lynn squeezed Amelia's hand. "What do you need first?"

"Lynn," called Marianna as she flung the kitchen door open. "Do you have any more information about--" She stopped as Amelia turned in her chair. "We're all so delighted!" Marianna hugged Amelia. "Tell me everything."

Lynn poured Marianna some coffee. "Amelia thinks she needs help learning to fit into Zachary's life, you know, fancy dress and entertaining and travel." She placed the milk jug, because it was adequate enough for family, and a sugar bowl on the table.

"That's no problem," began Marianna. "I'm a great

acting coach, we'll have her ready for the role in no time."

"Guys, I'm sitting right here." Amelia was looking up at the two women as they talked over her head making their Pygmalion plans.

"Anyone here?" called Penny as she nudged open the kitchen door.

"Come in," they all shouted.

"I came to--" Penny stopped when she saw Amelia.

"I know," nodded Amelia, "You want to know what Lynn knows. With all these interruptions, she doesn't know much." Penny gave Amelia a hug.

"I'll tell you what I know," she held Amelia's hand, "Buck and Nathan are delighted. Buck's mother must have been a terror. Even though she was Nathan's sister and Zachary is the in-law, they think you're quite an improvement." Amelia blushed.

"Please don't talk about her. His marriage is still very painful to him." Amelia's listeners nodded.

"Penny, you'll be the best help." Lynn started to explain as she found another cup, "Amelia needs a tutorial on high living. I bet Zachary has a tux and uses it." Lynn reminded Marianna and Amelia, "You know Penny was a successful environmental attorney before she married Buck."

Penny nodded. "It's not scary. I've adjusted to life in Palmer Mansion and so will you," encouraging Amelia as she explained further, "They *are* formal at the house. Nathan has standards and Buck and Zachary grew up," she swung her hand up, "on a higher plane than the rest of us. Boarding school, dancing classes, other homes."

"Anybody here?" shouted Piper. Since moving across the street last year, she sometimes entered the house through the front door.

"Back here," they all replied.

"What's the scoop on --" she spied Amelia. "Great, right from the horse's mouth." She kissed Amelia on the cheek.

Lynn started again. "Amelia says she needs help to learn to live rich." It was the quickest explanation. With all the interruptions, it had to be. Ignoring the coffee, Piper took a quick nose count and rummaged through the pantry for some wine and crackers.

"It's just learning how to spend money," offered Piper as she opened the crackers and dumped them into a dish then distributed wine glasses.

"It's a little more than that." Penny spoke from experience. "You can spend money and it shows, or you can spend money and it glows." She looked at the group. They all nodded knowingly as Lynn poured the wine.

Amelia squinted at them. "I don't understand."

Marianna sat beside her and began, "It's buying a great dress, but also knowing how to wear it, how to carry yourself, how to --"

"Look relaxed in a thousand dollar outfit," offered Lynn tossing some cheeses and old candy onto the table.

"Knowing how to be kind to us poor people without being condescending," supplied Piper as she pulled the cork from another wine bottle.

Amelia moaned. "It's also learning about which fork, which glass, and probably how to dance." The other women sipped wine and nodded.

"Did someone say dance?" asked Salley Connelly as she walked into the kitchen. Lynn's sister-in-law surveyed the group and kissed Amelia. "It's all over town. We're all delighted. No wonder you're talking about dancing." Marianna handed her a glass of wine.

Lynn got everyone back on track again. "Amelia needs help learning how to be rich. Dancing is just one of the things she thinks she has to know."

"Along with how to spend money and not be condescending," concluded Piper.

"Last Friday I was at a meeting with one of the hospital

volunteers. They're getting ready for their mid-summer under the stars fund raising gala at the country club." Salley looked at them all. "We've never gone, but I know they have dancing, and gowns and stuff."

"Who's on the committee?" asked Lynn.

"Millie O'Hara and Michelle Grayson," replied Salley as Penny and Marianna pulled out their cells.

After some quick consulting with the committee members, Marianna and Penny reported back to the group. "It's in June. And five hundred dollars per couple," offered Penny.

"Millie says they were wondering if they should lower the ticket price or advertise it as less formal," reported Marianna. "I told her to tell everyone, quietly," she raised her eyebrows and whispered conspiratorially, "that it will be Amelia's coming out as Mrs. Zachary Rawlings." She studied the group. "Millie was delighted. She knows this kind of gossip and social opportunity will sell tickets."

"I told Michelle the same thing and that Buck would buy a table."

"I said Jim would buy a table, too," admitted Marianna.

"But I can't dance," cried Amelia. They all looked at her, then at the acting coach.

"Dancing class begins Tuesday night." Marianna turned to Lynn, "We'll have to use your place. Our bungalow won't hold a crowd."

"Crowd?" they all cried.

"Amelia can't learn to dance while the rest of you just plod around the floor." Marianna looked them over. "Tuesday night at seven in The Heights, wear your dancing shoes."

~ ~ ~

True to his word, Wells got back into River Bend Sunday evening. It was dusk and he was driving slowly through Letitia's neighborhood because he was a cautious man. And he gasped. Stakeout cars. How dumb did they think he was? Then he studied the viewpoints. They didn't think he was dumb. If he were in the house, he wouldn't see these vehicles. He only found them because he took the cautious way home. Slowly Wells drifted through the neighborhood and continued as though his destination was in one of the streets branching off in the distance.

He meandered out of the neighborhood and pulled into a fast food parking lot. He texted Trong's phone: *"Staked out."*

*"What?"*

*"Someone watching house. Stay put. I'm back in town."*

*"Do what?"*

*"Let me think."*

~ ~ ~

Sparky was starting to enjoy life on the outside. Here he was sitting after dinner sipping coffee and reading a newspaper. Who did that in prison? But he had to go back. It was time for more chemo – he could feel his body looking for help. It would be soon, he told himself. He turned the pages of the paper, comics, sports, ads. It was so small town. He glanced at an ad for Spring Cleaning.

That took him back. He had been raised by his grandmother who turned the house inside out doing her spring-cleaning. He smiled at the memories. But a whole lot of other memories crashed in. He decided to read the sports pages again. And hoped his body could hang on until this job was wrapped up.

Trong came into the kitchen, glanced around. His demeanor told Sparky something was up. As they whispered about the texts, Letitia walked into the kitchen. "Anything wrong?" she asked.

With an acknowledgement that he was the spokesman, Trong said, "Wells says the police have us under surveillance."

She gasped. "What should we do? Close the curtains? Move someplace else?"

Trong sat her at the table and Sparky handed her a glass of water. After a nodding exchange with Sparky, Trong said, "He's working on a plan. He'll let us know. Let's watch TV and go to bed. Our movements should look normal." She nodded.

They spent the rest of the evening acting stressfully normal while waiting for Wells to text again. And they waited. Nothing. Sparky finally said, "It's late, we better look like we're in for the night."

Once settled in Sparky's bedroom the men waited until they thought that Letitia was asleep. In very hushed tones, a skill they had learned in prison, they huddled together at the far corner of the room and plotted. "We still got the money, right?" asked Sparky.

Trong nodded his head. "It's only three hundred dollars, remember?"

"But it's evidence if we get caught."

Trong rubbed his eyes. "I'm glad we didn't use weapons. We might already be dead."

"So you think Wells is telling the truth," asked Sparky, "about the stakeout?"

"Yeah, and he might want us to figure a way out and leave her behind," suggested Trong.

"What if there's no stakeout, just his way of letting us leave without her?" Sparky stared at the phone still waiting for a text.

Trong nodded. "That makes sense, too. Wells and I been together for years. He probably faked his granddaddy's funeral and took the time to set up our escape. Remember she told us to plan for success? That's what he did. He just needs us to meet up with him and we're golden." He yawned. "I don't want to take off tonight and we'd have to steal her car unless you got another idea?"

Sparky thought a moment. "I read something in that newspaper she gets. I got an idea." The two men grinned at one another. Convinced that the stakeout was a ruse, and that Wells was waiting for them and the money to run off to Kentucky, they climbed into their bunks and settled in for what they knew would be their last night in Letitia's cottage.

The last thing Sparky said, "She's okay, but he's probably got a wife or something in Kentucky."

~ ~ ~

"Dusty, we're going to have a ball," Lynn announced as she pulled the bed covers up to her chin.

"I was planning on it," he responded as he moved closer and began tracing his fingers over the contours of her breast.

"No, I mean a formal dance." Dusty pulled his hand away as though it had been singed.

"Don't we do enough of that dress-up crap?" He rose up on his elbow and looked at her.

"We're doing it for Amelia's coming out party."

"Why does that mean I have to go to a dance?" Dusty muttered in a voice that suggested he just got a ticket for the Gulag.

"You can stay home. But we're all helping Amelia feel at ease in fancy social situations. That way she won't be uncomfortable attending functions with Zachary, once they're married.

"Who's we?"

"Salley said she and Carl would come." Lynn spoke in her seductive voice.

Dusty stopped to think, giving consideration to his brother in a tuxedo. "Might not be a bad idea." He resumed his interest in Lynn's body, moving closer to kiss her neck. He stopped. "How much?"

"Five hundred dollars a couple." Lynn waited, holding

her breath.

"Who are you raising money for?"

"Does it matter?" Lynn knew that Dusty wasn't interested in this event. She waited for his next comment, hoping the conversation would be over soon. She liked Dusty's other plans for the evening.

But he was motionless for a moment. "I know there's something you're not telling me."

"We're going to start dancing classes for Amelia."

"Who's we?"

"All of us, Dad, Marianna, Piper, Will, you, me," Dusty swore. Lynn ignored his comments. "We could all use the training. You know that we don't have any style when we dance."

Dusty embraced her. "I thought we do just fine." He started to sing softly as he pulled her closer.

Lynn sensed she was winning this battle as she moved to Dusty's rhythm, because he said, "Hmmm, we can talk about dancing later."

# Chapter Twenty-eight

"You think this will work?" Sparky asked as they cleaned their bedrooms and stowed their few belongings in a small satchel with the stolen money. He had thought through a plan of escape and shared it with his partner.

Trong nodded. "You thought up a great idea. If we get caught we have some hostage to use as a shield. We don't want anyone firing guns at us. You can't get into a federal prison if you're dead."

Sparky thought about that logic. It was getting harder for him to think. The big C was distracting him. The pain wasn't too great but he knew it was time for another treatment, or at least some medications to keep him steady and focused on life. "Tell me one more time. How do you see this working?"

Trong could see that the disease was taxing his friend. He knew they hadn't much time. Sparky needed to get to a place where he could get care. "This was your idea, remember?"

Sparky nodded. "That's right. We take a hostage. Leave Letitia behind. That way no one thinks she had a hand in this. I think Wells wanted us to take care of her, but he isn't interested in taking her along."

Trong wasn't sure what Wells intended, but he wasn't a complex thinker, either. He had to get them out and Letitia was one more big worry he didn't need. "Sure, sure. We get away and we have money. Or we get caught and we give them the money and get you care." But Trong still had a question. "So how's anyone going to know that we have a

215

hostage?"

That was a good question.

Sparky gave thought to his plan, again, "When we get to that rest area on the interstate, we drop her off and we scram. We have money and she's free--"

"She? But how do we get her?"

"I called a maid service to come and look at cleaning the house." Sparky snapped his fingers. "We take her as a hostage. Easy as pie."

"But how will anyone know we kidnapped a hostage?" Back to the original question.

Sparky was pleased about this facet of his plan. "If there's really a stakeout, they'll see us leave, follow us and rescue her, arrest us and we go to prison. Or we drop her at the rest area and we go free. One way we get caught and one way we get the money and disappear." He felt like he was thinking through cotton fuzz, as his focus ebbed. Damn the big C.

"There you go," smiled Trong. "We start with Letitia."

~ ~ ~

A small town Memorial Day! The high school band was tuning up a few blocks from the courthouse. They would march to the front lawn following the veterans' honor guard. There would be the National Anthem, the pledge, a prayer and a speech and some songs. The band would then march in an orderly fashion back to River Bend High School and put away their instruments. It would be noon by then and the band members were looking forward to a free afternoon before finals started tomorrow.

At the courthouse, the microphone had been tested. The preacher designated for this year's prayer was in place with his ear cocked for the arrival of the band. The current sheriff was on hand to politic. Judge Dunn was available in her robes to lead the pledge. She was off to the side scanning her phone for fishing reports. She had a date with a trout up in the forest this afternoon.

Bev, as the newest county commissioner, was off to the side being bolstered by her friends. "You'll be great," murmured Annie, thinking she should have brought a flask for Bev.

Piper ambled over, scanning the crowd. "Have you two seen Lynn?"

Both women shook their heads. "She's probably at the bakery getting a cannoli."

"I didn't think of that," said Piper. "I'll get Janet settled. She's eating some hot dog she got from one of the street vendors." The other two women rolled their eyes. "I know what you mean." Piper gasped. "Now she's buying pop corn! I'll get her." And she dashed toward the very, very pregnant Janet as she tried to get Polly's attention, looking for some re-enforcements.

But Polly had been sidetracked by Jason and the teen crowd. The kids had found a perfect spot, close to the food vendors.

~ ~ ~

"Lynn," waved Amelia as she arrived at the small suburban house of her new client. "What are you doing here?"

Lynn walked over to Amelia's car. "I can't get that paisley dress out of my mind, the one we saw on the bank video. This is Letitia's house. I want to check on her. What are you doing here? This is a holiday."

"I know. I've gotten behind," she blushed as she admitted, "A few days away from the office can add up to more work."

Lynn smiled at her discomfort. "A few days away with Zachary, you mean. Where is he?"

"He's flying to Texas today to close out his apartment and close out his job." Amelia was thoughtful. "He really wants us to be together."

"Of course he does," Lynn stated, "and you know we'll help you with anything." Lynn looked at the cottage. "Did Letitia call for your service?"

"Someone called. I've come to do the walk through and set a date." The two women looked at one another, puzzled.

"Maybe she's cleaning this rental before she moves out. Who called?" asked Lynn.

"Harriette says I'm to meet a Mr. Jones." Amelia rechecked the cleaning order.

The house was in a subdivision that was situated outside the River Bend city limits, just past the entrance to the country club estates. The homes were in a tidy mid-market area, and the small yards were filled with spring and early summer flowers. Many large trees had been saved by the developer and lined the roadway. Lynn guessed that the neighborhood was about forty years old.

Without seeming curious, both Lynn and Amelia studied the house as they chatted, telling each other what they were seeing. "It looks normal," said Lynn quietly.

"There's someone watching from behind the curtain," cautioned Amelia.

"I think I'll come up to the door with you," Lynn offered as she stared at the quiet looking house on this secluded neighborhood street. Together they proceeded up the walkway.

At Amelia's knock, a man answered, smiled and stepped back to allow the women to enter.

Amelia said, "We're with *Amelia's Maids*, we had a call for our maid service. Are you Mr. Jones?" As soon as they were inside, he closed the door to reveal another man behind the door holding a knife.

"It don't matter who we are. We was just looking for a hostage and a ride out of here." The man holding the knife spoke.

"Gimme your car keys," the other man told the women

as he gestured with his open hand.

"What have you done with Letitia?" asked Lynn, as the man pocketed car keys. The other man prodded them toward a door with a knife at Amelia's back.

"You mean her?" The man threw open a bedroom door and they saw Letitia bound and gagged on the bed, her eyes in a silent panic and plea. Then he motioned the two women into another bedroom that was at the end of a short hall. The room had a small closet, a bed, a bureau and one shade covered window. The man pointed to a pile of cloth strips that had been made by shredding a bedsheet. With the knife he motioned to his partner indicating Amelia as the first victim, "You tie up her hands and then her feet." He finished the task and tested the knots, then pushed Amelia onto the bed. He turned to Lynn, "Now you." She placed her hands in front, the same as Amelia's hands. She didn't want to look at Amelia because she couldn't face the fear in her eyes.

After the men finished tying up Lynn they pulled Amelia back to her feet and then tied both women together, back-to-back. Once the women were trussed, someone stuffed a wad of clothe in each woman's mouth and secured it by tying bed sheet strips around each woman's head. Satisfied with their work, one of the men pushed them to the floor in a jumble.

As soon as the women were left alone in the room, Lynn began to struggle. Amelia did the same, but Lynn grunted in a tone suggesting that Amelia be still. Amelia stopped moving and waited. Lynn began to struggle again. This time Amelia felt them move.

Lynn struggled and twisted until she got Amelia to her knees, then, once Amelia understood how to help Lynn, she held her position until Lynn was able to get to her feet. Then Lynn stood and waited for Amelia to work herself to a standing position. Again Lynn grunted, trusting that Amelia would wait until she understood the plan. Lynn hobbled to the door and studied the locking mechanism. It was one of those knobs that had a button at the center to be pushed in to set the lock. Squirming and pulling Lynn managed to tilt her head toward the lock. As Amelia understood the purpose, she fell to her knees to show Lynn that she was closer to the button. Because Lynn was taller than Amelia, she was able to backbend while Amelia worked on the button with her nose and forehead. Once the door was locked Lynn pulled forward and allowed Amelia to get back on her feet. What to do next?

~ ~ ~

Bev stood behind the dais on Memorial Day and looked out at the crowd – the honor guard and the veterans with their weapons for the 21-gun salute, the veterans in wheelchairs from the nursing home. She took a deep breath and began her story about loss and service and those who were left behind. The crowd grew silent. Some older men poked one another, people nodded as she mentioned her father's name. When she concluded her brief presentation, everyone applauded. After the ceremony of laying the wreath and the final presentation of the gun salute and playing "Taps," the crowd was dismissed.

As Bev climbed down from the dais, she was stopped by many people, several of whom wanted to say that they remembered her father and other men who said they were not healthy enough to serve and understood now how her father felt.

"Thank you for telling our story," said an old fellow. He kissed her on the cheek. "I stayed behind, too. Bad asthma. Sometimes it was hard to even smile until my friends all came home."

Bev hugged the old soldiers and the old men who had stayed behind. It was a sad, and heartfelt tribute to all who had served, and in all the ways they had helped victory. Bev reflected on the moment and was grateful that her friends had helped her frame the meaning of patriotism and sacrifice.

~ ~ ~

At the cottage Sparky was having second thoughts. "Are we sure about this?" he asked Trong. "We got two women and Letitia. We ain't heard from Wells and we may be under surveillance." His mouth was dry and he sort of felt dizzy.

Trong's face reflected that he also had misgivings about the plan. "Let's just get out of here. We'll use the Bronco 'cause it's in the garage. If anyone is watching they won't see us put those women in the car."

"Letitia, too?"

"No, she'd take up too much space." Trong got their satchel and packed it in the Bronco. He walked back to the bedroom to get Lynn and Amelia. "Christ almighty, they locked the door." He raised his boot and kicked in the door finding Lynn and Amelia standing in the center of the room trying to figure their next step. So much for Plan B.

"Let's go, ladies." He grabbed at the bindings and dragged the women bundle down the hall, through the kitchen and into the garage.

Sparky stuck his head into Letitia's room. "We gotta go, sorry." He paused a moment, and added, "Thanks for everything." And he was gone.

In the garage Trong used the knife to cut the bindings holding the women together. He pushed both of them into the back seat of the car. Sparky closed the connecting door to the house and took his place in the front passenger seat.

Trong opened the garage door, climbed into the driver's seat. Over the seat, he said, "You ladies stay low and no one gets hurt." They sped away leaving the big garage door open.

~ ~ ~

On the courthouse lawn the investment club members stood off to the side and watched Bev in her triumph. Janet wiped a tear from her eye. "She'll be reelected forever."

"This wasn't about an election," snapped Piper.

"Everything is about the next election," said the politician's daughter. Her father had been the longest serving Sheriff in James County.

Piper opened her mouth to reply, but Janet's face turned white. She looked at a puddle at her feet. "Did my water just break?" she asked Piper and Annie. Each woman took an arm and guided Janet to a bench. Once she was settled, Piper ran to the emergency squad stationed at the edge of the crowd. With quick gestures she had them on the run in a matter of seconds.

Under a big pine tree a group of teens was sitting enjoying the excitement of Janet almost giving birth in front of the courthouse. "See, her water broke," explained Patti Ann, the pre-med student.

Jason poked Polly, Janet's adopted daughter and suggested, "Better let Uncle Tim know things are happening."

Patti Ann stretched to get a better look. "The baby is moving. She's probably going to have contractions soon as the baby's head moves —

"We don't want to know," cried Doyle, Piper's son, as the other boys plugged their ears and made noises over her explanation.

The investment club gathered around Janet. "Have you seen Lynn?" Piper asked Bev as she stretched on her toes trying to see above the crowd. "She was going to meet us after your speech."

Bev shook her head, distracted by all the attention Janet was receiving from the EMTs.

As the crowd gathered to watch the drama, the EMTs helped Janet to her feet and encouraged her to walk to the ambulance. "Take your time ma'am. But we're saving time this way." Piper watched them move across the courthouse grass and was certain Janet's feet never touched the ground. She was calling Lynn's cell but no one was answering.

"Oh my gosh," gasped Polly after watching the EMTs dance Janet to the ambulance, "It's really time!" She left her friends and dashed to the waiting vehicle. The other kids followed behind, not wanting to see an actual birth, but curious. Polly waved her arms and grabbed at an EMT. It was evident that she wanted to join Janet for the ride to the hospital. Everyone supported her request giving the EMTs no option but to take her along before the baby arrived on the courthouse lawn. The crowd scattered in the wake of the ambulance's departure.

Patti Ann tried to describe the birthing process but everyone scattered. Jason was the quickest, dashing toward the safety of the opposite curb.

~ ~ ~

As Piper was calling Lynn, Letitia's Bronco made a turn and meandered closer to the crowd leaving the courthouse lawn. "Where are we?" Sparky asked.

"I don't know," groused Trong. "I ain't never driven in town." The men watched as people crossed the street around them and the marching band assembled in the street in front of them, the solid rhythm of the drums getting everyone ready to march.

Lynn had been struggling on the floor of the car to at least look out the window, hoping to see or be seen. And there he was – Jason. He was standing in the street staring at his phone screen and thumbing responses. She glared at him using whatever telepathy a mother could manage, willing her son to look at her, at the car, in the window – anything!

Gradually the band assembled and smartly marched in place as each musician picked up the tempo. They moved out as they had been trained, and slowly, very sharply the synchronized body moved forward and the Bronco followed. As the car began to move, Jason looked over the top of his screen and into his mother's eyes – eyes as big as saucers over a mouth stuffed with a rag and muffled. He stared, frozen. The Bronco crept forward.

In the driver's seat Trong said, "I think we're part of a parade."

"No kidding." Sparky was not happy. "All the cross streets have barriers so we can't turn off." Trong was correct. They were in a parade.

~ ~ ~

Jason squinted at the woman on the other side of the window. His mother – with a gag in her mouth! The car slowly moved ahead, behind the band. Maybe he was wrong, Jason thought, maybe it was someone else's mother. More thinking. Maybe he should check it out. "Hey Ricky," he called to one of his friends who still used a bike. "Let me borrow your bike a minute."

"Sure." Ricky was a little distracted while he watched the EMTs hustle Janet to the ambulance as Polly left her friends and ran to scramble into the vehicle. It was a great pantomime as Piper gestured and Polly pretended to cry and the EMTs finally let her in. As Polly climbed into the ambulance Ricky wondered what Jason wanted with a bike. He scanned the crowded.

Wait, there Jason was making languid circles behind the band. As Ricky watched, Jason seemed to panic. He stopped, sent a text then raced back to Ricky. "Follow that car. They got my mom. I'll get Dusty." He thrust the bike into Ricky's hands.

Ricky took off in his bike keeping close to the Bronco, not knowing what else to do, or why he was doing it. He did know that if Dusty was involved it might be something exciting. So he made lazy arcs behind the car, waiting for ... something.

In the meantime Jason texted Dusty alerting him to Lynn's danger and gave a fair description of the car. Next he alerted his own posse to find bikes, suggesting anyone with a bike surround the Bronco. His plan – slow the car down. Soon the courthouse lawn was alive with younger kids screaming robbery and murder as their bikes disappeared at the hands of the older kids.

After seeing Jason Lynn tumbled back to the floor of the car and struggled to get to the window again. Amelia understood and managed to help her inch up then held Lynn in place. Lynn raised her eyes to the window as Ricky trailed the car, quickly joined by Jeff, the two boys not old enough to drive and still willing to ride bikes in public. They made lazy arcs, calling to each other and waving to their friends as the band marched down the street.

Back on the courthouse lawn, all the older kids grabbed, borrowed or stole bikes in their effort to support Jason in pursuit of ... something.

~ ~ ~

The FBI stakeout team had watched the Bronco leave Letitia's neighborhood. They noted that no one closed the garage door. An unusual occurrence. But what bothered the agents was that two men drove the car and there was no sign of Letitia. In a quick call to Claire, Agent Wilson explained, "The two guys left. We watched two women enter the house, two guys drive away and no sign of those women or the woman who owns the car."

Claire thought a moment. "Are you certain those women aren't inside having coffee and donuts?"

"One of the women was that detective's wife." The agent became more specific about his concerns. "And that other woman is the one who watched the tapes on Saturday. It's just that it doesn't feel right. Why is Dusty's wife paying a visit? And that other woman?"

"Knock on the door," said Claire, "but nothing else. I'll

give Dusty a call if you don't raise anyone."

Several minutes later Claire received a call. "No answer. The cars that the other women drove into the neighborhood are still here."

"I'll call Dusty." Claire skimmed through her contacts list on her phone, thumbed Dusty's icon and waited for him to answer.

And waited.

A few minutes later after she had stewed and cursed – her agents always took her calls – her phone vibrated. "We've got something going on here," said Dusty with no greeting. "Lynn and Amelia seem to be hostages of those men staying with Letitia."

"What can we do?" Claire knew how to change course in mid-air. "That's why I was calling you. My guys saw Lynn enter Letitia's house and they were uneasy because the Bronco drove off."

Dusty swore. "I don't know why she went to Letitia's but I gotta go, the Bronco is surrounded by bicycles and the marching band."

Bicycles and the marching band? Small town law enforcement certainly dealt out of the box! Claire called her agent. "Enter the house. I have just been notified that Lynn and Amelia are being held hostage in a parade."

"A parade?"

"Just enter the house," said Claire, "You have my authority and I'm sure this will all make sense at our wrap-up." She couldn't tell if Agent Wilson laughed or growled.

~ ~ ~

Lynn watched through the car's window with Amelia's knees holding her in place, her eyes barely above the rim of the window frame, as Jason's friends began to slowly drift in and around the car, delaying its getaway. She almost laughed when she saw Jason race into the mob on a pink, very girlie bike – pink woven basket included. And an angry little girl rushing after him, shouting. More kids with bikes seemed to be joining what was now looking like an impromptu parade. A parade with a lot of angry youngsters trying to reclaim bikes as the older kids pedaled faster. People along the sidewalk were waving and smiling. The angry little girl was getting closer to Jason. And the band marched on!

The driver of the car was almost as angry as the little girl, as he swerved to miss one bicyclist after another. The kids were keeping the car at a snail's pace without seeming to notice. The angry little girl wasn't giving up. And the band marched on!

As the parade got closer to the next intersection Jason went flying across the hood of the car. People rushed to him. He lay sprawled on the street in front of the car that was soon surrounded by pedestrians and cyclists. The little girl was on top of him, kneeling on his back and yelling.

"That's my bike," she cried and hit him, "You took it. That's not right." More hits.

As the crowd was entertained by the assault on Jason, two people quietly attached a chain to the rear bumper of the get-away car. Dusty sent Teniquia, who was the officer in uniform today, to talk with the driver about the "accident."

She knocked on the driver's side window and the man lowered the window a bit. "Sir, may I see your license?"

The man pulled out a wallet and handed her his ID.

"Sir, can you give me insurance information? This young man may need medical attention. You can't leave until the ambulance gets here." Tee was really improvising. It had been years since she had been on foot patrol. The little girl was still yelling at Jason.

As the man got out of the car, Teniquia held the door and quickly released the lock for the other doors. Immediately both back doors opened and officers grabbed

Lynn and Amelia. And the band marched on!

Dusty came rushing through the crowd as Teniquia shoved the man against the car and patted him down while Lynn and Amelia were cut loose from the ties. All the other youngsters who had lost their bikes in the escapade reached the crowd. Arguments and shoving. More uniformed officers appeared.

Dusty dragged Jason away from the little girl. He picked up the pink girlie bike, now twisted and useless. Before she could begin to cry Dusty took her name and address and promised that Jason would buy her a new bike.

Sparky and Trong were led away. The crowd was dispersed and four more bikes were found to be ruined. Dusty took more names and addresses. The newspaper reporter and press photographer were delighted with events. They had thought they would spend their day at a mind-numbing speech and little else. They took photos and got quotes and finally got some of Dusty's attention for the full story.

And the band marched on!

# Chapter Twenty-nine

Zachary missed the flight out in the morning. He had tried to leave Amelia early Sunday morning, then sort of tried after lunch, then, what the heck, he didn't want to take a red-eye. And here he was Monday morning, Memorial Day, watching his plane dash down the runway. He smiled to himself. He'd see Amelia tonight and make certain he was on that plane Tuesday – sometime.

Shuffling back to his car at the new airport parking deck, wondering what the gate attendant would say when he presented his long term parking ticket with only fifteen minutes as a charge, he was distracted by his phone with a new text message. This was strange – a message from Nathan? The man didn't text or use any of the up-to-the-minute communications – was something wrong? Buck? Little Olivia? Zachary stepped to the side of the parking deck entry and squinted at the screen.

*Amelia catnipped*

*What?*

*kitnipped*

*What?*

*df;gjprihp*

Clearly Nathan was upset. Zachary had to phone his brother-in-law for an explanation. "What?" he shouted as Nathan answered.

Nathan was just as upset talking as he was texting. He stuttered for several seconds before responding, "Amelia and Lynn have been kidnapped. Jason is leading the posse. On bicycles."

"What?"

"I have this..." Nathan seemed to sniffle into the phone. "Well, I don't know what I have. Jason added it to my phone so I could stay in touch during the football pool. And he's organizing his friends to ... . do something with bikes ... . on Main Street. ... during the parade."

"You're not making any sense," shouted Zachary while airport travelers tried to avoid him as he ranted and paced in front of the parking deck's entrance ramp. "Amelia was going to relax today." His phone chirped. "Wait. I have another call."

"Dad," Buck shouted into Zachary's ear, "Amelia's been kidnapped."

"I know. Nathan phoned. Can you explain it better?" Zachary was trying to get to his car, but the new parking deck obstructed his phone signal so he had to keep returning to the sidewalk.

"Mars called," explained Buck, "and ... then the kids ... that's all I know."

"Wait!" shouted Zachary standing firmly on the sidewalk, "tell me again. Never mind. I'm still in the airport. Where should I go?"

"Just get back to River Bend and call," replied Buck, "I'll have more information by then."

Zachary put away his phone and raced up the ramp. He hoped he could find his parking ticket or he would crash through the barrier.

~ ~ ~

The FBI searched Letitia's house and were surprised to find her bound and gagged in her bedroom. A quick call to Claire and details seemed to make sense. Clearly Sparky and Trong had intended to abandon her.

Letitia was helped into her kitchen where one of the agents made her a cup of tea as they initiated their soft, victim-focused interrogation. Claire relayed the information back to Dusty who was helping Mars release

Amelia and Lynn from their bindings.

Dusty never knew whether to bellow or punch something when he found Lynn involved in an investigation. Here she was again, this time trussed up to be used as a hostage. "Almost done, Chief," said Mars as he continued cutting the ties. The women had become the center of the parade crowd. They sat on a streetside flower planter as Mars tried to preserve their dignity and free them at the same time. They looked at Dusty and watched the cool detective melt. "What were you doing?" he demanded of Lynn.

"Ga, ma, ga," stuttered Lynn still struggling with her mouth stuffing.

"She was helping me," Amelia said as she pulled the last cotton strip from her mouth.

"Ga, ma, ga, ga," Lynn argued.

Dusty looked at Amelia. "She said you're lying to protect her."

"You understood that?" Amelia was amazed.

Mars helped both women to their feet while Lynn continued to pull pieces of fabric out of her mouth. Claire arrived at the scene wearing her official FBI windbreaker, followed by two of her agents. They helped the local police with crowd control, or as it appeared now, party control.

Claire made her way to Dusty and his two released hostages. She pulled two small bottles of water from her jacket and handed them to Lynn and Amelia. "Do you always use a parade to catch thieves?" she asked. Dusty swore.

"They took us as hostages," said Lynn after she had downed a nice gulp of water. "What about Letitia?"

"My team has her," explained Claire. "When they saw the Bronco leave and we heard from Dusty that he was already engaged with the Bronco, we entered her house and found her. She's having tea and answering questions, now."

~ ~ ~

Trooper Doug Fiori had volunteered for extra highway patrol duty this weekend. He had no life – divorced and not encouraged by his ex to spend much time with his son, he chose to work most weekends he wasn't needed at the family farm. Interstate duty wasn't bad, he could sit at one of the speed trap spots and catch some speeders, cruise through a rest stop, maybe–

A Mercedes flashed by as though the patrol car were not only standing still, but invisible. That driver has some balls, thought Doug as he engaged his blue light and stomped the gas.

Zachary Rawlings cursed as he pulled onto the shoulder of the interstate. He was just minutes away from the exit for River Bend. He powered down his window and began to babble as soon as the officer came within hearing distance.

"Officer," Zachary almost shouted, "I have to get to River Bend ... bank robbery ... fiancée..."

The man was making no sense to Doug. "Sir, would you get out of the car, please?"

Zachary opened the car door and reached for his phone before turning to exit.

"Sir, please drop whatever is in your hand," requested the officer.

"It's my phone," Zachary explained. He thrust the phone out ahead of himself and dropped it on the gravel. "I'm sorry, I was trying to show you." He scrambled out and fell to the ground to retrieve the phone.

By this time, Doug had assessed the man and car and concluded the citizen was very distraught, but not a threat. "Sir, may I help you?"

"She was kidnapped." Zachary punched his cell. "Here, he'll tell you." He pushed the phone into Doug's hand.

Being polite and not wanting to increase the man's anxiety, Doug spoke into the phone, "This is highway

**232**

patrolman Doug Fiori. Who is this? ... . Dusty? ... . I stopped this gentleman going about ninety on the interstate ... something about kidnapping ... wait a minute." He turned to the citizen. "Are you Mr. Rawlings?" He turned back to the phone. "Yes, it's him ..... Yeah ... Yeah ... Yeah." He handed the phone to Zachary. "He wants to talk to you."

Zachary took the phone. "Dusty? Is she all right? ... Yeah ... Yeah." He ended the call and looked sheepishly at the patrolman. "How fast was I going?"

"Fast enough that I've got to write you a ticket. I'm sorry about your fiancée."

Zachary smiled. "Dusty says she's fine. They got the men who robbed the bank."

Doug did the quick paperwork for the speeding fine and asked Zachary to sign it. "You show the lady the size of this fine and she'll know you care." Doug smiled at the man who seemed to be calming down.

"That's a great idea." He punched another number into his phone and said as the call was answered, "Meet me at Dusty's office with an attorney ... . No, I'm not under arrest." He glanced at Doug. "Am I?" Doug shook his head. "Just meet me. Dusty is keeping Amelia until I get there."

Now Doug was curious. "Why don't you follow me to Dusty's office. You'll stay out of trouble that way." He waited for Zachary's reply as several cars and trucks rushed by, sliding into the far lane.

Zachary heaved a sigh. "Sure. And thank you."

"The highway patrol doesn't want to stand in the way of romance." And Doug wanted this man to get to his fiancée in one piece.

~ ~ ~

Zachary got to Dusty's office but did not find Amelia waiting for him. Danny looked up as he entered the office. "She's at the hospital."

Zachary paled. "She's injured?" He gripped the side of a

desk and sank into a chair.

Danny jumped to his feet to assist the man. "No, sir, they all wanted to be there when Janet has her baby."

"Baby?"

"Janet, you know the one who married Lynn's brother-in-law from her first marriage and the daughter of the old sheriff?" Danny handed Zachary a glass of water. "Sir, do you know who I mean?"

Zachary sipped the water and tried to recall if he knew any of these people. "I know Lynn."

Danny grinned. "There you go. They're all at the hospital waiting for the baby. Do you want me to drive you there."

Zachary stood, a little shaky. "No, I'll find my way."

He got to the hospital and followed several older men helping a man in a wheelchair. "Where is she?" the wheelchair man demanded.

"Now, Sheriff," one man tried to calm the speaker.

Another man added, "Bergy, we got you here in time. That little Polly hasn't texted us. Her last message said the delivery room waiting area is on the third floor."

"We'll get there on time, Sheriff, don't you worry."

Zachary thought over what Danny had said about Lynn's brother-in-law and an old sheriff and decided to follow the wheelchair man.

~ ~ ~

"We'll have plenty of time," said Thel as Lynn paced the maternity waiting area. "I was in labor for two days with Janet." Polly and Amelia gasped. "Don't worry, honey, I don't remember it and neither does Janet. Bergy took a long time to recover from the ordeal."

"What's the doctor say?" Lynn asked Piper and Annie who had arrived with the ambulance.

"Dr. Rita's away," moaned Piper. "Does Janet have a sub?"

"Rita isn't Janet's doctor," said Thel. "She's been seen by

that ob-gyn that was in the play. You know, that chubby guy."

Annie slapped her thigh. "He was so funny in that part. Trying to look like a policeman and we all comparing him to Mars." They started talking about the play, *The Odd Couple* that had run for a weekend two years ago at the River Bend Little Theater.

"Any word about Janet?" Bergy interrupted the post play review as he wheeled off the elevator.

"Nothing."

The ob-gyn stepped into the waiting area. "Janet says you're all welcome to join us."

"What?" screeched Piper.

"It's the new family way system in our hospital. Lynn gave us the money to remodel," Dr. Avery reminded them.

"The Philanthropies gave the hospital some of the money." Lynn straightened him out.

"Whatever," he replied. "Are any of you coming? This is going to be fast."

Polly said, "I'm ready." She pulled an iPad out of her shoulder bag. "I'm supposed to record this for Tim. If you're wireless, I might be able to let him see it in real time."

The doctor scowled at her. "Does Janet know this?"

"It's her idea. I don't know if Tim agreed," frowned Polly. "He's a pretty queasy guy."

Bergy spun his wheelchair and directed all the men in the waiting area. "You all sit. The women will take care of this."

"We won't have to watch the movie, will we?" asked on unsettled former deputy.

Zachary had to silently agree. He took a seat as Bergy directed.

A nurse poked her head through the door and nodded to Dr. Avery. He pushed Polly ahead of him through the door as he glanced back at the rest of the women. They looked at one another and dashed through the door to dress for the event.

~ ~ ~

235

Letitia wasn't certain how to respond to the FBI"s questions as she sat, very confused, in her kitchen. She knew a lot, but she also knew that Trong and Sparky had certain goals and that she and Wells wanted no part of the robbery. She decided to stay focused on knowing nothing.

So when the agent asked, "Did you know what they were planning?"

She replied, "No, they were just staying here until the board found other lodgings." Her conscience pricked her, so she added, "They were fine men, no problems, helped with the cooking and cleaning."

"We understood that you were housing three men." The agent waited for her reply trying to look pleasant and un-accusing.

Letitia felt safer answering this question. "Yes, Mr. Wells. He borrowed my truck to go to his grandfather's funeral in Kentucky."

"When do you expect him to return?"

She didn't feel certain about the answer to this question. Were Trong and Sparky planning to meet up with Wells? Had they decided to take their money and leave her behind? That meant she was without a job, without a car and without a home because her landlord would certainly think an FBI raid somehow was in violation of her lease. "I don't know when he'll return. His things are still here."

The FBI agent had been considerate and, after assuring her that her car would be returned to her, left Letitia alone in her cottage. She kept hearing a distant buzz. Was that her phone? That's all she needed if the events of the day were already on the evening news her mother must be calling to gloat.

Her phone. Where had she seen it? Those FBI people left it once they concluded it belonged to her and she wasn't involved. Some consolation – no home, no job, but she had a phone. She found it resting beside her breakfast coffee mug.

Breakfast? She hadn't had any food since then. Her phone buzzed again. With a sigh she tapped the screen to talk.

"You alone?" whispered a voice. She looked at the screen. It wasn't Wells number, but it was his voice.

"Yes."

"You know who this is?"

"Yes."

"What happened today?"

"Don't you know?" she let the anger and disappointment work into her voice.

"No. I sent Trong a text last night to say the house was staked out and to stand by while I figured something out." Wells sighed into the phone. "What did those assholes do?"

Letitia's heart fluttered. Had she been mistaken? "They told me that you wanted them to leave me behind and they were leaving to join you. They sort of kidnapped two women as hostages and left me tied up at the house."

"Aw, shit," he moaned, "that wasn't the plan."

"What now?"

"Sit tight," he warned, "I'll come up with a plan. Can you stay there for a few days?"

"Yes."

"I don't want to talk too long if they're checking your phone. I got me a throw away. Delete this call. I'll call again." He was gone.

Letitia's heart was now pounding. He hadn't left her. He seemed to suggest that he would be rescuing her and taking her to some safe place. She'd wait and see. It was better than running back to her mother's place.

~ ~ ~

Dusty had Lynn wrapped in his arms as they finally snuggled in bed. He kissed her temple, held her tighter and said, "I can't get used to you in danger."

She yawned and got comfortable. "I wasn't in danger. They were really hapless."

"We didn't know that. You didn't know that." He kissed her again.

"I've been in worse situations."

He cursed, then said, "That's my point. I can't get used to you -"

"I didn't get myself kidnapped," she sighed, "or all those other things on purpose."

He mumbled, "I know."

She wiggled around so that she could kiss him. "Besides. It was a glorious day. Janet's baby is healthy. We were all there to welcome him. He looks just like Bergy, all red and bald and scowling." She could feel Dusty's laughter. "Even Tim called him a little Bergy when he skyped."

"The name will stick," predicted Dusty as he tried to get her attention. But he realized she was limp. She'd fallen asleep in mid-conversation. He held her tighter, burying his nose in her hair.

What a day it had been, he thought. And what a wife! She didn't understand his concern for her safety. Maybe he saw too much bad and she saw too much good. He worried and she didn't.

Susan Carmichael's death had been frightening to Lynn but several months of counseling seemed to have brought back her optimism. He only wished he knew a way to keep her safe without dampening her outlook and enthusiasm. He'd have to just be more vigilant, he thought, because he didn't want her spirit dampened. With that thought he wrapped them both in the sheets and fell asleep himself.

# Chapter Thirty

"That's some story in the paper this morning," said Jim as he walked into Lynn's kitchen. He handed his grandson twenty dollars.

"What's this for?" asked Jason who was huddled over a bowl of cereal.

"To help you pay for the bikes," said his grandfather, "A reward for saving my daughter." He tousled Jason's morning hair.

Will came into the kitchen and slapped a fifty-dollar bill in front of Jason. "That's the best parade I've ever seen. That little girl was really mad." He laughed.

"Hey, handsome," said Claire as she walked into the kitchen followed by two FBI agents. She plunked a big manila envelope in front of Jason. "We found the bank money. We took up a collection for the bikes." Jason grinned at her.

Jim and Will introduced themselves to the FBI. Claire pulled up a chair to join Jason at breakfast. The two agents felt comfortable in Lynn's kitchen and helped themselves to coffee.

"You caught your guys?" asked Will. He liked these early morning crime wrap-ups.

"Yeah," said Claire after she looked for her own bowl, "those two guys said they wanted to get some money and leave town. We're still trying to track down the third guy."

One of the agents buttered some toast and said, "He really was at a family funeral. So he may be coming back here. So far those guys say he was too busy," he looked at Jason, "ah, too busy getting to know Ms. Jacquet to pay attention to what they were doing."

"Yeah," agreed Dusty as he walked into the kitchen.

"She lost her job because the board found out she and Wells were getting to know one another."

"I'm in college," moaned Jason, "I know what your talking about."

"What who's talking about?" asked Lynn as she stumbled into the kitchen in her bathrobe. "I'm not going to work today." One of the agents stood to give her his seat.

Claire greeted her asking, "What's this I hear that you always manage to interfere with investigations?"

Will laughed. "Let us tell you!" And they spent an hour aggravating Dusty as Will, Jim and Jason detailed Lynn's crime solving exploits.

~ ~ ~

Tuesday morning found Zachary holding Amelia as they slowly awakened in her condo. "I want you safe. Do you feel safe after your ordeal?"

"Yes." She kissed his cheek. "That wasn't frightening." Her eyes saddened. "My marriage was much scarier." Zachary hugged her, wanting to cry himself.

"If you're uneasy, though, we can spend a few days at Palmer Mansion," said Zachary. "They'd love to have us."

"Thank you." Amelia and Zachary had gone to dinner at Palmer Mansion last evening. Once Zachary got back to River Bend and rescued her from the birthing hysteria, he had rushed to his family who had been texting with their concerns all afternoon.

"They love you," he reminded her.

"I'll be all right while you're in Texas."

"I don't have to return to Texas until after our wedding," said Zachary. "We'll go there as part of our honeymoon."

"Wedding?"

"We can have it organized in a few weeks," he outlined his plans. "We get married, attend some dance and leave town. Nathan says we have to attend some hospital dance because everyone bought tickets thinking we would be there."

"What?"

"Ask your friends." Zachary shrugged. "I think ticket sales were slow, so the committee let it be known you would attend as Mrs. Zachary Rawlings." He checked the date on his watch. "It's about three weeks from now. So we better hurry."

"Wedding?"

"Your friends will help you. We also have to go to the lake this weekend."

Amelia was beside herself with indignation. "A wedding? My friends will help? Three weeks?"

"Yes." He kissed her. "Yes," kissed her again. "And yes." He wrapped her in his arms and convinced her that three weeks might probably be too long a wait.

By the end of the morning, Zachary learned that he still had to leave town. But it was only a run down to Atlanta.

"Atlanta?"

"They have set up a transition office at our Atlanta location. They said it would be easier to close out my final tasks." He was throwing a few things in an over night bag. "You need anything, call Nathan or Buck."

"I will," agreed Amelia realizing that she had a wedding to plan in less than three weeks.

"I'll be back Thursday. And we'll go to the lake for a long weekend."

~ ~ ~

Wells wasn't certain about what the FBI could do with phones. So he had purchased a throwaway phone to contact Letitia. He kept his other phone, though, because his mother had that number in case she needed him. She had given him a quick call to make certain he had gotten safely back to River Bend. And that's how they found him.

Late Tuesday afternoon, the FBI surrounded an old

barn on the outskirts of Verona, a small farm community several miles outside of River Bend. "Mr. Wells, this is the FBI."

Wells sighed, then shouted, "I'm unarmed and I'm coming out."

And that's how he found himself in the James County jail with Trong and Sparky.

"What were you thinking?" Wells growled at his two cellmates. "Kidnapping? Weapons?"

"It was only a knife," moaned Trong. "We wanted to look scary."

"Scary?" snorted Wells. "I can't believe those women didn't punch you both."

"We showed them that we had your girlfriend tied up."

"Is she hurt? If you hurt her-"

Trong and Sparky stared that their partner. "What's going on?" asked a puzzled and confused Sparky. "She important to you?"

Wells hung his head. It was a question that he had posed to himself. "Maybe." That was the same answer he gave himself. "She kinda scratched an itch."

Trong snorted. "She did more than scratch. I thought you two would drive that bed through the wall." Wells gave him a look that made Trong gulp and quickly move to a far corner of the cell.

"I made plans. I was going to take her to my mama's place. We were going to leave this place once things cooled down." He glared at his partners. "Until you jackasses kidnapped that detective's wife."

"We didn't know," whined Sparky. "She looked too pretty to go for some cop."

"But we got a plan," bragged Trong. "It will get us all what we want."

"I'm listening."

"We been telling all the cops and the FBI that we acted

alone. You and Letty weren't a part."

"Do they believe you?"

"Since we only stole three hundred dollars and used a steak knife to scare the ladies, they think we're stupid." Sparky hung his head. As a career criminal he had a certain reputation to uphold. Being seen as stupid just rubbed him the wrong way – but he needed healthcare. "I think they're buying what we're saying. Have they talked with you?"

"I said I wanted a lawyer. I called Letty for help."

Trong eyed him speculatively. "Do you think she can get one?"

"I don't know, but I think she's smarter than we first thought."

"God, I hope so."

~ ~ ~

Lynn made Dusty and Jim move furniture to open up the living room floor for the first dance lesson to help everyone prepare for the hospital gala. The larger pieces were pushed against the wall while smaller pieces were carried into the dining room or the family office. Piper was busy directing Will's efforts to get the refreshments arranged on the dining room table and Marianna was reviewing a selection of music for the first dance night in The Heights.

Dancers began to arrive. Salley had Carl there, much to Dusty's delight. Buck and Penny arrived with Amelia and Nathan. "Dad had to leave town for a quick business trip," announced Buck. Everyone smiled at Amelia.

"I'm the lucky substitute," bragged Nathan. "I haven't danced with such a young and lovely woman as you in years, my dear." Amelia smiled. Lynn could tell that she was uncomfortable and not eager to be Nathan's dance partner.

"I hope I'll get an opportunity to be your partner this evening, Nathan," Lynn teased as she took his arm. After a sideways glance from Lynn, Piper pushed Will toward

*There's No Explaining Love*

Amelia.

Will looked back at his wife and received a complex series of eye movements which only a husband could understand because he said, "Great, and I can't think of anyone I want more for a partner than my oldest friend here." He grabbed Amelia's hand. "She won't laugh at me."

"No one," announced Marianna in her best director voice, "may laugh at anyone." She surveyed the class. "Is that clear?" They all meekly nodded. Marianna walked through the room examining her dancers as a general inspects the ranks. "Next class we all wear dancing shoes, the shoes you will wear to the gala. I don't care about the rest of your outfit. However," she swirled in her full skirt, "we ladies might enjoy practicing in a full skirt to learn to manage a dress while dancing."

"Manage a dress?" Amelia almost cried.

"Don't worry, sweetie," consoled Marianna, "I have a few things for you to use until we find the perfect dress for your coming out." Amelia moaned and everyone laughed until they caught Marianna's scowl. "Now, my partner and I will demonstrate a simple box step." She and Jim danced to a tune as everyone watched. When the song ended there was applause.

"Where did you learn to dance like that, Jim?" asked Will.

"Old Miss Lavinia."

"Miss Lavinia?" Nathan shook his head. "How old was she when she taught you? I thought she was at least ninety when I took her classes."

"Do you mean," asked Jim, "that she taught you, too? You're younger than me and I thought she was ninety."

"You took dancing lessons, Dad?" asked Lynn.

"Hell, yes. Your grandmother thought I needed to have manners. Miss Lavinia taught it all, forks and dancing and manners."

"Forks?"

"You know, which one to use for each course." Jim turned to Nathan. "Did she use that fake food when she taught you? And make you sip water from wine glasses?"

"She did it all," frowned Nathan. "Those classes were interminable. Sixty minutes of hell. She always had eight couples per class." Nathan looked at his audience. "Eight eager girls and eight reluctant boys, all eleven or twelve." He paused as he remembered. "My hands were always sweaty and I always thought my zipper would slide open."

"If you acted up," Jim said, "Miss Lavinia would be your partner until you demonstrated that you would behave. I think I danced with her more than with any of the girls in my class." Everyone looked at Marianna who nodded and then they laughed.

"One day we all wanted to be at a skating party in the park. So me and one of the other guys changed the clock in our classroom, which was her parlor. She came in, looked at the clock, looked at this little watch she had on a ribbon pinned to her dress, changed the clock back, then turned to me." Jim shook his head. "She always knew it was me. She said, 'Your mother pays for sixty minutes.' That was that, we all got to the park late."

After the Miss Lavinia memories, Marianna took control of the evening. She and Jim demonstrated the steps and watched as each couple worked at learning the pattern. Since Will and Lynn had other partners, Dusty and Piper found themselves as a dance class couple. At one point Dusty finally lifted Piper, her feet left the floor and he danced through the pattern himself while she yelped and complained. Marianna separated them and said, "Dusty, for misbehaving you have to dance with Miss Lavinia," and she placed her left arm on his shoulder and held out her right hand." She looked at the class and nodded. They all roared their approval. Dusty glowered.

Leaving the box step, Marianna took everyone into the world of the waltz, as she called it. "This is why you want a flowing skirt." She demonstrated as Jim swirled her around the floor. "This dance it best learned from the beginning with music. The rhythm is what drives the dancers. So begin." With this Marianna took Nathan's arm and Jim took hold of Amelia. All the other couples sorted themselves out and began counting to themselves as Marianna counted out loud.

Jim called, "Change partners." All the couples realigned as the music continued. Jim called, "Change partners," again. This time Amelia ended up with Nathan. They waltzed around the floor still concentrating on Marianna's count.

When the music ended, Nathan kissed Amelia's hand. "Thank you, my dear. The night of the gala you must save a waltz for me." Everyone grinned. The first lesson was a great success. Dusty handed out the beers.

# Chapter Thirty-one

**K**idnapped Monday, dancing classes Tuesday, Lynn hoped Wednesday would be boring. It was late morning and time for some tea and a nibble on that pastry Jason had dropped by on his way to deliver an order to the coffee shop in the business park. She was sitting at her conference table staring into her teacup when she looked up and saw Letitia Jacquet in the parking lot sobbing as she walked toward the Philanthropies office.

All sorts of negative comments tumbled through Lynn's mind. But the last time she had seen Letitia the woman had been bound and gagged. Lynn could be charitable.

Nelda stuck her head in the conference room, "There's -"

"I saw her, bring her on, I mean in." Nelda held her laughter as she opened the door for Letitia to enter.

"Would you like some tea?" Lynn asked as she got another small plate, disappointed that she would have to share her pastry. "I don't have any coffee made."

"Nothing, thank you," said the subdued woman, holding in a sob, barely.

A woman as large as Letitia crying? Lynn capitulated. "How can I help?"

"You don't even know my problem." Letitia wiped her eyes.

"You're in love." Lynn wondered at the idea even as she saw the evidence before her.

"I am?" Letitia took the offered tissues.

"Trust me, you are." Lynn patted her shoulder as she set a cup of microwaved tea on the table. "Is he good to you?"

Letitia nodded as she blew her nose in a tissue. "So how can I help?"

It came out in a rush of words. "They've got him in jail. They think he robbed the bank. He didn't. Those other two want to be in jail."

"I don't understand," said Lynn, perplexed.

"I don't either, but they think life outside is too hard. And Sparky's sick and needs chemo." Lynn gasped. Letitia continued, "They want to be guilty. But Wells wants to take me to his mama in Kentucky where we can be us." She heaved great sobs.

Jail. Innocent lives. Love. Where was a super hero when you needed one, Lynn wondered? And it came to her – Herbie! Several years ago H. Lawrence Grayson, pompous local attorney, had helped Dusty track a murderer. During a hard drinking evening, the gang learned he thought of his alter-ego as Herbie, the avenger of ... well, no one was certain of what. But he had proved himself brave and determined to seek justice.

Lynn called out. "Nelda when is Mr. Grayson due here to sign checks?"

"He just walked in."

Lynn grinned, the solution was at hand. "Send him in here."

H. Lawrence Grayson, prominent attorney and the Philanthropies board treasurer, walked into the conference room, being his usual pompous thirty-something self. "Yes," he smirked. Letitia sobbed. He looked at Lynn and knew his cushy pompous life was going to get sidetracked into one of her schemes. His alterego, Herbie, sort of felt excited.

"Herbie, this is Letitia." Lynn took his arm and led him to a chair. "Her boyfriend has been arrested as a suspect in that bank robbery and he's innocent."

"Innocent my eye." The pompous attorney was still in

charge.

Letitia sobbed harder.

Lynn continued the explanation as though no one in the room was a cynic and no one was sobbing. "The other two men are guilty. And want to be so guilty that they end up in a clean, well-run federal prison. Letitia's boy friend, Mr. Wells, wants nothing more than to take Letitia back to Kentucky to meet his family and build a new life."

"No."

Lynn ignored him. "Just stop by the jail and iron this all out. You only have to deal with the FBI. Everyone knows they like to see people caught and punished. They'll love finding reasons to be harsh and put those two men away for the rest of their lives. And they don't railroad innocent people so they'll appreciate your explaining what a nice man Mr. Wells is."

Letitia had stopped crying and was listening to Lynn. Herbie looked at them both and snarled, "You're just lucky I don't have any appointments this afternoon." He signed the checks Lynn placed in front of him and walked out of the office.

"Is he going to help us?"

"Of course," said Lynn.

"But he doesn't know us."

"He has a soft spot for love."

"Love?"

"Letitia, you and Mr. Wells have found one another. That's magic. We should help you. Herbie has lost a good woman and found another. He understands love."

"I can't pay him."

Lynn grinned at Letitia. "You go home and wait to hear from Herbie. Don't worry about anything else."

~ ~ ~

Dusty looked up as Zachary Rawlings entered the office. The detective stood because Zachary looked very focused.

249

*There's No Explaining Love*

"May I help you?"

Zachary looked around the office and nodded to Dusty. "Are those kidnappers in jail? Are they suffering?"

Dusty tried not to sigh out loud. "We have them stretched on the racks in the secret subbasement."

"I knew it," said Zachary as he flopped in the chair beside Dusty's desk. "You guys are so easy, lenient and too soft. Look what they did to our women!"

"Don't you mean womenfolk?" asked Dusty. "Although if you mean Lynn and Amelia, they already got past this. All I've heard for two days is weddings and dresses and dances." Dusty gave his visitor the evil eye. "And that means tuxedos and hair cuts and other things I don't even want to think about."

"And it's all my fault. Is that what you're saying?"

"If the dancing shoe fits," Dusty shrugged without finishing the statement.

Zachary rubbed his forehead. "I was so frightened when I got Nathan's text and Buck's phone call." He sort of smiled. "You be good to that highway patrolman –"

"Doug Fiore," offered Dusty.

"Yes, he could have shot me or something. I was out of control, babbling and falling down on the roadside."

The two men were silent for a moment. Zachary cleared his throat. "Can I take Amelia away for a few days? You don't need to question her any more or anything?"

Dusty smiled. He studied the man in front of him and knew what Lynn would be thinking – love! "She's free to leave town. The FBI is wrapping up. They'll have these fellows in court tomorrow. We won't need any witnesses. We're thinking they'll plead."

"They have a lawyer?"

"Do you know H. Lawrence Grayson?"

"They can afford him?"

Now Dusty was embarrassed. "Lynn convinced him to

do some pro bono work."

Zachary gasped. "But they threatened her and kidnapped her," he struggled for breath, "with a weapon."

"Yeah." Dusty shook his head. "They must have made an impression because she got them legal council."

Zachary stared open mouthed at that bit of news. Dusty stood. "Just get Amelia out of town. This isn't going to be pretty."

# Chapter Thirty-two

"Why did we have to get here so quickly?" Amelia asked as they finished breakfast on the deck at the lake house, watching the patterns of clouds reflected in the ripples in the water.

"I have a meeting with some subs." He didn't want to mention the court appearances.

Amelia stared out at the lake, "Submarines?"

He laughed, "No, subcontractors. We're starting the next phase of this development and my job is to interview subs, check their credentials, select those we want a bid from, and maybe even find a general contractor."

"Don't you already know who you want? I mean you have the people who built these houses." Amelia threw her arm out to encompass the neighborhood.

"These houses are ten years old. We're looking for people with experience in new techniques and materials." Zachary stood, taking the dishes back to the kitchen. "You're welcome to sit and listen to the interviews." He turned to Amelia who had followed with the remains of breakfast. "We better hurry. The first appointment is at nine-thirty. Let's have some coffee ready and have them sit in the kitchen."

"Do you really want me with you?"

"Yes. You have experience hiring people." He kissed her lightly. "We'll make a good team." With that they cleaned the kitchen and got ready for the first sub.

As the doorbell rang, Zachary and Amelia went together toward the front of the house with Zachary saying, "You get that, I need some notes from my office."

Opening the door, Amelia was surprised to see her brother, Miguel, standing there. Miguel's shock mirrored hers. "What are you doing here?" he asked. Smiling, she threw her arms around his neck and hugged him with enthusiasm. Miguel laughed and returned her hug with the same unrestrained joy and affection.

"Amelia?" They separated at the sound of Zachary's voice. Holding hands with her brother, Amelia started to speak, but Zachary raised his hand. "Same smile, same eyes, the brother who's a painting contractor?" She nodded.

Zachary looked at his list of scheduled interviews. "Miguel Santiago?" Miguel nodded.

"Please come in." Zachary led them into the kitchen, indicating a chair for Miguel. Amelia sat beside him and was still holding his hand. "Let's get down to business," began Zachary. "I suppose you want an explanation of your sister's presence?" Miguel didn't say anything.

Zachary stood and held out his hand to Miguel, "I'm Zachary Rawlings and I would like to marry Amelia." She giggled and Miguel started to cough.

"I swallowed my gum, " he gasped. Amelia got him a glass of water. Miguel stared at both of them. "When? How?" He told himself that he would call Will in River Bend to catch up on things as soon as this interview was over.

~ ~ ~

Lynn got an afternoon text from Letitia. "He's free. Come to my house."

"Nelda, I'm running an errand," Lynn shouted as she dashed from the office. She arrived at Letitia's small house within minutes, glad that she had avoided that speed trap by the country club entrance. Wells and Letitia were packing the Bronco. They waved as she drove up.

Wells helped her from the car and said, "Thank you, ma'am, for all your help." He was very formal. Lynn gave him a quick hug and watched his surprise.

"Mr. Wells, we always help our friends."

Letitia ran into Lynn scooping her up and swinging her off her feet. "Now, Letty," cautioned Wells, "we can't kill her with affection."

Letitia released Lynn and wiped her eyes. "I'm so happy. You didn't have to help. I was so mean to you."

Lynn patted her arm. "I'm sure you would have helped someone in need." She wasn't certain that were true, but it sounded good and Letitia was sobbing now as Wells tried to console her.

"Letty, honey, it's all right." He wrapped his arms around her. "We'll be at Mama's tonight and you can help my whole family with their problems."

"What are you to planning?" asked Lynn.

They looked at her, not knowing what to say. She was a detective's wife and they were planning on living together. Wells wasn't certain if that was legal. And neither had a job, or plans for one. The more they thought about their situation the more they didn't know what to say to Lynn.

She smiled at them, sort of understanding. She remembered those early days in her romance with Dusty. She had no idea what was in her future. And that's what she said, "You two remind me of me and Dusty. We wanted to be together ... we just had to figure out the details." Now she grinned. They were so cute – really big, but cute. She gave each of them another hug and said, "Be careful, and if you come back to visit family, you stop and see me." They nodded. And she waved as she drove back to her office marveling at love in all its forms.

~ ~ ~

Dusty went through his usual routine as he entered the house. Weapon locked, phone on charger. He walked into the kitchen and went straight to the refrigerator. Noticing Will and Piper sitting at the kitchen table he brought three beers and sat. "No kids?" he asked.

255

"They said to text when we had the food," replied Piper who looked like she was starving.

"Jim and Marianna?" asked Will.

"They agree with the kids," explained Lynn as she walked into the kitchen. "We make the decision and they'll all eat."

"What are you hungry for?" Will asked Dusty. "Because I know my wife will eat anything."

"After seeing Herbie in court, I don't know what I can stomach." Dusty surveyed the group. "He outdid himself. It took us all day to wade through the paper work."

"He got Mr. Wells out." Lynn announced as she sipped her wine. She had seen him and Letitia off.

"What do you know about this?" Dusty gave her his best interrogator's stare.

She grinned back at him. "I asked Herbie to help Letitia."

"You don't even like her," muttered Dusty. "You said she was hostile, fat, unfriendly—"

"Now she's my friend and in love." Lynn smirked as she made her point.

Will spattered beer all over the table as he reacted to this conversation. Piper got a cloth and wiped Will and the table down. He said, "You two aren't making sense."

"Yes, we are," said Lynn and she explained, "Letitia was running that early release program and got caught having an affair with one of the felons."

"Is that legal?"

"They're consenting adults," groused Dusty.

"And in love," added Lynn.

Piper returned the beery cloth to the kitchen sink and sat at the table. "What does Herbie have to do with felon love?"

"When the FBI arrested Mr. Wells for the bank robbery—"

"He robbed the bank and Herbie got him out?"

"Will you let me finish?" Lynn was losing patience with her brother. "Mr. Wells got arrested. Letitia asked for my help."

"What did she expect – you'd organize a jail break?" Will laughed at his own joke.

Lynn gave him a squinty-eyed look. "He was innocent. The other two robbed the bank because they wanted to go back to a good prison."

"A good prison?"

Dusty interrupted. "Let me explain." First, he got another beer and tossed Will a bag of corn chips. Piper rushed to the refrigerator for the guacamole before he started his explanation. "Wells was a prison leader. He had a reputation for looking out for his friends," Dusty paused for a moment to crunch a chip, "He protected them inside and was probably still feeling responsible for them once they were released. That's why I think he planned this robbery – to help his friends get back in prison."

"What?" gasped Piper and Will.

Lynn sighed. "Trong and Sparky wanted back in prison because they're old and have no family. And Sparky has cancer. But they weren't scary enough to rate a federal prison," she kind of shrugged, "because it was just a little bank robbery. So I asked Herbie to help."

"Herbie got them all out of jail? What about the man's cancer?"

Dusty held up his hands signaling time out. "Herbie got everyone where they want to be. That's what I meant about outdoing himself." His audience was all ears. "He got Wells off by pointing out that the FBI had no evidence that he had anything to do with the robbery, he had really been at his grandfather's funeral, and that he was rehabilitated by his romance with Letitia." Dusty shook his head is awe or something. "If he could have managed, he would have had violins for that defense." Sipping his beer he continued, "He did have one of the early release board members willing to swear that Wells had been helping her move furniture the whole time of the robbery. The judge agreed. Then when the other two came up for their hearing Herbie joined the DA and argued as a representative of the victims, the kidnap victims," here he glowered at Lynn, "that these two were hardened criminals who had taken two women at knife point, one a wife of a detective and the other the fiancée of one of the wealthiest men in town. Herbie made the felons sound like two insane perps who planned to take their victims to another state and do despicable things using the money they had stolen -"

"Only three hundred dollars," offered Lynn.

"And torture them with disgusting weapons—"

"A steak knife." Lynn corrected the story.

"So?" Will and Piper were enthralled.

"What did Claire say?" asked Lynn.

Dusty got another round of beer for everyone. "Claire agreed with Herbie and the DA. Privately she said Herbie is up for a secret FBI award for best drama for the least amount of crime. Wells was last seen climbing into Letitia's Bronco."

"They've run off together?" asked Piper as she found a take-out menu on the kitchen counter. "I'm hungry just listening to all this romance and robbery."

"I'm hungry and happy for Letitia," said Lynn as she looked over another menu. "She needed some love in her life. She was so unhappy and lonely."

"So what happened to everyone?" asked Piper as she scribbled an order to call in.

"Everyone is living happily ever after," grinned Lynn.

Will laughed and grabbed up the take out order. "I'm buying. It's the least I can do for all the entertainment I get here." He called the order and texted the boys to pick up the food and texted Jim and Marianna to bring dessert.

The evening got even more entertaining as they waited for the boys to deliver the food. Will's phone rang. "Miguel? What's up? ... Yeah ... yeah ... yeah..."

Everyone stopped to listen and they all grinned as Will tried to get Miguel's attention, "Pal, I didn't know until ... yeah, a bank robbery ... Dusty got them ...Yeah. Just a minute, I'll ask." He turned to Lynn. "Miguel wants to know how rich Zachary is."

"He's Nathan's brother-in-law," said Piper."

Will repeated, "He's Nathan Taft's brother-in-law." Will held the phone away from his ear. "Wait, I'll put you on speaker."

"Hey, Miguel," shouted Lynn over the Spanish coming out of Will's phone, "Did Amelia call you?"

They all listened as Miguel went on to detail his surprise this morning when he called at Zachary's lake house to interview for a job. They all laughed. "Honest, pal," Will apologized, "we didn't find out anything until the FBI came in to solve the bank robbery."

Miguel shouted something about accusing his sister of robbery.

"Calm down," Dusty said, "I never accused her of robbing a bank, or him." Once he heard Dusty's side of the story Miguel began sounding calmer, so Will said to everyone, "I'll finish this call with a little privacy." He took his phone and wandered out of the kitchen.

Shortly the boys came in with bags of food while Jim and Marianna juggled two cakes as they came through the door. "Umberto said these would do. He was closing the bakery as we got there."

Will came back into the kitchen as he shoved the phone into his pocket. While everyone set out the meal, he provided the entertainment relating Miguel's phone call and general astonishment regarding Amelia and Zachary. And after that

*There's No Explaining Love*

Jim and Marianna and the boys wanted the low-down on the robbery. It was a lively meal. Then Patti Ann and Ricky came in to help finish off the food.

Patti Ann, Herbie's sister-in-law, asked Dusty, "Did Herbie really dazzle the FBI in court? He's telling Dad and Dr. Rita all sorts of stories."

"It's all true," said Dusty and he gave an abridged version of the day in court with Herbie the lawyer who both defended and prosecuted in one day or as Dusty put it – typical lawyer, both sides of his mouth.

Dinner finally ended, with everyone sated and the cleaning almost done. The six adults sent the kids into another room, the better to gossip about Amelia and Zachary.

As they whispered and chuckled at the new romance, they heard whoops come from the living room. Lynn rolled her eyes at Dusty. He had made a copy of Jason's footage from the bank security cameras. In one of the camera angles viewers were able to see Jason standing in the bank parking lot staring at his phone, texting, while the robbers scurried into the bank and then back out. During the time it took for the robbery Jason had walked about ten feet, never taking his eyes off his phone.

And the whoops and catcalls belonged to all his friends who delighted in watching the tape, over and over and over...

"How long do you think this will entertain everyone?" Lynn asked.

Dusty smiled, "Maybe by the time he has kids of his own." Dusty shook his head. "No, then it'll start all over again, like the way the boys like to hear about you and Piper and all the trouble you caused."

Lynn scowled. He was correct. The boys never tired of listening to those stories that her father embellished. But wait, she would be the parent who would get to embellish Jason's stories. She smiled just thinking about the future and possible grandchildren.

# Chapter Thirty-three

"**...S**o we need a bigger house." Amelia's voice carried into the kitchen through the open window.

Nathan stirred uneasily in the kitchen, caught eavesdropping but unable to move without giving himself away. Zachary and Amelia were walking along the kitchen garden toward the house.

"You're learning to spend my money quickly," said Zachary.

Nathan frowned as he listened to the private conversation. Was Amelia a grasping spendthrift just like Zachary's late wife, Cynthia? Nathan pursed his lips thinking about the implications for Zachary.

"The lake house." The sound of Amelia's voice showed impatience with her husband. She continued, "We have room for Penny, Buck and Olivia. But where will we put Nathan?"

"At the lake?" asked Zachary.

"Yes. He has to be with us. He has to see Olivia at the playground and all the other places we plan to take her," she explained.

Zachary said something Nathan couldn't hear. Startled by Amelia's concern, he was caught standing in the kitchen as they entered.

"Here he is," said Zachary. "Do you want to sleep on a sofa-bed, a sleeping bag or on the deck on a lounger?"

"What?" Nathan was embarrassed, but warmed, by the discussion he had heard.

"When you all come to the lake," Amelia began, "we'll just give you our bed. Zachary can spend the night in a sleeping bag."

"My dear," said Nathan, "I would sleep at your feet like a faithful old dog." He kissed her hand.

The rest of the evening was spent planning the big family outing to the lake. Nathan enjoyed every minute of the evening and marveled at the way the family had changed, had blossomed, come together, with the addition of Amelia.

~ ~ ~

The baby had arrived. What an experience! Polly had to "talk" with her mother. She was sitting on her bed, holding the charcoal, but still too distracted by the birth to begin sketching Susan. But her hand began its own sketch. It was the baby, all scrunched and new and perfect. Polly grinned. Then she drew her mother, whose face reflected the awe Polly felt in this new life. "See, Mom. That's Little Bergy." Susan smiled. "I knew you'd like him. He looks just like big Bergy. But Janet says he'll get better looking. I think he looks perfect now." Susan's head seemed to nod.

Polly kept talking and seemed to delight Susan with her stories of Janet adjusting to parenthood and Bergy and Thel enthralled with their grandchild. Susan's face reflected her affection for the Bergman family. "I'm glad I'm here," admitted Polly. "They're good to me."

Polly continued to sketch and another emotion appeared on Susan's face. "I did give Lynn the plants from the garden. What else?" Susan's new face gave Polly a look that all mothers used. It meant 'you know what I expect.' "I know. I haven't talked about drawing yet. I have time." Susan's face indicated that she disagreed. In fact, it seemed to tell Polly that enough was enough, get going on developing her talent. Polly looked at that face and sighed. "OK."

This time she didn't stretch out on her bed and reflect on this recent conversation. She began to draw. It became a portrait. Her charcoal danced and swooped across the large sheet. Soon there was a sketch, a portrait, and the answer. Polly knew her mother had taken control. How else could she draw such a perfect sketch. They were all there – Bergy and Thel and even Tim surrounding Janet as she held Little Bergy.

Polly knew what she had to do. She tore the page from her sketchpad and walked downstairs to find the family.

Back in the bedroom Susan's sketch smiled when she heard the gasps of delight and admiration as the Bergmans viewed Polly's art – her gift.

~ ~ ~

Lynn looked up as Nathan tapped on her open office door. She briefly wondered what good having a receptionist was if everyone just barged in. But she welcomed Nathan with a smile.

"I have to tell someone," he confessed.

"Gossip?" Lynn asked in a hopeful voice.

Nathan frowned at her. "No, a secret."

"That's even better." She put down her papers.

Nathan sat on the chair in front of her desk and reached across for her hand. "I overheard Zachary and Amelia talking yesterday."

"Eavesdropping?" accused Lynn.

"Yes," he admitted. He sat, embarrassed at his own venality.

"Well?" Lynn had different standards than Nathan.

"Amelia asked Zachary for a bigger house and I thought Zachary had moved from one grasping wife to another. Cynthia was my sister, but she had her faults. Anyway, as I listened further I found I was the topic of discussion." Nathan related the conversation he had overheard. "I don't think I've ever been the subject of any sort of discussion. And to have it be so loving and caring has me enjoying a guilty pleasure."

Lynn squeezed his hand. "It's something you deserve to know. You heard Amelia express what we all think." Nathan withdrew his hand and pulled a handkerchief from his pocket. He wiped an eye and ran the cloth under his nose.

"So tell me," asked Lynn, "are they building a new house?"

"For our first visit, I'll sleep on the sofa-bed in Zachary's office." Lynn laughed as Nathan anticipated the adventure. "But, " he continued, "Buck may purchase a home there for his family." Nathan raised his eyebrows and stared at Lynn.

"Another baby!" she guessed.

"Yes. It was quite a dinner last evening and the most delightful family meal I've ever had." Nathan beamed at his friend.

~ ~ ~

Lynn got home in a panic. There was another dance class tonight. Trying to keep up with Zachary's timetable for the wedding was making everyone breathless. Of course, this whole adventure wasn't without comic relief. They were all still laughing at Miguel. He had placed a panic call to Will hours after meeting Zachary.

According to Will, Miguel had no idea that his sister was even thinking about dating let alone marriage, and as Miguel put it, marriage to a bundle of money. Will was still delighting everyone with the story.

Lynn smiled to herself. Zachary had been out of town for a few days and was returning this evening to attend dancing class. That thought brought her back to her time crunch – she had to get Dusty and Jason fed before the gang showed up to dance! And there was a strange car in her driveway as she coasted to a stop. Claire climbed out of the driver's seat and waved.

After giving Lynn a quick hug, she said, "I couldn't leave town without thanking you for everything."

"What did I do?" asked Lynn as she led Claire into the

kitchen.

"You were responsible for the bust."

"Me?" She and Claire settled at the table to drink a beer.

"You were so certain about that dress," said the FBI agent, "that I got interested in your friend, Letitia. We put a stakeout on the street Sunday morning." She toasted Lynn with her bottle.

"What's for dinner?" asked Jason as he walked into the house smelling of his usual sugar and spices

"Dusty's bringing home pizza because we're having a dancing class tonight," Lynn explained to Jason.

"Dancing again?" Jason was puzzled by the family interest in dancing. He had made a quick exit the first dancing class evening.

Lynn explained all the latest gossip about Amelia and Zachary, concluding with the need for a dancing class. Jason just shook his head in disbelief, or was it resignation. "This is the norm for this family," he admitted to Claire.

"And you're *my* partner tonight, handsome." Claire tugged at Jason's arm. "Just remember I didn't have you arrested for your part in the robbery."

"My part?"

"If you had been paying attention instead of glued to your phone, you might have saved us all sorts of problems."

Dusty heard her remark as he came in with dinner. "Yeah, all your friends wouldn't have had to steal bikes from little kids."

Claire laughed. "That's why you're my partner tonight." Jason grinned at the agent.

Lynn invited her to stay for dinner as they all enjoyed rehashing the last few weeks. They finished dinner just as the dancers started to arrive.

Tonight Zachary was back in town. He came as Amelia's escort. Nathan had convinced Patti Ann to join him. After two dances the college crowd arrived to collect their friends.

## There's No Explaining Love

Jason and Patti Ann waltzed right out of the house and were soon with the gang at Pedro's Casa talking about dancing class night. While back in The Heights, Nathan and Claire showed the class a thing or two about the tango.

# Chapter Thirty-four

Lynn watched Amelia climb out of her car wrestling with a garment bag on her way toward Lynn's office. She had been looking for a wedding dress for days, at all the nearby shops and all over the Internet. She must have found her dress, Lynn thought, as the bride-to-be exclaimed breathlessly, "I want your opinion." She thrust an old-fashioned dress across the conference table.

"It's lovely," said Lynn, "Where did you get it?"

"It was my mother's," explained Amelia, "I didn't wear it at my first wedding because she said she wanted to save it. I think she didn't like my husband and didn't want her dress involved." Amelia shrugged. "But I remembered that I had it. After she died, I stored it away at Miguel's. I put together mementoes I didn't want to lose or have my husband take," she hung her head, "and when I remembered I called Justine and she sent it to me."

"Let me see how it fits," said Lynn as she closed the drapes to the conference room and closed the door.

As Amelia stepped into the dress, Piper burst into the room. "What's going on? Something secret?"

"What are you doing here?" asked Lynn.

"I knew it," challenged Piper, "I was at the office supply store and saw Amelia come in here. You're up to something."

"I am not," scowled Lynn, "Amelia's showing me a dress."

"What do you think?" asked Amelia as she spun around.

"It's beautiful," smiled Lynn. She looked at Piper who was wiping a tear from her eye.

But one tear never stopped the tiny principal. "Now your hair and we have to get your make-up right. I'll call Bev and Marianna." She pulled out her cellphone.

"Wait!" gasped Amelia.

"Too late," said Lynn, "we all want to help you look the best for your wedding."

Piper ended her calls. "We're all meeting at Lynn's after dinner tonight." She looked at Amelia. "You'll have to tell Zachary that he can't come. Let Nathan entertain him." Piper had everyone's evening arranged.

"What a perfect dress," said Marianna as she made Amelia spin around in Lynn's living room later that evening. "It doesn't need any alterations. A good dry cleaning and you're all set."

"Now for your hair," announced Bev. The current county commissioner, and successful salon owner, was opening a small toolbox on the dining room table.

Amelia gasped, "Leave my hair alone."

"I'm not cutting it," promised Bev, "I'm just going to show you how to twist it up and then Lynn and Marianna can help you thread small flowers through it on your wedding day." With that Bev began hair styling training class, and the ladies spent a delightful evening organizing Amelia's wedding day look.

~ ~ ~

When Amelia arrived home, Zachary was sprawled on the couch watching a baseball game. He jumped up as she entered, "Your hair," he gasped, "it's beautiful"

She blushed at Zachary's compliment. "That's how Marianna and Bev said I should wear it for our wedding."

"What else did they decide?" he teased. He knew Amelia well enough to know that she hated to be the center of attention.

"They like my dress," she said.

"Did you have enough money for it? I don't know why

you won't let me pay for it." He sort of scowled because he wanted to give Amelia so many things and she kept his generosity under control.

"My dress is priceless," said Amelia. "It's my mother's wedding dress."

Zachary drew her into his arms. "What a perfect choice! I want to see it."

Amelia shook her head. "Marianna took it home and is taking it to be dry cleaned, so you won't see it until our wedding day."

Zachary kissed her cheek. "I like all of your friends. They know you're someone very special."

"They're your friends, too," she told him. "They would do the same for you. I mean they would come to your rescue if you needed them."

"I know that years ago Dusty and Lynn did everything they could to help me and my family through horrible times," he nodded in memory, "So, yes, they are my friends, too."

They walked into the kitchen where Zachary had opened a bottle of wine. They collected glasses and moved out to the screened porch as had become their evening custom. As they sat and looked into the night and listened to the crickets and frogs, Zachary said, "I heard from Nancy. She says she can't be with us. She was very apologetic and wanted you to know that she is still pleased that we'll be married."

Amelia took his hand. "Do you feel bad?"

"No, just puzzled. I believe she's sincere. But she's pulling away from the family. You've noticed how she'll phone but never visit. Buck says Mars never talks about her any more. And we all thought they would be married by now." Zachary kissed her fingers. "I think Nancy is not the girl I raised any more."

"What do you mean?"

269

"I think she runs with a wild crowd. I hear rumors and have some suspicions." He kissed her cheek. "But we'll get married without her and be ready to help her if life doesn't go her way."

"That's what parents are for," agreed Amelia.

# Chapter Thirty-five

Not many plans for the family this evening. Although it was Friday everyone seemed to agree that the trip to the lake for Amelia's wedding tomorrow would be enough family time over the weekend for everyone. Or as Piper put it, "Three hours each way on a bus, I may have to kill someone."

So Lynn was making a big summer salad for her, Dusty and Jason to share. The guys didn't mind because Dusty would attack the snack shelves about nine tonight and Jason would eat, then join his friends at Pedro's for what was referred to as summer friend fare – a basket of tacos. Lynn planned on a few snacks herself later but she enjoyed her summer salads, getting more creative each year. Tonight she had harvested some of her early lettuce, added strawberries, pecans, a few stray things hanging out in the vegetable crisper and salmon. A light dill vinaigrette, she was on a roll!

Dusty came in, put away his gun and phone, washed his hands. "Where's Jason?" He kissed her cheek and grabbed a beer.

"He's a little late," she replied as Jason tumbled into the kitchen with several paper sacks in his grip.

"We're supposed to test this stuff." He flipped the sacks onto the table and several loaves of bread and individual rolls skittered onto the tabletop. "Umberto's experimenting with artisan breads." He shrugged. "I don't know what it means but the shop smells great." And now the kitchen was smelling great.

They all stared at the bread, noses twitching. Dusty

said, "Butter." As if by some secret signal, they all moved. Dusty grabbed a fresh stick of butter from the fridge, Jason washed his hands while Lynn brought small plates and flatware to the table. As an afterthought, she placed the salad there, also. The three of them settled in staring at the aromatic bounty.

Jason pointed. "I think that's sourdough, those rolls are white, those long things are something crispy that you break apart and the round loaves are wheat." He grabbed a roll and broke it apart, slathering it with butter.

Lynn watched him put away the chunk in three bites. If he ate like that she would barely get any, so she encouraged him, "Eat some of the salad too." She said this as she broke apart one of the long things. Dusty was silent as he found a knife and began slicing chunks off a round loaf.

"Fresh bread?" asked Piper as she entered the kitchen. She used the front door often now that she and Will lived across the street. So she had snuck up on them. Dusty's instinct was to hide all the loaves from the marauding principal, but he wasn't quick enough. She had her hands on a sourdough loaf before he could stuff a slice in his mouth and grab the rest. "Where is this," she hacked off the end and bit, "stuff from?" Then she took the remains of the chunk and covered it in butter. "The boys are having dinner with Mom and Dad. Will's -"

"Right behind you," Will announced as he walked into the kitchen, smelled the bread, grabbed a beer and sat at the table reaching for a crusty roll. "From Umberto?" he asked before stuffing it in his mouth. Jason nodded.

Piper jumped up and opened and closed cabinet doors in the kitchen. She returned to the table with two small plates filled with olive oil seasoned with oregano, basil and other herbs. The gang groaned in ecstasy as they took turns tracing bread chunks through the oil.

The salad disappeared so Lynn dug several hunks of

cheese out of the fridge. She was a sucker for weird things – lemon white cheddar, goat and cranberry, gorgonzola with pine nuts. She brought it all to the table.

Will finally spoke for all of them when he pushed back from the table and stretched out his legs. "Ahhhhhh." The bread was gone. The butter a memory. The oil plates dry and the salmon salad bowl holding the sad remains of the early lettuce.

"I guess we were hungry," ventured Piper. "Is this something Umberto is selling?"

Jason gulped his soft drink, thinking he should have had the wine like Piper and Lynn. "He's experimenting with breads." Jason looked over the table. "I guess I can tell him we liked it all." Everyone nodded. He stood. "I guess I'll shower and go meet the guys." He trotted out of the kitchen.

"I think this was a great way to prep for Amelia's wedding. You know the food will be great." Lynn poured more wine for herself and Piper. She turned to Dusty who didn't seem to be able to move. "Can I get you another beer?"

"I'll get it. If I sit here, I'll never move again." He brought more beer to the table for himself and Will. "Besides, I need this after our marathon board meeting today."

"What do you mean?" asked Lynn. "Letitia's gone. What more is there to do?"

Dusty gaped at her. "We have a program to organize or the state threatens to come in and run it." He took a long drink. "They still require us to provide this service." He looked at three sets of eyes. He couldn't tell if they were interested in his story or just in a bread induced coma. But he had to talk. "We had to straighten out our finances and make it look like we spent our money legally. We had to hire a director and we had to clean up any lingering evidence of stuff."

"Stuff?"

"Yeah, stuff." He didn't want to get into that much detail – bank robbers, sex and the staff.

"So how did you clean things up?"

"Since a nonprofit board is responsible for financial management, three of our board members, the Baptist, the Presbyterian and the guy from the synagogue went to a meeting with the county finance officer and-"

"Leaned on him to fix the books," finished Will.

"No, more like prayed over him. He goes to church with one of the board members." Another gulp of beer. "We were all surprised that things were pretty well organized. Those few weeks Letitia had to establish the office, she made certain the money was spent legit, even if just on paper. She got the paperwork to the state for creating our nonprofit and did all those other things we learned we had to do after our retreat." He shrugged. He didn't need to tell them that the board only cared that it looked right on paper. "Then today we hired a director. Bergy and Judge Dunn recommended a retired probation officer. He had done that work for years and then moved over to the DA"s office as an investigator. He has good credentials."

"What about that woman, Sasha, who was interim?" asked Lynn.

"She's happy," replied Dusty. "She told us that having this responsibility was taking time away from her service to her church."

"Sounds like you're a fully functioning agency now," Lynn summed up.

"We are," Dusty admitted. "We even adopted a policy that says our staff can't date our clients. The fellow we hired said that was no problem because his wife has a gun with the same policy."

They all laughed. Then they all wondered if they should go for a walk or something.

# Chapter Thirty-six

*I*t was a beautiful day at the lake. Amelia and Zachary had chosen this June Saturday afternoon to be married. The yacht club was decorated with flowers, a small canopy set out on the deck for the ceremony, and afterward everyone would dine before Zachary and Buck took their guests out for boat rides.

To get everyone there from River Bend, Zachary had chartered a bus. It was a small, intimate group who all became more friendly during the ride – Lynn and Dusty and Jason, along with Will, Piper and her three sons, Jim and Marianna, Harriette and her son, Sherry and her family and three of Amelia's long time employees. Zachary only invited his two children and Nathan. Sadly Nancy chose not to attend, saying she had a client to see in Greece.

Doyle and Jason were delighted to be included because they were anxious to spend some time with Miguel's daughter, Lori. The three youngsters were all in college, Doyle and Lori attending the state university.

Buck was his father's best man, and Sherry Vonder, Amelia's oldest and dearest friend, was the matron of honor. Amelia was walked down the aisle by her two brothers, Miguel, the painting contractor, and Diego, the surgeon. The rest of Amelia's family, two sisters-in-law and a half dozen nieces and nephews waved from the front rows. A soft breeze fluttered the canopy as butterflies danced around the flowers decorating the area. A small string quartet played softly as Zachary grinned at his bride.

The ceremony left everyone in delighted tears. No one more so than Nathan, who with tears in his eyes, asked

Lynn, "Is there anything more beautiful than a happy bride?"

"Nathan," she teased, "you're an old softie."

"I know, my dear," he said as he sipped champagne, "but it's more than that – Penny, Amelia and our little Olivia have transformed Palmer Mansion. We have laughter and gaiety." He handed Lynn his glass and pulled a handkerchief from his pocket to swipe at his eyes. "I am so delighted."

Lynn laughed. "You and your family deserve the laughter and fun. Your hearts are so welcoming."

"Now we're getting maudlin," Nathan said as he reclaimed his glass. "But I do look forward to family dinners and holidays from now on."

"Are Zachary and Amelia planning to stay in town?" Lynn hadn't been able to get the final word from them."

Nathan sort of shrugged. "Zachary is building more homes here at the lake and Amelia has her business. I think they will be spending time traveling between their two homes. I do know they plan on staying here a few days for what Zachary likes to call 'Phase I' of their honeymoon. I've made Zachary understand that they must be at the hospital dance next weekend. I just can't seem to explain how he and Amelia became the main attraction."

Lynn laughed as she and Nathan stood aside to watch the celebration lakeside. After the ceremony, a marvelous dinner and early evening boat rides, the guests were all invited to Zachary's lakeside home for wedding cake before they would get back on the bus to return to River Bend.

Relaxing on Zachary's deck overlooking the lake, Will and Miguel stared into the twilight. Will said, "We haven't had the chance to talk about this." He poked Miguel in the ribs then pointed to Amelia. "So, what do you think?"

"Things have moved pretty fast." His old friend shook his head.

"Yeah," agreed Will, "they disappear one weekend and are married a few weeks later."

"No, I mean with me." Miguel grinned. "Zachary wants me to be the general contractor and site manager and head guy at the new phase of his development. He says he can't take Amelia on a honeymoon if he has to be on top of things here." Miguel shrugged.

Will's eyes grew big. "What are you going to do?"

"My painting business will have a big role in the development. Justine and the boys are excited about moving to live on a lake. It's a big opportunity. And he's so good to my sister."

"That's the important part," said Lynn as she joined the men.

~ ~ ~

The wedding was on Saturday and a week later, everyone was ready for the big hospital dance. All the women had new summer dresses, purchased with dancing in mind. All the men were in tuxedos, and some of them also wore a scowl. But as Lynn reminded Dusty, the chief scowler, "We're doing this for Amelia."

He couldn't object. He remembered all those years, from the time he was a rookie on the police force, being called to Amelia's place to intervene at domestic assault situations. Today, she was truly free and looking forward to a life that would never again be scary or dangerous.

So he waited with everyone else on the country club dance floor as Zachary and Amelia made their entrance. There was some polite applause, then it grew louder and soon there were cheers and whistles. This was River Bend after all, the place were friends let you know when life was right!

The gang danced up a storm. Miguel and his wife had stayed in town for this event and thrilled everyone with their Latin dances. The hospital committee was thrilled at the ticket sales and everyone felt they got their money's worth. The dance committee members wondered what they would do as the hook next year to sell tickets.

It was a great night!

~ ~ ~

The bar was a dive but the folks were the same as he remembered from his youth. Wells sat at a corner table watching Letitia. In just a few weeks she had changed her wardrobe from tent dresses to jeans and big billowy tops often with some sort of glittery design. She wore her hair all piled on the top of her head and was even wearing make-up. She didn't look bad. She was a lot of woman and he thought he would enjoy being with her in his retirement from crime.

And much to his surprise, she was fitting right in with the family. His mother liked her. They even wore the same size clothes and shoes. Wells laughed to himself. Those two women had bonded over big feet.

She had found a job working for a local tow trucker as a dispatcher. Wells, himself, was working for his cousin who managed a local store that was part of a big building supply chain. He was a cashier at the general contractor's check out and was considering working toward some management position.

He had heard from Trong that Sparky was on chemo. He was getting good care. Trong was enjoying federal prison. He said it was much better that a state pen. He had closed his last letter by saying, "I can spend my days here. No hassles or bullies. Mostly a bunch of old white guys who embezzled."

Wells waved to the bartender for another round of drinks. Letitia sashayed back to the table. She liked dancing and never lacked for a partner. Wells' old friends and family members always saved a dance for her. They all agreed. She was the reason he came home. And they appreciated her for it.

278

~ ~ ~

Lynn followed Dusty up to bed, picking up pieces of his tuxedo as she climbed the stairs. She had to wrestle his bow tie from the dog who had caught it in mid air as Dusty undid it and tossed it behind him.

She dumped all the odds and ends on a chair in the bedroom, knowing it all had to go to the dry cleaners – because she also knew that the dog would sleep on it in the chair this evening. Dusty's theory was that the tux had such an assortment of foul smells that it appealed to the dog and one night nuzzled in the jacket was like dog heaven.

"Are you sure you don't put snacks in your jacket pocket?" she asked as she turned so that he could unzip her dress. They watched the dog growl and burrow deeper into the jacket lining.

Dusty wasn't paying attention, he was kissing her shoulders as her dress slipped to the floor. She turned to face him, placing her arms around his neck. "She was beautiful."

"Not as beautiful as you." He was on a mission and soon had her on the bed.

"And Zachary will make her so happy."

"Not as happy as you make me."

Lynn pushed him on his back and got up to wiggle out of the rest of her clothing. Dusty did the same. Within minutes they were washed and flossed and returning to the bed spot bookmarked for affection. "That's better," sighed Lynn. My feet aren't used to all that dancing."

Dusty stopped in mid-kiss. "We all looked pretty good," he mused. "I heard some fellow complain about Hoefler's friends showing off."

"Dad did look good tonight. And you all danced with Amelia. I think Zachary was pleased. He told me he valued all her friends." She scooted closer so that Dusty wouldn't forget his plans for the rest of the evening.

And he didn't.

= = =

# About the Author

**Renee Kumor** has lived in North Carolina for over thirty years. The setting for the River Bend Chronicles series reflects her early life in Ohio and her later years in western North Carolina. She was a stay-at-home mom for several years developing a personal ethic of community service. Through the years as her children aged, she became active in the political and non-profit life of the community. She began writing a political opinion column for the local newspaper, but retired from writing when she announced her candidacy for local political office. After eight years as a county commissioner, she returned to non-profit service and began writing a monthly column for the newspaper on non-profit management and service issues. Renee has been married to her husband for fifty years. They have four children and four grandchildren.

# COMING NEXT:

# Brewing Terror
## *The River Bend Chronicles*
### Book 13

Lynn gets ready to celebrate the Fourth of July in Boston. She has been accepted into a two-week program at Harvard for nonprofit fundraising professionals. On the plane to Boston she chats with Eloise, a River Bend friend. Eloise is going to visit her daughter, Julie, a high tech government worker with Top Secret security clearance.

Homeland Security agents enter the picture to guard Julie when they learn she has come to the attention of a terrorist cell. When Lynn takes some time off to enjoy the Fourth of July with Julie in Boston, they are assaulted by terrorists and rescued by Homeland Security agents. Julie returns to River Bend to heal from the assault.

In the meantime Mars has invested in a micro-brewery run by three disabled Marines. As the Marines work on their new business, planning on an October opening, they meet the agent guarding Julie.

They had worked with him in Afghanistan during an investigation a few years ago. They are happy to help him chase and capture the terrorists who have come to River Bend in their continuing pursuit of Julie as an asset to be compromised or captured.

www.ingramcontent.com/pod-product-compliance
Lightning Source LLC
Chambersburg PA
CBHW070444030726
47503CB00004B/881